THE AETHER

SENTINELS OF MAGIC BOOK 1

T.M. CROMER

ISBN: 978-1-956941-14-2 (EPUB)
ISBN: 978-1-956941-39-5 (PAPERBACK)
ISBN: 978-1-956941-40-1 (HARDBACK)
ISBN: 978-1-956941-41-8 (LARGE PRINT)

Cover Design: Deranged Doctor Designs
Edits: Trusted Accomplice

PROLOGUE

The sun was setting on his life, yet the brightness of the morning light was hard to stomach. Over five hundred years he'd lived. Roughly a hundred and fifty more than he'd cared to.

He halted before the tombstone where his beloved's name and death date were etched.

Vivian Dethridge née Stephens
Beloved Wife of Damian
b. February 24, 1981 — d. December 29, 2181

Because of his gifts, she'd lived a century longer than any average human. But it still wasn't enough, and he missed her like hell. All these lonely years, he'd been forced to continue without her. And it had been a miserable existence. With a glance at the stones for his remaining family, he sighed. But not as fucking miserable as outliving his children and his children's children.

All but one.

"Papa?"

He'd never hear her voice without imagining her as a youngster.

As his wild Beastie, never doing as she was told, always running into the thick of things with no regard for danger.

"Almost ready, Sabrina," he replied. His voice was gravelly, giving hint to his deeper emotions. Yet she could feel them because of what she was, the power she wielded. In a short time, she'd be more powerful still. All that was his would transfer to her so he could be reborn—with Vivian.

A crack rent the air, and a retina-searing golden light slashed across the fabric of the veil, opening a portal from the Otherworld to theirs.

The Goddess had arrived.

With one last glance at the headstone, he turned away, belatedly catching movement out of the corner of his eye. He didn't need to look to know the letters of his name were forming next to Vivian's, along with today's written date. His death was foretold long ago when he once worked for the Authority and had the balls to confront the Fates. When his misfit band of Sentinels, who defied him at every turn, finally stood as a single unit behind him, ready to burn the entire magical community to the ground if that was what it took to rescue him from his crimes.

Damian smiled at the memory.

Goddess, he loved those fuckers, the men and women who'd become his best friends. He'd see some of them today. Not as who they were, but as who they'd been reborn to be.

Perhaps it was a good day to die after all.

But it was an even better day to be reborn.

CHAPTER 1

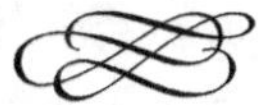

SUMMER 2011

"*A*re you planning to attend the gala tonight?"

Damian Dethridge glanced up from his cards to study his distant cousin and longtime friend, Alastair Thorne. "Why? Do you need a date?"

An amused smile curled Alastair's mouth, but he never looked up from his hand. Damian knew from experience for anyone to beat him at poker, they needed every bit of concentration to block him from reading their thoughts. He always tried to play fair, but when an opponent was particularly excited by what they'd been dealt, their strong emotion transferred. This was also true in life.

As he watched Alastair, Damian felt a sense of kinship mixed with melancholy. Golden-blond hair, perfectly sculpted features, and a strong jaw made Alastair classically handsome. With his pristine suits and unrelenting etiquette, he presented like old Hollywood royalty. The warlock version of Cary Grant and the exact image of the man Damian called his father—Alastair's great-grandfather, Nathanial Thorne.

Nate and his wife, Evie, had provided Damian a home when he was only eight years old and gave him, a young orphaned boy, the love and life lessons he desperately needed. He owed the Thornes a debt he could never repay.

Perhaps that's what fueled their friendship. Alastair's humor was similar enough to Nate's to keep Damian entertained.

"To answer your question, Al, *no*."

At one hundred and ninety-one years of age, balls, galas, and the like had ceased to entertain him. Most days, Damian preferred to remain at his ancestral home, Ravenswood, where he could avoid the dregs of society and read to improve his mind. Although, it did seem that over the last few decades, novels had become no more than deadly dull drivel. There wasn't anything unique. No story idea that hadn't been rewritten and expounded on ad nauseam. No talent was able to touch the greats—Wilde, Fitzgerald, Dickens, Austen, and the like.

Perhaps he should author a book. He certainly couldn't do worse than what passed for literary works these days, and it might help to pass the time.

Alastair brought him back from his side trip when he topped off their drinks.

"Why not go, Dethridge? It might be fun."

Damian snorted. "If you believe that, your idea of fun vastly differs from mine."

He peered into Alastair's mind, only to be mentally smacked away. Laughing, he nodded his head.

"Well done, Al. Not many can keep me out."

"You were the one who showed me the surefire way to repel you." The considering expression in Alastair's narrowed sapphire eyes wasn't surprising. The man didn't miss a trick. "Clearly, you did it for a reason."

"I needed a challenge."

"Life must be awfully boring for you if reading my tedious thoughts is challenging."

"Yours are more interesting than most."

Alastair nodded and raised the bet. "Still, a certain young lady will be in attendance," he stated casually as Damian called and raised the stakes higher.

"I'm too old for her, and we both know it."

"You're too old for anyone." Alastair barked a laugh. "But look at you. You're a woman's wet dream, my friend."

"That doesn't matter in the least."

Irritation prickled, and Damian quickly shut down the emotion, knowing if it got out of hand, others—namely Alastair—would feel the sting. He'd won the genetics lottery and abhorred the fact that he was, for lack of a better description, drop-dead gorgeous. Seduction had been his mother's game after the Darkness consumed her. As an Enchantress, she'd leveraged her looks and sexuality to steal magic from the unsuspecting. Long ago, Damian had sworn he'd never resort to luring others with his natural-born gifts.

"What really has you out of sorts, Damian?"

He looked up to see Alastair's concerned gaze focused on him. With a toss of his cards, he folded the game and shrugged. "I don't know, Al. Maybe it's because no one should exist as long as I have. See what I've seen. Have the power to restore or remove magic from another at will. The power to annihilate a soul for all eternity."

"It sounds pretty good to me."

Tugging up his slacks, Alastair crossed his legs and leaned back in his seat, scotch in hand.

Damian half expected to see a naughty saying on his crew socks like Nathanial was so fond of wearing. Alastair, however, would never dilute his impeccable fashion sense with novelty items.

"That's because you are a fraction of my age," Damian replied dryly. "Give it another hundred and twenty-plus years, then we'll circle back to this discussion."

"I feel as if my life is one long sentence as it is," Alastair said in a suddenly somber voice.

"No change in Rorie's condition, then?"

"None."

Aurora Fennell-Thorne, the love of Alastair's life, had been in stasis for several years with no hope of waking.

"I can attempt to bring her back, Al. Say the word."

"And turn you into an enemy of the Authority for breaking their protocol?" Alastair's mouth tightened as he shook his head. "No, Damian. I'll find another way. She still has time."

"Al—"

"It'll be a death sentence for you. They'll send the Death Dealers."

"So what? Let them. Even if they *did* manage to defeat me, which we know is doubtful, I have nothing to live for but this pile of rocks and that blasted garden containing my mother's tomb."

A wicked grin transformed his friend from morose to mischievous. "And perhaps Vivian Stephens?"

Pausing in the middle of lifting his tumbler, Damian narrowed his eyes and pointed a finger in his direction. "Get that thought out of your head, or I'll pluck it out for good."

"Spoilsport."

"Besides, she's engaged to Sebastian Drake."

"An arranged marriage in this day and age is barbaric."

"Just because their parents encouraged the match doesn't mean it's arranged, Al," Damian said with a light laugh. But amusement was the last thing he was feeling.

Two months ago, he'd strolled onto the Drakes' estate in search of their butler, Leopold. On the far side of the back lawn, Damian had encountered Vivian, who'd been admiring the giant oak just outside the forbidden garden that held the Enchantress entombed.

She was ethereal with her long platinum hair, peaches-and-cream complexion, and large silver-blue eyes. The white sundress added an air of innocence, as did her bare feet, and she looked like a virginal sacrifice for the gods.

One glimpse, and Damian had been a goner. His lungs had ceased to draw another breath, and his heart had left his chest to settle in the palms of her delicate hands to do with what she will.

Only she didn't know it.

Their first meeting was nothing short of disastrous, however, and her impression of him had been blackened by his sudden irrational fear that his mother, Isolde, might escape by using Vivian. Unfortunately, that fear had been disguised as temper.

"What the hell are you doing?" Damian snapped.

She gasped and drew her fingers back right before touching a plate-sized matte-black rose, whose vine—unnoticed by her—had inched down the side of the stone wall. When she didn't answer, he ordered her away from the garden. Of course, she didn't run away fast enough for his liking, and he used his magic to give her slow-moving ass a boost.

Her second gasp was more indignant and distracted him momentarily.

It almost cost Damian his life.

The deadly vine barreled toward him at a blinding speed, and had he not caught the movement in his peripheral, he'd have been a human shish kabob. With a fisted hand, he halted time and stopped its forward motion. Drawing on ancient family power, he decimated the vine with a fiery blast, channeled the wind to gather the ashes, and dumped them on the cursed side of the wall.

Time snapped back with a resounding pop.

Keeping his gaze locked on the stone ledge, he addressed Vivian over his shoulder. "Go! And send the senior Drake to me immediately." When she again didn't react fast enough, he bellowed, "Move, woman! This is life and death."

She hissed a breath and disappeared with the faintest glimmer of light in her wake.

Belatedly, he realized he hadn't been able to hear her thoughts, which was highly unusual. As the Aether, he was subject to everyone's inner dialogue, magical and non-magical alike. The idea that hers might remain a mystery to him was intriguing.

Resentment flared in her eyes when she returned with Sebastian and his father.

"I only required one," Damian told her with raised brows and a slight smirk.

Sebastian's immediate unease tickled his mind, and Damian stalked forward, invading the man's space.

"Why didn't you warn her, Drake? That garden is off-limits to every-one. No exceptions."

"I wasn't in that garden. I was on this side of the wall," Vivian retorted, an underlying challenge in her cold tone.

One Damian was happy to accept.

He spun to face her, pinning her with a stare.

But she didn't react with fear or caution, as expected, and her pointy chin shot up in defiance.

"Do you know who I am?" he asked silkily.

Her sense of self-preservation finally kicked in, and she shot a questioning glance at Sebastian.

"I asked you a question, woman." Crossing to her, Damian used his fingertip to draw her face around to his. Mentally, he shrugged off the little voice taunting him, telling him he wanted all her attention for his own. "Do you know who I am and what I'm capable of?"

His voice had been whisper soft. Seductive in a way he's sworn it would never be. But she appeared immune to his spellbinding charm, and the impact of her frosty gaze punched him right between the fucking eyes.

"Who are you?" he asked. "And what have you done to me?" he wanted to add.

"Vivian Stephens." Her tone had lost its former chill and now had a breathy quality able to blank his mind.

Damian let the sound wash over him and found the effect pleasurable. Enough that he wanted to talk to her forever. "Viv—"

"Get away from her!" Sebastian barked the order, his unease growing and wrapping around Damian like a python. Belatedly, he recognized the emotion as jealousy edged with fear.

"Watch your tone, Drake," he replied casually. They both knew he could kill the man in an instant. "I'm simply gathering facts."

"And yet you still haven't removed your bloody hand."

Rarely was Damian surprised, but Sebastian's comment disconcerted him. Heat crept up his neck as he dropped his arm, and for the first time in his life, he felt true embarrassment.

Bowing his head in apology, he said, "I beg your pardon, Miss Stephens. I meant no offense."

What she would've replied, he'd never know. From the terrace, Leopold's warning shout rang out.

Acting instinctually, Damian threw his balled fists in the air and encased them all in a protective bubble a mere instant before the vine struck. Like a fingernail tapping glass, its inches-thick thorns clinked against the barrier, then drew back to try again. Harder and more frenzied with every attempt.

"Mr. Drake, I need you and your son to hold my protection spell in place while I deal with that damned vine once and for all."

"Where did you go?" Alastair asked with raised brows. "You certainly weren't here with me, old man." Squinting, he watched Damian. "You were recalling your meeting with her, weren't you?"

"Sod off."

In a highly irregular action for him, Alastair made smooching noises and laughed at Damian's promise of retribution.

"Whether you go to the ball or not, this dance of yours is going to be fun, my friend."

"There will be no dance."

"I hate to be the one to rain on your self-isolation parade, but I believe you won't have a choice." Alastair nodded toward the terrace.

On the other side of the French doors, Vivian stood in a shimmering pale-blue, off-the-shoulder ballgown, her hand poised to knock. Her distraught, tear-stained face propelled Damian out of the chair and had him yanking open the door to get to her.

CHAPTER 2

"**M**iss Stephens! What is it? What's wrong?"

Damian's frantic concern cemented Vivian's decision to break her engagement to Sebastian tonight. From the moment the Aether touched her face, she'd been obsessed in her desire to know more about him, to learn how he had ruined her engagement without trying. If she could be swayed by a simple admiring glance and become obsessed by a brush of his fingertip against her skin, she had no business marrying another man.

"I..."

How did she explain her instant attraction? He'd think her insane. Hadn't she discovered nearly everyone who ever came in contact with him was instantly enchanted? Why did she believe she was any different?

"Vivian?" His tone was gentle, as if attempting to calm a child.

Embarrassment consumed her, and heat infused her body, traveling at the speed of light to her face. No doubt, with her telltale complexion, she resembled an overripe tomato.

"Forget it, I—"

Then he touched her.

A simple clasp of her hand to draw her in out of the chilly

English air, and all thoughts flew from her mind as she allowed him to lead her.

The click of the door woke her from her trance. Unable to meet his penetrating stare, she sought a distraction, and across the room, she found just the thing. Or rather, the person. *Alastair Thorne.* Outside of the Aether, he was the most dangerous warlock in existence. One never to be trifled with, lest he smite the person foolish enough to get on his bad side.

Apprehension for her recklessness caused her heart to take flight. She'd foolishly sought Damian out, never expecting he wouldn't be alone, and now she was faced with not one powerful being but two. Both strangers. Both men with reputations that should've made her think twice before crossing their paths.

A slight frown tugged at Alastair's dark-blond brows, and with an elegance not usually reserved for men, he rose to his feet and set his glass on the table.

"Miss Stephens, I don't believe we've been formally introduced, and however rude it seems, I'm afraid I don't have time to correct that unfortunate oversight. I must return home at once." After bowing his head in acknowledgment of her, he cast a wry smile at Damian, then teleported away in a shower of golden light.

And then she was alone with the man who sent her heart into overdrive from their first meeting.

What had she done?

"Why don't you have a seat and tell me what the problem is, Miss Stephens?" Damian suggested with a wave of his hand toward a leather sofa on the far side of the room.

"This was a mistake," she blurted. "I... I... This was definitely a mistake."

"Why don't you let me be the judge of that, hmm? Now, tell me why you're distraught."

"Distraught?" She touched a hand to her cheek, and the dampness reminded her that she'd been crying as she fled the Drakes' maze. "Oh."

"Are you quite all right, my dear?"

He sounded like a kindly grandfather. Someone, somewhere, had told her he was close to two hundred years old. Yet he appeared no older than her thirty years, and hands down, he was the sexiest man she'd ever seen. His features were perfectly symmetrical, and his firm jaw held not an ounce of softness. Black hair fell over one of his perfectly groomed brows in a cavalier style. Penetrating almond-shaped eyes, obsidian in color with silver slivers, seemed to see to the depths of her soul. Knowing, they called eyes like his. And they were. All knowing.

"Yes," she said on a breathy exhale, her attention caught by the V of his white button-down dress shirt and the exposed skin of his throat.

"Why are you here, Vivian?"

Caught by the smooth cadence of his voice, she glanced up, meeting his mesmerizing gaze. How could he produce a sound so soothing and seductive at the same time?

"You."

The lightly tanned skin at the corner of his exquisite, dark-as-sin eyes crinkled, the only sign of his forming amusement. Had she glimpsed a brief flare of satisfaction?

She was such a ninny.

Gathering her courage, she lifted her chin and asked, "When we met by the garden… Did you, um, *feel* anything?"

His brows shot up, and for an unguarded second, his expression showed she'd surprised him. Her stomach dropped.

He hadn't experienced the same connection.

Self-conscious and convinced she'd imagined everything, she jumped up and rushed for the door. "Never mind. I've got… to go… a thing… to do."

Stop babbling, Viv!

"Wait."

His commanding tone halted her in her tracks, but she didn't dare turn around. Attuned to his every movement, Vivian felt him close in behind her. Her breathing bordered on panicked, and every inhale or exhale resembled a racehorse crossing a finish line, the sound harsh to her ears, competing only with her pounding pulse.

Damian hadn't touched her, but his encompassing presence surrounded and pressed into her.

"I did," he said in a low, sinful voice that triggered the fine hair on her neck to lift.

"Oh, thank the Goddess!" Shoulders dropping in relief, she faced him. "I, uh, broke it off with Sebastian."

His grin set off a thousand butterflies in her belly.

"Excellent," Damian murmured. "You had no business marrying him. You're out of his league."

She wanted to protest on Baz's behalf, but two of her three sisters had said the same, and a tiny part of her knew their relationship didn't have the fire she'd secretly longed for.

Lifting a hand, he asked, "May I?"

Unsure what he intended, but not truly concerned, she nodded.

His thumb brushed across her bottom lip, and the tingle it created went straight to her core, causing a rush of desire. Awed by his ability to get her juices flowing with a simple light touch, she shook her head.

Immediately, his brows dipped together, and he withdrew.

"I beg your pardon."

"Oh, no! I didn't mean for you to stop. I…" Vivian slapped her palm against her forehead and groaned. "I'm making a complete fool of myself."

"How so?" he asked smoothly, almost curiously.

Again, she shook her head. "When we met, I felt connected to you. Yes, I was irritated by your arrogant dictate about the garden, but Mr. Drake explained why." Unable to look away from his hypnotically beautiful face, she swallowed hard. "The truth is, from the second you touched me, I had the oddest sensation that I somehow *knew* you."

His mouth softened into a hint of a smile, but he remained silent as he watched her closely.

Licking her lips, she cast a longing glance at Alastair's forgotten beverage.

Would it be gauche to guzzle it down and relieve her parched throat?

"Go on," Damian urged.

For a whole three seconds, she thought he meant drink the booze. It belatedly registered he was indicating she should continue her confession.

"I've been obsessing for the last two months. Believing I saw interest. Wanting you to be interested." Swallowing hard, she met his admiring eyes. "How do you do that? How do you seduce with a look or a touch?"

In a flash, his expression hardened, and the room's temperature dropped a good ten degrees.

Goosebumps pickled her skin, and she rubbed her arms against the chill.

"What did I say wrong, Damian?"

"Go back to your young man, Miss Stephens. See if you can salvage your relationship," he ordered in an awful voice. "I don't have time for children's games."

"Games? What games?" Her sense of fairness prevented her from walking away without defending herself from whatever slight he'd imagined. "I asked you a legit question."

"Do you know what true seduction is, Vivian?" he asked. The husky rasp was accompanied by a look so hungry and hot that had she been wearing underwear under her tight gala gown, it would've gone up in a poof of smoke. As it was, the unconscious shifting of her thighs caused the material to rustle, drawing his gaze downward as if he could see the beginning of her freakish arousal.

Who got turned on by a probing question?

Speaking of probes... her eyes traveled the length of his torso, pausing briefly on his crotch before she dragged them back up his body to meet his stare.

"I thought I did," she replied when he seemed to expect an answer.

"Hmm. I wonder."

Me, too.

"Are you attending the gala tonight?" Again, his gaze swept her body, heating her to the point of uncomfortable.

"I'd intended to, but now, I'm not sure it's a good idea."

"Because Drake will be there?"

"Yes. He's presenting a check for some charity or other."

"I see." Shifting closer, Damian held out a hand. "It seems a shame so lovely a gown will go to waste. Will you dance with me, Vivian?"

How did she say no when he asked like he had? As if her agreement meant everything to him.

Placing her hand in his, she audibly sighed as he wrapped an arm around her waist.

"I'm not interested in games, Damian," she said as she studied his inscrutable visage. "This is me telling you that I'm drawn to you on a deeper level. It's more than sex or curiosity. It's a feeling I can't account for and one I've never experienced."

"Would you believe me if I told you I feel the same?"

Raw vulnerability shone in his eyes, and oddly, she did.

"Yes."

"What should we do about this unexpected attraction?"

Her heart thudded painfully in her chest. This was a deciding moment for their future. "Can we explore it? Is that an option?" she asked, daring to hope.

"It would be a travesty if we didn't."

Her smile came from her blindingly happy soul, but he didn't glance at her mouth like most men would. Didn't kiss her as she'd expected. Instead, he grinned and twirled her away from him, then guided her back and dipped her.

When he drew her up, he released her and bowed. A gentleman of another time, with courtly manners appealing to her romantic daydreams.

"I intend to marry you, Vivian Stephens," he said, determination and promise in his eyes. "If that isn't what you want, walk away now."

"I'm not sure walking away is an option," she replied in all honesty.

CHAPTER 3

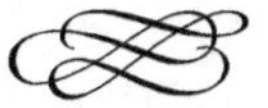

5 YEARS LATER

"*D*on't do this, Viv. Please, don't leave me."

Damian hated the begging quality to his voice, but if she left, he'd lose everything. His wife, his daughter—*his humanity.*

"I can't be here anymore. I just can't," she cried.

As he reached for her, intending to calm, she flinched, and his fucking heart broke all over again. Like it had the moment she began pulling away. The moment she stopped loving him.

Dropping his arms, he stepped back.

"What have I done to make you believe I'm such a monster?" he asked in a moderately neutral tone, pleased he hadn't given away his inner turmoil.

"I'm not saying you are, Damian. Not in the least. But you have the potential to be, and you know it. Your mother went crazy. What's to stop it from happening to you, too?"

Coldness invaded his soul, and in a detached manner, he watched her pack her things. A search of his memory couldn't produce a single episode in their past to spook her. Yes, the possibility was always there for him to lose his mind, to become a danger to those around him, but he would never hurt her or his perfect child. *Could* never. He didn't have it in him, and the fact she believed he might absolutely killed him.

"If you leave, you risk Sabrina. There are those who would seek to take her power." He was pathetic, reaching for any excuse to keep her with him, and not above using their daughter's safety as leverage.

"She has no magic for anyone to steal, Damian. Not yet."

"But she *will*, and then they'll come."

"There is no guarantee she'll be the next Aether, and no one knows she exists. You've made sure of it by keeping us hidden here at Ravenswood."

Her accusing tone stung, and it felt as if he were seeing her for the first time. Where had his loving wife gone? The woman who had sought him out to form a relationship. The one who had stood before the Goddess and promised him all her tomorrows. The one who had agreed keeping the birth of their daughter a secret from everyone, friends included, was what was best for her safety.

"You said you understood the need for secrecy, Viv."

"I thought I did. But you're the fucking Aether, and if you can't protect her whenever we go out, who can?"

After slamming the lid on her suitcase, she skirted his frozen form. She left him blindly staring at nothing and wishing he could find the words to make her see what was in his heart. Yet it sounded as if she was scrounging around for any excuse to leave him, and nothing he could say would make a difference.

"Did you ever truly love me?" he asked dully when she returned.

"How can you ever doubt it?"

And for the first time in months, she appeared as tortured as he felt.

"That's not an answer. Did you ever truly love me, Vivian? Or was it simply a challenge to win the famously reclusive Aether?"

Frowning, she hugged herself against the cold permeating the air. "Pull your anger back, Damian."

"It's not anger. It's *hurt*! And maybe you should experience what it's like, hmm?" He lifted his hand, palm up, and met her suddenly fearful eyes. "Should I crush your heart like you're doing mine, my love?" he taunted.

"Think about Sabrina. Think what it would do to her to not have a mother."

The tremble in her voice was telling.

She was terrified of him.

Him, the man who adored her and who had given her absolutely no reason to be afraid before that moment. Weary to his ancient soul, Damian let the fight drain from him. There would be no winning this war for her love. Even if she stayed, she'd forever fear him. He dropped his arm and turned away.

"Thank you," she said softly.

Meeting her gaze in the wall mirror, he blanked his expression except for the chilly disdain he reserved for those who thought to cross him.

"We are at an impasse, my dear. Should you leave this house, I'll hunt you down. You'll not take my daughter away." There was no pleasure when she paled, just an ache in his chest that she could ever think he'd be so monstrous as to hurt her.

Her chin came up, like the day they'd first met, and she faced him down with more courage than a person in her position should possess.

"I won't be a prisoner, Damian."

No. Butterfly that she was, her wings would droop and her sparkling beauty would dim with the blow to her spirit.

After a long minute of internal torture and debate, he nodded slowly.

"You can go out and flit about to become the social butterfly you so long to be, but Sabrina stays hidden here. *With me.* Do I make myself clear?"

"I'm not leaving my child alone with you.

"I didn't say you had to. Since you hate me so fucking much, we'll maintain separate bedrooms, and you may do whatever your heart desires. Leave the confines of the estate if you choose. However, when it comes to Sabrina, she stays." He returned to stand before her, staring down at her and putting up a false front. One of dominance and power. Of uncaring. "And you'll pop back here to tuck her in and kiss her goodnight before you resume your evening activities or chase sleep."

"I want her away from you. That's the point of our leaving," she protested.

Desperation rolled off her in waves.

He ruthlessly ignored it.

"She'll stay where I can protect her, Vivian. That's nonnegotiable."

"Damian, please."

Her whispered plea was agonizing, cutting him to the quick. If it was within his power, he'd grant her anything. Anything but taking Beastie away from him.

"You fear the monster, Viv? That child is the only thing keeping it at bay right now." He stalked to the door and, without looking back, said, "Remember that."

Vivian sagged down on the bed and buried her face in her hands. Her sister Josie had warned her Damian had the potential to go mad. She'd said she heard from those in charge that the almighty Aether hated to be crossed and that he tended to take another's power on a whim.

When Vivian initially asked him about it, he'd chuckled and told her she'd nothing to fear. Almost condescendingly. She hated that he'd avoided answering, and she'd been left to wonder if the rumors about him were true. After all, his mother had gone insane and amassed power at an alarming rate. What was to stop him from doing the same?

One of the very last things Sebastian had said to her was framed as a warning. "Be careful, Viv. You've fallen hard and fast for an extremely dangerous man."

The wounded look on his face still haunted her after all this time. Yet he'd been honest in his concern when he had every right to be spiteful or try to sabotage her relationship. Baz had been the one to tell her the tale of the Enchantress—Isolde de Thorne—Damian's mother. It was rumored that she'd been as beautiful as her son, a thousand times more cunning, and lethal to anyone who encountered her. Yet she hadn't started out that way, and in the beginning, her power wasn't equal to what her son currently possessed.

"Who am I to believe?" she asked aloud.

In her heart, she wanted to side with Damian, but his cold question almost stopped the organ he'd threatened to crush.

"Should I crush your heart like you're doing mine, my love?"

Vivian would never get that image out of her mind. Never be able to sleep at night without picturing the burning anger in his eyes or the disdain on his face when he'd told her he'd hunt her down. The promise of retribution was there, and she didn't dare defy him.

Yet she had her toddler to protect. Sabrina. Her beloved daughter.

But she was Damian's beloved daughter, too.

Vivian picked up her cellphone and dialed her sister.

"Josie?"

"Viv. I thought you were coming home. What's going on?"

"Damian won't let me leave."

There was a long pause on the other end of the line, then a moment later, Josie said, "You'll have to sneak away. Make everything seem normal and wait until he least suspects it, then take Sabrina and run."

"Where am I supposed to go that he won't find me? He knows the location of our house. Knows all of my friends. We'll never be able to block him if he decides to scry for us."

"Let me worry about blocking him. If we have to, we'll appeal to the Witches' Council or the Authority."

"Oh, Josie. What if we're wrong?"

"He's erratic, Viv." Josie's tone became cajoling. "You've told me so, remember?"

Frowning, Vivian tried to recall what she'd said to give her sister that impression. Had Damian been erratic? Today had been the only true indication he could turn on a dime. Hell, he never punished Sabrina when she was bad. He'd merely snuck her candy whenever Vivian put her in time-out.

"Viv?"

"I'm still here," she replied absently.

"You can't stay where you aren't safe," Josie said in that same persuasive tone, and deep down Vivian agreed. "At least not alone. Do you want me to come there for a while?"

Did she? Not really. But why the sudden reticence to have her sister visit?

"What about *The Elements Shop*? Won't Taryn and Soleil need your help?"

The four sisters had built up the small-town store their great-grandmother opened two centuries before, and they'd made it a viable business, both locally and online. The residents of their tiny town always looked to the sisters for a spell or two, believing they were the standard Wiccan variety of witches. The townspeople didn't realize the true power the four sisters held. Each possessing her own elemental magic: air, earth, fire, and water.

"I'll be sure it's stocked before I go, and if the girls need me, I can teleport back," Josie said with little regard for the work involved in running a business. She'd never taken an active part if she could help it, but she did love to spend the proceeds.

Vivian shoved aside the uncharitable thought. "In that case, I'd love for you to come."

Truthfully, she wasn't sure what protection her fiery sister could provide. If Damian was truly after more magic, he could do worse than steal from the Stephens sisters.

She eyed her luggage. Should she leave it packed and store it in case she ever needed to get out quickly? What was really in there that she couldn't conjure if she needed to?

With a heavy sigh and a wave of her hand, she said, "Put yourself away." The unpacking spell was one of her favorites after a long vacation.

Her toiletries disappeared in a poof, and her clothing drifted back to their hangers. When the case was empty, she shoved it in the bottom of the closet and closed the door. If she had to stay at Ravenswood, she'd keep the room nearest to their daughter. Damian could move his things to another.

She only had to work up the courage to tell him so.

The king-size bed reminded her of all the passion-filled nights they'd shared over the last five years. Reminded her of his worshipful gaze and loving gestures.

A sharp, stabbing pain in Vivian's head caused her to cry out. When it passed, she firmed her resolve to leave. She didn't want to believe he could go insane, but what choice did she have? The thought slithered through her mind that his behavior in recent months had become erratic and that she, along with her daughter, was in serious danger. There was only one option—*they must escape.*

CHAPTER 4

3 YEARS LATER - BELTANE 2019

Damian swiped a hand over the scrying mirror to conjure the image of his wife with her sisters. Tonight they were to celebrate Beltane, and the women were dressed in loose flowing gowns, with their hair ranging from straight to curly and spilling down their backs. Each wore an amulet about her neck to represent one of the four elements—a ruby stone for the daughter of Fire, sapphire for the daughter of Water, emerald for the daughter of Earth, and moonstone for the daughter of Air. The amulets had begun to softly glow as their magic ramped up closer to the upcoming ceremony. Each of the sisters was as different as the next, but to a one, they complemented the other.

It was Vivian, though, with her white-blonde hair that matched the shade of her moonstone amulet, who captured and held his attention the longest. Since returning to her family home, she seemed lighter, flitting from place to place, alighting on people and places, bringing joy wherever she went.

It disturbed Damian that she was happier away from him.

The night she absconded with their daughter, he'd been true to his word and hunted them down. She hadn't gone far, just to her family's estate on an island off the coast of Massachusetts.

In a rare act of bravery, the four sisters had stood up to him, defiant and bold. It had occurred to him that if Vivian was truly terrified he'd hurt Sabrina, terrified enough to take a stand, then perhaps they were better off away from him.

Leading up to that moment, he and Vivian had done their jobs well when they hid Beastie's existence. So after extracting a promise from Vivian to let him know the moment Sabrina's magic bloomed, he'd allowed them to cast their wards on their home and left for the mental well-being of mother and daughter.

For the last three interminable years, he'd been a fucking bear. No one had dared approach. No one other than Alastair and Sebastian Drake's butler, Leopold, could stand his surly moods.

With a tired sigh, Damian shifted the scene from his estranged wife to his daughter, and his heart spasmed at the look of loneliness and longing on her face as she watched her mother and aunts prepare for the Beltane ceremony.

"I want to be like you," she said forlornly. But for all the emotion Sabrina packed into the confession, there was no one to hear her. No one but him.

"Oh, Beastie." Moisture stung his eyes, and his throat ached with his grief. To see his child so lost and alone, similar to how he was after his mother had been entombed, was pure agony. He wanted nothing more than to ease her suffering. But he'd promised Viv not to interfere unless Sabrina showed signs of developing abilities.

Now, as the sisters laughed and gathered their supplies for their celebration, Sabrina squeezed her eyes shut.

"I wish," she whispered from her hiding place on the stairs. "Oh, Goddess, please, please, please, give me powers!"

On the heels of his daughter's fervent plea, Damian became supercharged, as if he'd touched a live wire and was absorbing its energy at warp speed. Lightning flashed and thunder boomed simultaneously, reverberating and shaking the walls of Ravenswood.

The image of Beastie blurred, and he felt fear cloud his mind, but an instant later, he could see her witchy glow.

Goddess Almighty! Sabrina had willed her own magic into existence!

That kind of blast would be felt around the globe, and the single thought, utmost in his mind, was that he needed to get to her before anyone else discovered the source. She was no longer safe in her mother's care. Visualizing Vivian's lawn, he teleported outside the doors of the Stephens' old Victorian home. Unthinkingly, he touched the doorknob, and the metal burned his hand. Not enough to blister his skin, but enough to sting and piss him off.

How dare Vivian ward her house against him!

Channeling the air current, he harnessed it into one tornadic blast. The entry door flew back on its hinges and slammed into the wall behind it. The rainbow-colored glass that had once represented a tree of life shattered into hundreds of tiny fragments. But he didn't care. He had to get to Sabrina.

As he stepped through the opening, his furious gaze locked onto her, and the terror in her eyes was a fucking wrecking ball to his chest.

His child had been taught to fear him.

Right as he was about to speak, he noticed her glowing aura flicker as if it couldn't make up its mind whether to attach to her or not. As if her magic was fighting against another to return to her. And suddenly, he knew. Vivian had bound her powers.

It was the only reason she hadn't come into her legacy six months ago when she'd turned five, as all Dethridge children had throughout history. While it was true not all his potential children would or could hold the title, any destined to become Aethers inherited their gifts at the age of five. His daughter had lost six months he could've used to help her learn the craft.

Without removing his focus from her, Damian understood what he had to do.

"Vivian! Get out here!"

Sabrina's elfin-like face contorted with fear, and she screamed, *"No, Mama!"*

When she would've called out again, Damian raised his hand and, clenching his fist, locked the sound in her throat. Although she would experience no actual pain, she was heartsick, and he could feel her angst. Tears pooled in her eyes and slowly dripped over her lower lids, finding their way down her cheeks and neck, dampening the collar of her pale-pink unicorn pajama top.

The sight of her helpless visage was tragic.

Christ, this moment was torturous for him, too. If he wasn't mistaken, she was able to see what he was about to do. Her inner Oracle was developing and attempting to culminate as her greatest ability. From here on out, she would catch glimpses of the various outcomes of his confrontation with Vivian. And if he wasn't mistaken, in all of them, she'd see her mother die.

Vivian, fierce, tall, and more beautiful than imaginable, charged into the room. She summed up the scene in seconds.

"Damian!" she gasped.

"You lied to me," he spat as he stormed farther into the room. "You swore to me she had no magic."

"She doesn't," she squeaked.

"Liar!" he shouted. Fear for Sabrina and an aching sense of betrayal fueled his anger, and the air around them contracted. "You bound her powers."

"With good reason, Damian." Her voice trembled, but she stood her ground. With her chin up and the arrogant tilt of her head, she resembled a warrior queen. Damian respected her courage.

"So you don't intend to deny it?" he asked, chillingly soft.

He stalked her, and for every step she backed, he took one forward, until he judged the distance to the wall would be adequate for his needs.

"No," she said defiantly.

Damian almost hated her for her confession. Not only had she denied Sabrina and him the years together that would form a tight father-daughter bond, but Beastie had lost essential training time she needed to learn how to protect herself until she became the reigning Aether. Vivian had foolishly risked Sabrina's life with her antics.

"You heartless bitch." His voice was low and lethal, the last Vivian

would hear as he flicked a wrist in her direction, effortlessly flinging her against the wall. Killing her.

"No!"

The horror behind Sabrina's emotion-packed cry overpowered Damian's hold on her voice. Her raw anguish echoed around the foyer and created destruction to the century-old house. The chandelier shook, decorative paper curled back from the walls, and the solid wood door cracked down the center. The floor slats buckled beneath his feet, and he had the damnedest time remaining upright.

With narrowed eyes, he tilted his head and carefully watched his daughter, prepared to mitigate her grief-based destruction.

When Sabrina would have run to Vivian's side, he grabbed her by her sparkling Unicorn t-shirt. Stopping her was essential to his plan. If she was as strong as he suspected, she might be able to revive her mother with little effort.

Fueled by her hurt and fury, Beastie fought him with every ounce of strength her young body possessed. Kicking, hitting, biting. She was ineffectual against a grown man like him, but Damian still held tight to her wiggling form.

Vivian's sisters huddled together in the double doorway to the sunroom, afraid to make a sound for fear of drawing his notice and rage down upon themselves. He paid them no mind, instead focusing all his attention on his spitting-mad daughter.

With a suddenness that caught him unaware, her body convulsed, and for a heart-stopping second, he knew true fear. Had he made a mistake in unleashing her magic by killing Vivian? Had the binding Viv created been to protect their daughter from harm? And the most pressing concern: was it too much power for Sabrina's small body to absorb at once?

Her dark eyes, identical to his, stared off into the distance as her tiny frame trembled under his hold. Right when he was about to summon the Goddess for assistance, Sabrina snapped out of her trance and glared at him.

"You'll pay for this," she spat, her young voice quivering. Her pain seared his insides, and he wanted to ease her suffering more than he wanted to draw his next breath, but she wasn't done. "You'll burn like the devil, and the Darkness will get you."

He felt the blood drain from his face, and he eyed her warily.

Had she cursed him, or was her knowledge straight from the future? Would he suffer the same affliction as his mother?

Ruthlessly, he tamped down his flash of uncertainty. He'd seen none of that for himself, and he had to put her words down to a distraught child's rebellion.

"Be quiet, Beastie. If you don't want your beloved aunts to suffer the same fate as your duplicitous mother, you'll do exactly as I say."

"If you hurt them, I'll kill you," she swore.

Where she found her courage was anyone's guess. No one in their right mind would go against so formidable an Aether as he. Damian observed his daughter with pride, though he'd never let it show to the outside world. She not only had her mother's courage, she had her temperament. Reckless and daring to the end.

Vivian's binding spell had ruined his plans. But not in the way any of the Stephens women believed. Unlike his mother, he'd never had any intention of harnessing his daughter's powers for his own. Instead, his intent was to teach her to work side by side with him—to learn to control *all* the elemental forces. She had it in her to one day be stronger than him, and Vivian shouldn't have interfered. Beastie would be further along by now if she'd been at home with him, where she belonged.

Deep down, where his humanity still existed, Damian regretted his temper. Vivian wasn't exactly as dead as they all believed; however, she wouldn't be waking anytime soon. Or at least, not without his supernatural assistance.

"Calm down, child," he ordered.

Sabrina's response was to kick him in the shin.

The trio of women cried out their shock.

Tears again welled in the large dark eyes staring up at him, making them appear wider and more tragic because she refused to shed a single drop this time.

"Gather your things, Sabrina. You'll be coming with me," he informed her gently.

Desperately, she looked over her shoulder toward her aunts. In response, the three siblings cast their eyes to the floor.

None of them would stand up for their sister's daughter.

"I'm not leaving Mama," Sabrina declared, her voice shaky and small.

Damian did something seemingly uncharacteristic for him. He squatted in front of her, smoothed back her wild black hair, and lifted her chin. Although she showed no fear, he could sense it brewing beneath the surface. He'd be sure to teach her how to cloak her emotions better in the coming years.

Pitching his voice so only she would hear, he said, "Run and wash up, then pack your things, Beastie. I'll see to your mother." With a deep frown, she studied him, and he let down his barriers, giving her a glimpse of what he wouldn't allow another to see—how much he truly loved Vivian and his immediate plan to heal her.

"Go, now," he said more gently.

Her decisive nod almost made him smile.

After she'd gone, he made his way to where his wife lay. Bending, he scooped her into his arms and pushed past the sisters to enter the solarium.

"Soleil, I need these herbs from your garden. Taryn, a cauldron and crystals." A snap of his fingers produced a laundry list of exactly which items he desired. "Be quick about it."

As expected, Josie lingered after her sisters made haste. Shifting closer to him, she tiptoed her fingers up his bicep and cast him a flirty smile.

"If you let her die, the child's powers would revert back. You and I—"

Suspicions confirmed, Damian sneered down at her. "Do you honestly believe I would want anything to do with you, Josie? After you convinced my wife and daughter I was a demon bent on acquiring magic at any cost? This"—he gestured to Vivian—"is ultimately *your* doing. Don't for one moment believe I'll forget it."

CHAPTER 5

Damian inwardly shuddered at Josie's attempted seduction. He should absorb her abilities and make her live like the ineffectual mortals she so despised and mocked. It would serve her right after the devastating mischief she'd caused.

"Leave me," he barked, taking satisfaction in her sickly pallor.

She was right to be afraid, the conniving bitch. If it wouldn't cause his wife untold heartache, he would murder the treacherous woman on the spot.

After Josie beat a hasty retreat, Damian smoothed back Vivian's pale, shimmering hair. She would remember the attack on her person when she woke, but there would be no memory of pain—she'd felt none. He'd struck too fast, taking great care with his magic. His plan was only to retrieve Sabrina, not to kill his wife with any permanence.

Vivian would, however, wake angry as a tiger with a sore tooth.

His lips twitched at the idea of his fired-up wife.

She'd be magnificent.

His left thumb worked the platinum band on his ring finger. Involuntarily, his gaze was drawn to her left hand, and he was startled to discover she still wore her diamond wedding set. When she'd initially confronted him a little over three years ago, stating she was leaving with their daughter, she'd also said she no longer loved him. Damian had never experienced pain of that magnitude. Not even when he'd watched his mother's takedown and eventual entombing.

His hurt wasn't because of Vivian's lie. *That* he'd felt instantly. But it cut him to the core that she'd felt the need to run from him and take their daughter with her.

As if he'd ever hurt Sabrina.

She was his life's blood.

That first time, Vivian had relented, but her fear never did, and she'd snuck away one night, a few months later, while he was off seeing to Witches' Council business.

"Papa?"

He faced his daughter and held out his hand.

Trepidation welled in her large, dark eyes.

"Despite what you may have been told, I won't hurt you, my little love. Come," he ordered gently.

When she slipped her tiny hand in his, he smiled his profound relief. That tiny bit of trust was a start.

"What did you do to her, Papa?" she whispered.

"Can you keep a secret?"

Sabrina gave him a solemn nod, and he mourned the vivacious toddler she'd been. He'd help her get back what they'd lost and find a way to strengthen their relationship in the process.

"I simply put her to sleep."

"Why do you need those things to wake her?"

"I don't." He flared his eyes wide and grinned. "Watch."

Damian ran a finger along Vivian's lush, rosy lips.

"This time, you'll recognize the truth when confronted with it, Viv," he told her softly.

Bending at the waist, he kissed life into her, breathing Aether magic into her lungs. Her bones knitted as his healing power coursed through her bloodstream, restoring her to her previously uninjured state. As his wife's lids twitched and her lashes fluttered, he straightened.

He lifted Sabrina into his arms so she could get a good look.

"See? Sleeping Beauty awakes."

His daughter gasped, and the arm around his neck tightened. "Oh, Papa!"

Vivian's pale silvery blue eyes cleared and zeroed in on the two of them. Her confusion fled, and in its place was horror.

She would always believe him a monster.

Damian's heart literally ached at the loss of trust between them. Neither he nor his beloved said a word, lost in the emotional torment.

Sabrina's small hand patted the side of his face and urged him to look at her. In her too-serious eyes, he saw understanding and what appeared to be compassion. The overwhelming need to declare his love for his little darling closed his throat.

She tilted her head slightly to the side and gave him a tentative smile.

"It's okay, Papa. I'll go with you."

"No!" Vivian surged up and grabbed his free arm in a death grip. "No, Damian. Don't take her from me. She's all I have left."

He easily broke her hold, then tucked Sabrina's head against his neck. With one hand rubbing her back, he murmured, "Sleep, Beastie."

She was out in an instant.

"Damian? *Please.*" Pure terror coated Vivian's plea.

Gutted by her constant distrust, he glared at her.

"You should've thought of that before you lied to me. Before you took her away and brought her here, where your horrid excuse for a sister could influence her." He leaned in slightly so Vivian was forced to meet his fierce gaze. "While you were unconscious, Josie propositioned me. She said if I let you die, we could be together. What say you to that, wife?"

"She wouldn't. You're lying to strike at me."

Hurt and betrayal flashed in her eyes, and the brilliant silver-blue dulled to a murky gray. A witch's tell was her iris color. The happier she or he was, the brighter the color. Vivian was thoroughly distraught.

"Josie would never—"

"Josie *would* and *did*," he snapped. "You know I never lie. *Never.*" He let his words sink in. "When I told you I loved you, I meant it. Yet you believed her over me. Every single time."

"But you're the Aether. If you gain Sabrina's power…" She trailed off as the truth dawned.

Damian remained quiet as she answered her own silent questions.

"You never intended to steal our baby's magic, did you?" she croaked.

"No."

"But you told me you're stronger with us by your side. I began to feel weaker by the day. If you weren't siphoning off mine to feed yours, why was I experiencing such an epic drain of my power?"

"Love makes us strong, Viv. Not the other way around. It doesn't cause the destruction of one another if it's as true as ours was." His words sank in, and tears flooded his wife's devastated eyes. Then he hammered the nail in the coffin. "If you experienced the loss of power, you should look closer to home." He didn't blink as he let it sink in. "I'm taking my daughter where she'll learn to be a proper witch."

"But I've bound her. Only my death can free her."

A half smile twisted his lips. She would find out soon enough that her binding was never going to hold Sabrina's inner Aether for long. In the meantime, he couldn't resist a parting jab. "It's a good thing I built in a contingency with the spell to take your life."

"I… was… *dead?*"

"As a doornail." He walked to the exit and picked up Sabrina's godawful lime-green suitcase. "Goodbye, Viv."

"Damian, wait!"

Her cry went unheeded. With Sabrina held tightly in his arms, he folded back the veil separating Vivian's home from his own estate, Ravenswood, four thousand miles away. Not sparing a backward glance, he stepped through the opening and sealed the rift behind him.

Vivian sat, shell-shocked, as she watched her husband and child disappear into the pulsing gold rift he'd created in space. Before she could force her body to respond to her mental commands, Damian was gone.

And Sabrina with him!

An anguished cry was torn from the deepest part of Vivian's soul.

He would never let her close to Sabrina again. Not the way they had been. Never alone together without a guard. This much she knew about the Aether—*he never made the same mistake twice.* Which meant he'd never allow Vivian back into his life.

"Sister?" Josie's cloying perfume preceded her into the room, and Vivian raised a hand to cover her nose and mouth. When had her sister started to wear such a gag-worthy scent?

"We thought you were dead!" Josie exclaimed as she moved to her side.

With an odd little jolt, Vivian recognized the calculating look in her sister's cold eyes.

When had that happened?

When had Josie turned toward darkness? Was this a trick Damian was playing on her?

As soon as the thought flitted through her mind, Vivian dismissed it. The facts were much more brutal. The moment he'd kissed her, he cursed her with clarity. Now she'd be able to see the truth behind everyone's actions, whether she wanted to or not.

Her stomach lurched.

"What have you done, Josie?" Vivian whispered achingly, fancying she could hear her heart as it cracked within her chest. "Why would you do this to me?"

Any pretense dropped away as her sister sneered. "All that

incredible strength, that beautiful man, and you have no idea what to do with him. You are *weak*."

Their sisters came in on Josie's insult, and Vivian was somewhat mollified to see their surprise, followed by a severe disapproval, take hold.

"What have you done, Josie?" Taryn demanded, anger causing her normally pleasant voice to vibrate. "If you brought the Aether's wrath to our door, I'll never forgive you."

"As if I require your forgiveness," Josie scoffed and crossed her arms over her scantily covered chest. "You walk around all day with your face crammed in a book and your head in the clouds." An ugly sneer curled her lips. "You wouldn't have known it was Beltane if we hadn't told you. And do you even remember your niece's name?"

Distress clouded Taryn's stunning visage, but it didn't last long. She was a fighter, and she intended to go down swinging. "You're so damned power hungry and sex starved that you can't see the blessings the Goddess bestowed upon you."

"Blessings? What blessings, Taryn? Please, tell me, because I don't see anything other than a decrepit old house in a podunk town, on a disappearing island, with needy-ass people." Tears filled Josie's eyes, but she angrily blinked them away. "The female-to-male ratio is three to one, and unless any of us want to steal a miserable excuse for a man away from one of the all-too-desperate women here, we are going to die old maids."

"As if you don't already steal them," Taryn muttered.

Ignoring her, Josie gestured to Vivian. "She ran away from the only good one. And why, you ask?" Her lip curled again. "She feared he'd become like his deranged mother and murder people for their magic."

"The fear *you* perpetuated, Josie!" Indignation gave Vivian the strength to stand and confront her sister. "*You!* All because you wanted Damian for yourself. But he rejected you, didn't he? How many times did you make a play for him over the years? How many times did you go behind my back?"

"I've *always* made it clear what's available should he wake up and realize you aren't enough for him, Viv." The smug grin on her face bordered grotesque. "*Always.* And are you so sure he was faithful?"

Fury consumed Vivian, making her insane with the need to strike out. Without conscious intent, she gave in to the urge and punched her sister in the nose.

Soleil screeched even as Taryn shouted a laugh, and Josie pinched her nostrils together to stem the flow of blood.

"'Bout time, Viv," her youngest sister cheered. "About damned time." To Josie, Taryn said, "If it was me, I'd throw your ass out."

"You don't need to bother. I won't stay where I'm not wanted."

Josie teleported away before the other three could comment.

Knees weak, Vivian fell back against the table. "I've been such a fool. How could I miss it?"

"No, Viv." Soleil placed a hand on her arm. "She conned us all."

"He took my daughter, Lei," she cried. "He took Sabrina."

"He'll relent in time," Taryn assured her, rubbing Vivian's back soothingly. "You just have to make him see this wasn't your doing."

"You didn't hear him. The finality in his tone. The disgust in his eyes." Shaking, Vivian swiped at the tears streaming down her cheeks. "He hates me."

"I don't believe that." Soleil shook her head and stared off into space. "He'll come around. He has to."

Vivian wasn't so sure. No one was as prideful or as uncompromising as her husband. And he'd had three years to plan his revenge.

CHAPTER 6

*D*amian experienced a pang of remorse as he watched his wife through the scrying glass. Yes, he wanted her to experience what it was like to have her spouse disappear with her beloved child into the night. Wanted her to know the helplessness and pain of betrayal. Wanted her…

Hell, he just wanted her, period. With every fiber of his miserable being. He desperately missed the sunshine of her laughter and the sparkle of mischief in her shining eyes.

"I'm hungry."

Sabrina's tentative voice brought him back to himself, and he turned to face her. She stood in the doorway, looking small and unsure. A trail of previously shed tears stained her cheeks. His heart broke all over again, but he didn't allow it to show.

"Then food you shall have, Beastie."

She cocked her head to the side and gave him a curious look. "Why do you call me that?"

"Beastie? Because when you were this big"—he bent to hold a hand down by his knee—"you were a holy terror." He grinned. "Once you'd made up your mind to do something, you did it despite my best efforts to keep you from trouble."

The hint of a smile teased her lips, but disappeared just as quickly. "Mama makes me pancakes when I'm hungry."

He barked a laugh, knowing perfectly well Vivian was the more health conscious of the two of them. If anyone was inclined to spoil Sabrina and feed her sweet tooth, it was Damian.

"Does she, now?"

"Sometimes she adds chocolate chips and whipped cream." His daughter tucked her hands behind her back and stared at the tip of her slouchy sock as she swung her foot back and forth. A sure sign she was lying.

"Come, let's go conjure your chocolate-chip pancakes."

Her chin jerked up, and she met his indulgent gaze with shock.

"Did you think I'd be a harder sell, Beastie?"

Her elfin face was scrunched in her worry, and again, Damian felt the blow to his heart.

After crossing to her, he squatted to make their faces level.

"You've naught to fear from me, my love. Regardless of what you've been told, I'm not a monster. I'm just your papa." He brushed away the single tear that trickled down her cheek. "Can you remember when you lived here before? When we would play and laugh the days away?"

She shook her head, and her lower lip trembled.

He held back his frown. Although it made sense that she couldn't remember all her time here—she'd scarcely been out of diapers, after all—he had expected her to retain *some* memories of their earlier lives. Perhaps that wasn't the way it worked with children. Having rarely been around them, he had no experience to draw from. The pain of regret lashed his very soul. He should've retrieved her immediately and not allowed Vivian to convince him Sabrina was safer away from him.

"Where do you think you developed your love of pancakes?" he teased, attempting to keep his darker emotions at bay. Chances were, she'd begin to develop her empathic ability soon, if she hadn't already when the magic infused her system earlier. "You get that from me."

The doorbell rang, indicating an unexpected visitor.

Sabrina inched closer to him.

"I think it's an old man," she whispered as if worried the visitor could hear. "I see it here, in my head." She tapped between her eyes.

Reaching out with his senses, Damian probed for the essence of the person on the other side of the front door. He smiled his pleasure, happy to see her abilities were forming as they should. "I believe you're right. Let me introduce you to Leopold." He held out a hand, silently hoping she'd take it without hesitation. When she didn't, he smiled to cover his disappointment and to ease her sense of insecurity. "It's all right, Beastie. This seems strange to you now, but you'll understand with time."

"I miss Mama."

"I know. Me, too."

"Then why can't I go home?"

Sabrina's tearful question was torturous. No sane person wanted to hurt their child this way, but he didn't have a handy answer. How did one explain adult feelings to a five and a half year old?

"Your mother and I need to work out a few logistics. We'll get there. But this is your home from now on."

Uncertainty flashed across her face, and she opened her mouth as if she wanted to say something.

He waited her out.

Finally, she nodded her head and followed him toward the front door.

"Damian! My boy!"

"It's good to see you again, Nate." Damian glanced out the door to see if Evie was with his adoptive father. She wasn't, and he swallowed his disappointment. It was harder for Evie to sneak away from her role as doty old aunt to the Drake siblings. "Or should I call you Leopold since you're in disguise?"

With a twinkle of lights, Nathanial Thorne revealed his true form, causing Sabrina to gasp.

"Never seen that done before, sweetheart?" Nate asked with a deep chuckle.

She shook her head, wonder lighting her pixyish face.

"I can teach you if you'd like. As long as your father says it's okay."

With an inquiring look, she gave Damian a shy smile. "Papa?"

"I think it's a fine idea," Damian said, trying desperately to keep the gruff emotion from his voice.

"Then moving forward, that's our plan. And you, young lady, may call me Grandpa Nate." Nathanial dropped to one knee to meet her gaze. "You don't know it, but your Papa came to live with me when he was just a bit older than you." He glanced up. "How old were you, my boy? Seven? Eight?"

"Eight."

"That's right." He winked at Sabrina. "My Evie and I raised him. Turned into a fine man, don't you think?"

She frowned up at Damian, then shrugged without speaking.

"Fine?" He forced a laugh and held out a hand to help Nate to his feet. "Are we stretching the truth now?"

"Pfft. I couldn't be prouder if you were my own son, Damian. You know Evie and I consider you ours."

The warmth of unconditional love spread through his chest. Where would he have been without the Thornes to take him in and raise him? Likely abusing his position or dead at his mother's hand back when she'd been alive and consumed by evil.

"As I consider you and Evie mine," Damian replied with a tight hug. "You're the only true family I've ever known."

After a series of rapid blinks and a hearty clearing of his throat, Nate grinned down at Sabrina. "You may not remember, but my Evie adores you. If you want to be thoroughly spoiled, I'm the one to seek out, though. Now, how about those pancakes your dad promised you?"

"How—" Damian shook his head. Appointed as Guardians by the Goddess, Nate and Evie had untold abilities. He'd probably tapped into Sabrina's tumultuous thoughts without trying.

Nate held out his hand, and she took it with no hesitation, causing Damian's stomach to flip and envy to cloud his mind. Once, she'd been free with her affection, but since living in America with her mother, his daughter was no longer the lively spirit she'd been. He only hoped he could reverse the damage losing her formative years had wrought.

"I love pancakes," Sabrina told Nate with a small smile.

"That's good to hear because I'm the best pancake maker in the land," he declared proudly.

Not one to ignore a challenge, Damian protested. "I hate to disabuse you of your notion, but *I'm* the best pancake maker in all the land."

A giggle escaped Sabrina when Nate gave him an affronted look.

"Can you believe he has the gall to claim he's number one?" Placing his palm over his heart, he shook his head and closed his eyes. "It's a good thing my sainted mother isn't here to witness such a travesty."

"Your sainted mother?" Damian laughed. "You always pull out that one whenever you know you can't win." He unbuttoned his shirt sleeves and rolled them to his elbows. "Watch and learn, old man."

"Are you challenging me to a pancake war?"

"I believe I am."

He placed a hand on Sabrina's shoulder and tried not to feel hurt when she jerked away. "We'll leave it up to Beastie to judge. What are the rules?"

"No rules. Best pancake wins," Nate replied.

They shook on it, and Nate ushered Sabrina toward the kitchen as he chatted on, insisting it was his organic, homegrown vanilla bean that made all the difference.

Following behind, Damian grinned. The more time spent in Nate's company, the more talkative Sabrina became. It was as if his adoptive father had known exactly what she needed, just like he'd instinctively known what Damian needed as an orphaned boy.

"It's no use, Viv. You can't get through his wards." Taryn's sympathetic look was a kick in the gut.

Refusing to shed the tears building behind her lids, Vivian nodded and swiped the back of her wrist over her brow to wipe away the sweat. "Thanks for trying. I'll call him again. Perhaps he'll pick up this time."

Soleil hugged her. "He'll relent. A child belongs with their mother."

"I don't know, Lei. I let Josie convince me he was evil incarnate, and I ran away with his child. Then, I bound Sabrina's powers and lied to him. I told him she had none, so she'd be safe from him." Vivian sniffed. "He's been denied his daughter for three years. I doubt he'll forgive me for my lack of trust."

"He will," Soleil insisted. "And you gave him access to see her through scrying. He has to understand you did what you thought best. Just give him a few days to calm down. Think of it as shared custody and Sabrina is spending this week with her father."

"How do you always remain so positive?" Vivian shook her head and gave her sister a rueful look.

With a single-shoulder shrug, Soleil smiled. "I'm just blessed, I guess."

"Have you never seen her lose her shit over a wilting orchid, Viv?" After rolling her eyes hard enough to see her brain, Taryn snuffed out the candles and collected them.

Laughter came unbidden, and Vivian was surprised she could feel anything after such a heart-wrenching and emotionally draining day. "I honestly don't know what I'd do without the two of you."

"It's a good thing you'll never have to find out." Soleil followed up with a squeeze of Vivian's hand. "Would you like me to call him?"

"As tempting as it is, no. I'm the one who made a mess of this. I'll be the one to fix it."

"Sabrina will understand, sister. And if I know my niece, she'll pester Damian to death until he relents."

"Lei has a point, Viv." Taryn grinned. "Your kid is a force to be reckoned with. Like her awesome mom."

"Yeah, I only have to keep the faith. Easier said than done. But we need to discover why Josie betrayed us the way she did."

With a snort, Taryn led the way down the stairs from the attic. "It isn't enough that she's a tramp?"

"Don't slut shame," Viv scolded absently. Taryn had sexual appetites like any of them, but her excessive dislike of what she believed were Josie's "loose ways" always triggered her scorn. "If it was a guy pulling the same crap, would you feel that way about him?"

Her sister stopped short and turned around, jutting her chin in the air. "Yes! Because it isn't about scratching an itch. Josie always has to push boundaries, and she doesn't care whose partner she's sleeping with, male or female. It's like she's got a vendetta against happiness, hers or anyone else's."

Frowning, Viv considered Taryn's reply. She glanced back at Soleil, who simply raised her dark brows. "You agree?"

"I do. You weren't always here, but for the last three and a half years, possibly longer, she's been determined to sabotage people's relationships. She slept with Taryn's—"

"Lei!"

"I'm sorry, T, but she did, and Viv should know the truth." Soleil passed Vivian on the steps and hugged their youngest sister. "You cared about Morgan. She had no right to do that to you, and I get why you're constantly angry with her."

"Oh, Taryn!" Vivian felt sick to her stomach that she'd missed her sister's pain because she was too wrapped up in her own. "I'm so sorry."

"It was nothing, Viv. Morgan wasn't worth the heartache. Not if he could be so easily swayed by a pretty face and a hot-as-fuck body."

"Have you seen yourself?" Scoffing, Soleil shook her head. "You've got it all over Josie, sister. She doesn't hold a candle to your looks. None of us do."

When Taryn opened her mouth to object, Vivian cut her off. "It's true. You're the true smoking-hot Stephens sister. The rest of us are attractive, but you... Girlfriend, you're the shit!"

After her initial shock wore off, Taryn laughed. "Shut up. Let's go find Josie. We'll tie her up in the attic if we have to, but I want to know what her drastic change is all about."

"You don't think it's magical in nature, do you?"

Thoughtful expressions crossed her sisters' faces. Finally, Soleil answered. "It would make the most sense, unless someone broke her heart and she's allowed her bitterness to fester. But you know Josie, she keeps her cards close to her chest."

"Then we definitely need to discover the root cause. Despite what she's done, we need to help her if we can."

"Good luck," Taryn muttered.

CHAPTER 7

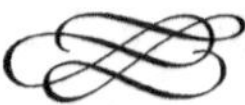

$\mathcal{A}$s Josie paced the bell tower chamber just below the belfry, she allowed her frustration to take hold. Once again, she'd failed in seducing the Aether to her side. This time, with drastic results. Vivian had somehow seen through her act to the truth, or rather enough of the truth to know Josie had designs on Damian.

She shuddered.

Not by choice.

The Aether scared the ever-loving hell out of her. Yet she needed his amped-up abilities to block the evil stalking her.

"Josephine."

Correction, the evil that had found her.

Pasting on a welcoming smile and trying to mask the sick dread consuming her, Josie turned toward the approaching warlock.

Morgan Black.

The name he preferred over the Welsh one he'd been born with, Morcant Thywyll. There was meaning in a name, and she intended to find out why he shunned his. It could be he was simply trying to stay off everyone's radar. But perhaps if she discovered his deepest secret, it would lead her to his weakness and she'd find a way out of her predicament.

The evil fucker had been around almost as long as Damian. At least a hundred and seventy years, if he was a day, Morgan had grown in magical strength, and Josie wasn't sure how he'd achieved it. After a particularly tedious night between the sheets, he'd boasted about avoiding detection by the Witches' Council by faking his death a time or ten. But he'd never told her exactly how.

Because he monitored her actions, he felt free to confess to a few heinous crimes in his past that would require him to stay hidden. Perhaps it was to instill fear in her, which he had, or perhaps he thought she was as lacking in morals as he was, which she wasn't, but nevertheless, he loved to brag.

Thank the Goddess she'd been able to save Taryn from his clutches. Had he succeeded in turning her sister toward the darkness, Josie would never have been able to forgive herself.

Sidling up to him, she planted a boner-raising kiss on him. His thin, cruel mouth opened under hers, and she tried to hold back a gag as the rising smell of decay filled her nostrils.

Goddess! She needed a shower after every touch from his corpse-like hand. How he'd managed to glamour long enough to fool Taryn, or any other unsuspecting witch, Josie would never know.

She'd seen through him from day one, and all her attempts to alter Taryn's opinion of him had fallen on deaf ears. It was as if her sister had been spellbound. Soleil, too, for that matter. Both of them had thought the sun rose and set with the man. They'd raved about his handsome face, his bodybuilder physique, and his charming manners. None of which Josie saw. The one time she'd tried to talk to Vivian, she failed. Viv had been just as enchanted with Damian, and it hadn't sat well with Josie.

"Morgan, darling. I've missed you," she purred, waiting for the lightning bolt to strike her lying ass dead.

If her ancestors in the Otherworld could see her now, they'd be weeping copious amounts of tears for the sinner in their descendants' midst. The Stephens were pillars of the witch community and held to a higher standard. Or so her parents had loved to drill into her head whenever she didn't walk the straight and narrow.

"Did you, pet? I wonder."

Her blood turned to ice in her veins, but she never lost her seductive mask.

Please, Goddess, tell me he didn't acquire the ability to read minds!

"Of course I did, darling." She cast him a coquettish smile, batting her lashes and praying it wasn't over the top.

"Where is the child?" he asked, his tone silky and menacing. "You were meant to bring her to the festival."

Josie inhaled sharply and almost choked on her own spit.

"The Aether came for her, Morgan." Internally cringing at the hint of fear in her voice, she stepped away from him with a careless shrug. "We'll have to find another way."

She hadn't anticipated his instantaneous rage or the whiplash she received when he gripped her hair and flung her to the floor.

"You had one job, Josephine. *One.*" Each step he took toward her echoed through the chamber with sinister intent. "To bring the girl to me."

He held out a hand as if he intended to help Josie up, and though she knew it was a mistake not to teleport away immediately, she needed to find out his plans for Sabrina before she could. No way was this asswipe going to hurt her niece.

Placing her hand in his, she smiled up at him. "I still intend to, darling."

For a man with bony limbs, he packed a punch, and the one he delivered to her left eye had her seeing stars as it broke the orbital bone.

"Not good enough, you bitch!"

He followed the punch with a kick to her ribs, and Josie curled into a ball to protect herself as best she could. Envisioning the coast of France, her cells warmed. The first opportunity she got, she'd warn Damian, but in the meantime, she needed to teleport to safety.

She hadn't expected to land in deeper shit.

Damian stared down at Josie, his arms crossed and brows raised. When her swelling eye and the gingerly way she held her ribs became apparent, it registered she needed his help. It required all his willpower, but he managed to refrain from rushing to assist her. First, she needed to confess to whatever games she was playing, then he'd let his protective nature take over.

All the while he and Nate had been entertaining Sabrina with their pancake contest, Damian had a niggling feeling he'd missed something about Josie's seductive performance when she believed he'd killed Vivian. It finally dawned on him. Her overtures were exactly that. A performance. He'd felt no desirous intent behind the action. No real concern for Vivian's welfare. It was as if Josie had already known he would never take her offer or let Viv die.

"Why are you here, Josie?"

She glanced around as if confused.

"I thought I was heading to France," she muttered with an edge of disgust in her tone.

He barely suppressed a chuckle. She was fiery to the end.

"Care to tell me who did that to you?"

Tenderly, she probed her eye socket and sighed. Without answering, she rolled, placing her hands on the stone beneath her and pushing up to her knees. Unable to take another second of her painful progress, Damian gripped her elbows and helped her rise.

She was quick to step back, all pretense of a femme fatale gone.

"Thanks."

"You still didn't answer my question, Josie."

"Morgan."

It only took a brief moment for him to remember the man Taryn had dated.

"I didn't realize you'd taken up with him, other than the one time you foiled your sister's relationship."

She didn't reply and merely lifted her chin. The defiant gesture was similar to Sabrina's when she was hurting, and Damian experienced a pang. Josie, whatever her faults, appeared to be misunderstood.

"What's going on?" he asked coolly, hoping to frighten her into a confession.

She blanched but firmed her resolve. "Nothing."

"Give me your hand," he ordered.

Alarmed, her gaze shot to his. All the smooth sophistication and practiced seduction she wore like a cloak was gone. In its place was apprehension.

"Josie, it isn't a request."

Closing her eyes, she inhaled deeply, then winced and grabbed her ribs.

"He'll kill me if I tell you, Damian."

"Are you sure I won't if you don't?"

He wouldn't, but he wasn't beyond putting the fear of death into someone.

Heaving a tired sigh, she raised weary eyes to his. "He's evil."

"I believe that's a given, considering he struck you and broke your ribs."

With a nod, she limped over to the patio set and sank down with a gasp.

Unable to take another second of her discomfort, Damian strode forward.

"If you don't want me to know what's going on, blank your mind. But give me your damned hand, Josie."

"Why?"

"So I can heal you."

Her amber eyes shimmered with tears she was too stubborn to shed.

"Thank you, Damian." Placing her hand in his, she shut her lids and let her other arm fall to her side.

Recalling the spellwork his mother had taught him from an early age, Damian summoned the enchantment from deep within his cells and drew a series of sigils in the air around her. Taking the time to merge with her energy, he used his to slide over her from head to toe, testing the battered bone and tissue. When he was confident there were no life-threatening injuries, he began the healing process of knitting her eye socket and ribs, calming any inflammation he encountered, and providing an extra boost of health through her system.

"Better?"

"I wish I knew how to do that," she murmured.

Pulling out a chair across from her, he sank down and crossed one leg over the other. After hooking his arm over the back of the seat, he asked, "Do you have a desire to become a physician, Josie?"

"Not necessarily, but it's a handy ability to have."

He grinned, unable to help himself. She was deeper than anyone gave her credit for, himself included. With Vivian around, he'd never been able to look at anyone else or delve into their psyche. Never cared to, because his wife fascinated him to the point of distraction.

"Tell me about this Morgan."

She frowned. "You've never met him?"

"No. I always believed it was poor timing, but now, after"—he motioned to her with a swirl of his finger in her direction—"I think there is something more sinister at play. As if he's been avoiding me." He cocked his head. "Am I right?"

"Yes."

"What's his full name?"

"He goes by Morgan Black, but his real name is Morcant Thywyll."

Damian swore viciously but smothered his annoyance when Josie winced in pain.

"Sorry. Are you *certain* it's Morcant Thywyll?"

"He didn't tell me, but I overheard one of his asshat friends call him that."

"Trust me, they weren't friends. Morcant doesn't inspire that type of loyalty." He watched her for a moment, absorbing the emotions she tried to hide from him. The fear, the worry, and the fierce protectiveness.

"Who were you trying to protect, Josie?" he asked, not unkindly.

"My sisters." Lifting her sincere gaze to meet his, she added, "Sabrina."

It took an effort, but he quelled his swift rage, or at least enough to not hurt Josie.

"How does he know about my daughter?"

"Taryn and Soleil." The second she saw the thundercloud forming overhead, she held up her hands. "They didn't tell on purpose, Damian. I swear. It's like he had them under a spell. They couldn't see through his glamour."

"Glamour?"

"To Taryn and Soleil, he appeared to be a damned Adonis. It was freaky. I think he fooled Viv, too."

He frowned as he watched the distaste flash across her lovely face. "But not you?"

"No. Never once. I couldn't understand what my sisters saw in the creepy fucker."

"How did you get him away from them?"

Her expression dropped to one of hopelessness.

"Josie?"

"I seduced him, and in doing that, I somehow chained myself to him. He eventually finds me wherever I go."

CHAPTER 8

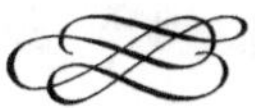

"*Bloody hell!*"

"Damian, I'm sorry." Josie jumped to her feet. "I'll go to France right now. Maybe he didn't pick up on this location."

"You'll do no such thing," he growled. "You're going to stay right here and tell me everything you know and why he tried to seduce Taryn."

"He thought she was the weak link in our family."

"Taryn?" Damian actually chuckled. "Did he not research your family first?"

"Well, Viv was in love with you. I'm rebellious. And Soleil…"

What could she say that wouldn't sound derogatory about her flighty sister? Soleil loved her plants and romance novels. Technically, she should've been the easier to lure to Morgan's side, but he'd once claimed he didn't have it in him to seduce a "fatty."

Josie had wanted to rip his eyes out with her fingernails, but she'd laughingly agreed with him that Lei was the most unattractive and could stand to lose weight. Personally, Josie thought her sister was perfect just the way she was, but of course, she couldn't reveal that in any way. She'd gone so far as to mock Lei whenever Morgan was visiting.

The hurt on her sister's face wounded Josie's soul.

"Say no more." A grim smile tightened Damian's mouth.

"Soleil is beautiful, Damian." Where she found the courage to snap at him, Josie would never know, but she was floored when he grinned.

"I never thought otherwise. However, I'm happy you recognize her worth."

"I always have," she said quietly. "I just wish she knew that."

"She will. You'll tell her when this is over."

"If I survive Morgan."

"I'm going to make it my mission to see you do, Josie. I promise."

Tears burned her eyes. It was the second time she'd almost cried in the Aether's presence, and she didn't understand why she was so emotional. The last time she wept was the day of her parents' funeral, twenty-two years ago. As an eighteen-year-old girl left to care for her teenage sisters, she'd been distraught and scared shitless.

But they'd made it work.

In recent years, she'd tried to distance herself, allowing her siblings to take over more responsibilities by acting as if she were too good to run the family store. She wanted to make sure they didn't rely on her, but on themselves, should anything happen to her like it had their parents.

She was doubly glad she did because she'd never anticipated Morgan.

"Tell me everything."

She did. Whatever she recalled, she regurgitated and let Damian draw his own conclusions.

Horrific tales of Isolde de Thorne had prompted Josie to protect Vivian and Sabrina on her own. She didn't care for the way her sister had become so enthralled with the Aether or how quickly it had happened. It was as if Viv was under a spell. Belatedly, Josie realized she should've never tried to save them without getting to know Damian better, but the man was reclusive by nature. Although courteous, he'd never been overly friendly with Josie or her sisters. His primary focus was always Vivian.

Josie could admit she was probably wrong about him. Yes, Damian was one scary motherfucker. But he'd healed her when he could've left her to suffer. He'd resurrected Vivian when he could've easily left her to her fate and absconded with Sabrina, as he would've, had he truly desired her abilities. And now, he was offering to shield Josie when anyone else would've told her to fuck all the way off after what she'd done.

She'd misjudged him.

"First things first. We need to get your family here," Damian said after a long silence. "They aren't safe from Morcant. He'd just as soon kill them to steal their magic as look at them."

"Why do you think he hasn't already?"

"My protection wards—" Swearing viciously, he stared at her with something akin to horror. "I destroyed them to bring Sabrina home. Do you know if your sisters restored them?"

Josie's heart seized in her chest. Her only thought was to get to her sisters before Morgan, and she teleported straightaway.

The sight greeting her was terrifying. Viv, Taryn, and Soleil were all physically bound to chairs centered in their living room. Two additional chairs remained, and Josie could only assume one was for her. But who was the fifth one for? Damian? Sabrina?

"Ah! Josephine, you're just in time," Morcant said as if he were hosting a tea party.

Vivian was fucking terrified—and heartsick. Morgan, that lying sack of shit, wanted her daughter and was willing to sacrifice her entire family to do it. It wasn't surprising someone from outside her circle would betray her, but her own sister? When had Josie become so self-centered and evil that she'd contrive to hurt a child?

Hatred burned in Vivian's chest, and she'd never believed she was the type of person to despise another. Yet she did. Oh, she might not murder her sister outright—unless she had no choice—but she would definitely cut Josie out of her life for good, with a middle finger raised to show she meant business.

Vivian could only pray Damian would protect Sabrina as she'd so foolishly believed she could. Thank the Goddess he'd come when he did, foiling Morgan's plan. Trying to shove down the overwhelming angst she was feeling, Vivian sat straighter and stared coldly at Josie. If it weren't for the gag, she'd curse her sister to hell.

As if he could read her thoughts, Morgan slowly faced her and smiled.

She shuddered.

With his glamour gone, he was gruesome. His hollowed-out features, sunken eyes, and pallid skin were positively frightening, and Morgan was a far cry from the handsome character he'd presented himself as when he was wooing Taryn. What the hell did Josie see in him?

Their gazes locked, and firm understanding took root in Vivian's mind.

Josie had done it for them! She'd seen through the glamour all along and found him just as distasteful as Vivian did.

Thank you for your gift of insight, Damian.

"You're welcome, my love."

At first, she was convinced she'd imagined his voice, but the warming sensation she always experienced in his presence settled over her, and she *knew* he was close. Purposefully blanking her mind, she gave a nearly imperceptible nod in case he was watching her.

"Beastie is safe," he whispered to her.

Vivian almost jumped when she felt his invisible hand brush her shoulder.

How did you read my mind? You've never been able to before.

"Sabrina's power." When she tensed, his fingers tightened on her shoulder. "Not like that, Viv. She and Nate gave my magic a boost when I prepared to come here."

You're not really here right now?

"Yes and no. I'm here through you. Different than a standard cloaking spell." His lips felt as if they were a hairsbreadth from her temple, as if he wanted to kiss her but held himself in check. "You are about to experience the magic of an Aether. Be prepared to let me take over. Can you do that?"

If it will save my family, yes.

"Courageous to the last."

A compliment? Perhaps, but she didn't have time to mull it over. Morgan was stalking Josie around the circle. When her sister passed by, Vivian felt the bonds at her wrists loosen.

"Why hasn't Damian followed you?" Morgan asked. For a second, she thought he was questioning *her*, but his focus was locked on Josie, who kept a healthy distance from him. "That's where you went, isn't it? To seduce your sister's husband and get him to heal you?" Morgan narrowed his beady eyes. "Looks like it worked."

"She sought help, Viv. All isn't what it seems. Don't be taken in by his lies again," Damian warned.

His lies? Not Josie's?

"I'll explain when this is over, but for now..."

Her husband's spirit stepped into Vivian's body. It was the only way to describe the shocking merging of his abilities with hers. Incapable of hiding her reaction, she convulsed. Her cells weren't made to accept the type of power Damian's held.

"What the fuck is wrong with her?" Morgan demanded.

Her sisters all stared as if they'd never witnessed a seizure before. Maybe they hadn't, but either way, it was scary as hell. Both for them and for Vivian, who couldn't seem to get control of her own limbs.

"Let go, my love," Damian encouraged.

She did just that. She simply inhaled deeply and mentally stepped away from herself. It seemed to do the trick, and as her spirit watched from a safe place in the corner, the bonds dropped and her body surged to its feet with Damian at the helm.

With no warning, the entire house went dark, and lightning continually crackled in the room, giving it an eerie blue cast.

Morgan's thin-set, small eyes grew three times their size, practically bugging out of his skull-like head as Damian gathered the molecules from the air. He wasn't fast enough to escape the wrath of the Aether, and a bolt hit him center mass before he could get away.

Like Vivian a minute earlier, Morgan's body convulsed as it absorbed the impact. The smell of burning flesh drifted to the others. Taryn's and Soleil's skin turned a sickly shade since they were unable to cover their noses and mouths to avoid the ghastly smell.

"Now, Alastair!" Damian shouted through her.

From nowhere, Alastair Thorne appeared and clapped manacles around Morgan's wrists.

Josie dashed to Taryn and untied her bonds, then did the same for Soleil. Grasping their hands, she jerked them up and ran for the exit.

"No!" Soleil pulled back. "We can't leave Viv."

"That's not Viv," Josie replied in a low voice. "She's exchanged places with Damian."

"What the fuck—"

Slapping her hand over Taryn's mouth, Josie scowled. "Shhh! Let's get to safety, and I'll explain everything."

"Not that, Josie," Soleil whispered. *"That!"*

Vivian spun back to see the chains drop from Morgan's hands.

"That shouldn't be possible." Josie wasted no time and ran forward to stand beside Damian and Alastair. "How did he do that?"

"He's stronger than I expected," Damian replied grimly. "Al, get the women to safety."

"They can do that on their own, Dethridge. I'm not leaving you."

"Go, you stubborn bastard. I can't remain in Vivian's body for long." He shot Alastair a grim look. "That means you and Nate are Beastie's protectors."

"I don't understand," Josie said frantically.

Not bothering to spare her a look, Alastair said, "He'll be left weak, but he'll return to save your sister. With Morgan's heightened powers, he might be able to defeat Damian and Vivian."

From her corner, Vivian hugged herself. No way was she allowing this to happen. Thinking about Sabrina, she allowed her spirit to find her daughter.

CHAPTER 9

From where she sat on the floor and played with her dolls, Sabrina glanced up the moment Vivian's spirit arrived.

"Can you see me, baby?"

Her daughter nodded.

"You have to help your father. I don't think he's strong enough inside my body. My magic is considerably less than his."

"What can I do, Mama?"

Vivian squatted and lifted her hand, intending to stroke her daughter's cheek, but in her celestial state, she had no form. Frustrated, she sighed.

"You're the Oracle. Can you not see what's going to happen?"

Sabrina's dark eyes looked haunted as she gazed back at her. "Morcant is a bad man."

"Morcant? Do you mean Morgan?" After her daughter nodded, Vivian replied, "Yes, he is, baby."

"Do you want to take Papa's body to him? I can help you."

Vivian had seriously underestimated her daughter's abilities when she'd thought she could bind her magic. "Wait, you mean take Damian's body to *him*, not to Morgan, right?"

"I can go with you and Grandpa Nate."

"It's not safe for you." The fear she was experiencing turned crippling. How did she save Damian and protect her child at the same time?

"You can't, Vivian," Nathanial said from behind her after reading her troubled mind.

She whirled to face him. "You can see me, too? How did I not know this was possible for all of you?"

He shrugged, but half his mouth curled in a mocking smile.

"Never mind." She waved a hand as she approached him. "Damian's in serious trouble."

"Stay here. *Both* of you." With a stern look for Sabrina, he teleported away.

"Where do you think he went?" Vivian asked her.

"To get Grandma Evie." With a shrug, Sabrina picked up her doll and beheaded it. "That's what he's going to do to Morcant."

Shocked and more than a little horrified, Vivian collapsed on the carpet and stared at her. "You received a vision?"

"Morcant must die, Mama. Grandma Evie knows, and she hates him."

She stared at her daughter helplessly. "Do I return Damian's body? Are you safe here alone?" She was incredibly confused and terrified for her sisters. "And why am I asking a child?"

A twinkle lit Sabrina's near-black eyes, lightening them and making the silvery flecks more noticeable.

"Because I'm the Oracle now, Mama," she said as she cocked her head. "Grandpa Nate is waiting for you in your bedroom."

"My...? The one here or at home?"

"They look the same." Waving her hand, Sabrina repaired her doll and returned to playing.

"Logic tells me Damian's body is here, so let's go that route." Closing her eyes, Vivian visualized the primary suite she'd shared while living here. Sure enough, Nate and Evie were in deep discussion as they stood guard over Damian's physical form.

"I think I'm meant to inhabit Damian for the teleport," she told them. "Which one of you is staying with Sabrina?"

"Neither," Evie replied. "You will, in his body." She nodded to the bed. "There's enough juice left for you to maintain the wards here in case Morcant gets through us."

"Morcant? That was the same name Sabrina used. I thought his name was Morgan."

"He's one and the same."

If she were corporeal, Vivian's heart would be in her throat and her stomach would be churning. As it was, her ghostly energy was abuzz with anxiety. "How long do I need to inhabit Damian's body?"

"As long as you need to. Ten minutes or ten years," Nate said grimly. "You can conjure whatever you need to survive, but never leave these grounds should Damian not return. Sabrina will be strong enough to take over after she reaches her majority."

"You're scaring me!"

"You should be scared. Morcant is a rotten sonofabitch." Evie exchanged a wary glance with her husband. "He's also a con man, Vivian. A shapeshifter of sorts, capable of glamouring into whatever he wishes you to see. Very few are able to discern the real warlock from the one he presents. Trust no one who approaches you, even if you believe they are your friend."

"Will Sabrina be able to tell the difference?" Please, let it be so.

"She should, but I don't know. We've no more time to waste," Nate said. "You need to possess Damian's body."

"I don't know how."

He held out a hand. "Place your palm over mine."

Vivian did as he ordered, and she could feel the pulsing power wrap around her as she connected with his aura.

"Concentrate, and imagine yourself merging with him. Your body filling his."

She did, but the result was unexpected.

In a flash, she was facing down Morgan.

Weak from the energy exchange, Vivian blacked out.

Damian came to the moment his spirit entered his physical form.

"Goddammit! What did you do?" he thundered. "Where's Vivian?"

Evie gave her husband a small shove. "Go, Nate! Take Damian. I'll protect Sabrina."

Nathanial shook his head. "The wards…"

"I'll weave a layer over top of the old ones, and I'll take Sabrina to the Goddess if they fail. Go!"

The sight of Damian's petite adoptive mother pushing around the towering form of Nate was amusing. He might've laughed had he not been so fucking worried about Vivian and Alastair.

"Let's go, Nate. Time is of the essence."

"You should go *after* him, Grandpa Nate," Sabrina piped in.

Damian crossed to the doorway and knelt in front of her. "What did you see, Beastie?"

"He needs to cloak and take the long sword from your special room." Wide-eyed, his daughter watched him as if she feared he'd not take her seriously.

"And if he does? What's he to do?"

Lifting her doll, she snapped the head off.

"Morcant is a bad, bad man, Papa," she whispered.

"That he is, my love." He brushed the black curls from her brow. "Anything else to give us the upper hand?"

With shining eyes, she shook her head.

"Stay with Grandma Evie. She'll take care of you if I don't return."

A stiff wind could've knocked Damian over when she flung herself at him and wrapped her arms tightly around his neck. "Watch out for the potion, Papa."

"Potion?"

"He makes smoke with it, and people get weak."

"Duly noted." After kissing her temple, he hugged her to him. "Go with Evie, Beastie."

"I don't like the sound of the potion. What do you suppose is in it?" Nate asked after Evie and Sabrina exited the room.

"Doesn't matter. We'll have a protection spell at the ready."

"But if it seeps into the skin? And what about the others?"

"Christ, Nate! One problem at a time. Go retrieve my grandfather Stephan's sword—the one in my ceremony room—and join me at Vivian's place. Her room is identical to this one. Teleport there and cloak yourself before coming downstairs." Damian rubbed the spot between his eyes, trying to disperse his tension. "Perhaps you'll get the jump on Morcant, that wily bastard."

"Go. I'll be there momentarily."

Damian arrived to see all five chairs filled and a gloating Morcant standing in the center of the circle with his arms crossed and a smug expression on his grotesque face.

"Good of you to return, Aether."

"I realized I forgot something," he replied flippantly with a careless shrug. A fleeting side glance showed Vivian was out cold, but he suppressed the concern. Rage radiated off Alastair, and the air around him crackled with his indignant energy.

Years ago, Damian and Alastair had created matching pinky rings with tanzanite stones to boost telepathic communication for situations like these. Hoping their bond was still working, Damian spoke through their link. *Take it down, Al. He's an Arcane Devourer and feeds off the strife.*

Alastair immediately stilled and shot him a sharp look. His nod was barely perceptible but a definite signal he understood.

"I suppose I never got around to asking what you were after, Morcant." Damian wandered over to the chairs, testing for magical traps. Feeling none, he ventured closer.

"Isn't it obvious? As much power as I can amass. I'll start with yours, and then take theirs." A grin of pure evil intent curled his misshapen mouth. "Then I'll go for your daughter's."

Ruthlessly, Damian cut off his rush of fury. If he gave in to it or the fear for Sabrina or Vivian, Morcant would feast on it as he had with Alastair's anger.

"Why?" Damian asked simply. Seeing he'd disconcerted Morcant, he elaborated. "I don't understand why everyone feels this endless need to obtain more than their fair share of magic. Of anything, really. When is enough, enough?"

"Spoken like someone who's held all the power for centuries." A sneer curled Morcant's thin lips. "One who can give or take what isn't theirs with a snap of the fingers and who's held the favor of the gods and goddesses."

"Perhaps they favor me because I don't abuse my gifts."

"What about these women?" Morcant pointed at Alastair. "Or him? They haven't abused their gifts, but they're not going to live forever like you or me."

"I'd hardly say Al hasn't crossed the line, but I understand what you mean." As Damian edged closer, he called to mind a protection bubble for himself and the others in the room. "Really, though, who wants to live forever, Morcant? Do you honestly believe Alastair hasn't already seen enough tragedy and sadness to last him an eternity?"

"But I live for the tragedy and sadness, as well you know."

Nodding, Damian acknowledged the claim. "You're the first person I've encountered who's able to feed on another's negative energy. How did you come by this extraordinary ability?"

The megalomaniac's cruel eyes narrowed briefly as if he couldn't understand Damian's lack of reaction. "Radioactive spider. Similar to Spiderman."

Damian laughed. He'd forgotten how quick-witted the man was. "Good one. But you're aware, whatever your superpowers, you can't defeat me, correct? I was designed by the deities for the sole purpose of neutralizing villains like you, Morcant."

"But you're as human as the rest of us, Dethridge." The man produced a small bottle and shuffled closer to Vivian. Inside the glass, the liquid churned, crashing against the sides as if attempting to escape its confines. "With hopes and dreams, feelings of affection, no?"

Again, Damian suppressed his unease. This was the potion

Sabrina had warned him about. Casually, he clasped his hands behind his back and shrugged, as if choosing to ignore the implied threat to his wife. "I am human, yes. Harder to kill than most, but for someone as determined as you, it's doable."

"I want to repair my body. With your heightened abilities, I can heal myself."

"Your human form is wasting away, Morcant. You were never meant to live as long as you have. Even my magic can't fix you for long."

Waving the bottle of poison around like a drunken sailor with a tankard of rum, he gestured to Damian. "I'm going to cry foul, Aether. Look at you. You appear no older than thirty-five, and yet you're at least three decades beyond me in years. I can be young, too."

"That's not how it works." Placing his palm on Alastair's shoulder, Damian removed the spell holding his ropes in place. Adding a little charge to Al's already formidable gifts, he encased his friend in the invisible protection bubble. Next, he sauntered to Taryn and did the same. "Being an Aether requires your DNA to be altered from a normal human. Anything you steal from me would cause you to age even faster than you are, since you don't have that altered DNA."

"I don't believe you," Morcant snapped. "And I know what you're doing. Stop now, or I explode this bottle in your wife's pretty face. You wouldn't want to see her marred, would you?"

"Estranged wife," Damian replied dispassionately. A pang struck his heart as he saw Vivian's lids flutter open and hurt fill those glorious eyes of hers.

Cocking his head, the other man studied him. "Do you feel her pain, Dethridge? I do. It's like ambrosia." Breathing deeply, Morcant smiled. "Pure ambrosia. Oh, and the strength it gives me."

"I'm surprised Viv can be upset by me at all. She has ice in her veins and feels nothing at all." Damian hoped like hell she'd take the hint and shut down any stronger emotion.

Soleil, who'd been silent until that moment, gasped. "That's cruel, Damian, even for you."

"But accurate," he said, as if bored by the conversation.

Understanding dawned in Vivian's ice-blue eyes, and she shot a quelling glance at Soleil. "Don't waste your outrage, sister. For as many women as Damian's had, I'm surprised he can keep all our names straight."

Well done, my dear!

As if out on a morning stroll, he casually circled the ring of chairs and paused next to her. With his knuckle, he tilted her chin up. "I'll always remember you, Vivian. You are, after all, the mother of my Beastie."

Bending, he kissed her, infusing her body with a preemptive antidote for any toxin Morcant intended to unleash.

He lifted his head. "Mm, yes. I'll most definitely remember you, my love."

CHAPTER 10

Not only did Damian's spell sizzle Vivian's cells, but so did his steamy-as-fuck kiss. Breathless, she could only stare when he raised his head and winked.

"Mm, yes. I'll most definitely remember you, my love."

Goddess, how she wished it was so.

With one last lingering brush of his fingertips across her lips, he moved away.

"I'm not a fool, Aether," Morcant hissed. "I know what you're doing. Trying to calm everyone. Provide protection." He gestured with his head toward Alastair. "Set them free."

"I never mistook you for a fool, Morcant. Not once," Damian replied smoothly. "But I'd be remiss if I didn't protect my own."

Lifting the bottle high, Morcant shook it. "This isn't just to poison you all. It's to separate you from your magic. Long enough that I can claim it for my own."

Vivian's heart rate rocketed straight into the stratosphere the second Nate appeared on the stairway. Those old steps creaked most times, and he was seconds from giving himself away.

"How do you hope to hold all that you steal, Morgan?" she asked coolly. "You're *two steps* from the grave, you creaky old fool."

She purposely used the insult she'd previously heard Evie jokingly hurl at Nate.

From her peripheral, she saw him pause, glance down, then look at her.

She nodded vigorously. "Yes, you heard me correctly. So, Morgan, you may hold the advantage now, but how long before your muscles atrophy and your fetid breath precedes your arrival?"

"Long enough, you ignorant bitch!" Spittle gathered at the sides of Morcant's mouth, and he reminded Vivian of a rabid animal.

"No name-calling, Morcant," Alastair said as he shifted in his seat. Dropping the pretense of being tied, he straightened his suit jacket and tugged each of his cuffs. "It only shows your lack of intelligence, man."

Josie, too, dropped the act of being bound and rose to her feet to approach Morcant. "And I don't particularly care for people calling my sisters 'bitch,'" she snarled.

Vivian wondered if he ever saw the punch coming.

One moment, he was glaring down at Josie, and the next, his head was snapping back from the force of her blow.

"Suppress your anger, Josie," Damian warned. "Remember, it strengthens him."

Seeming to recognize he was outnumbered, Morcant threw the bottle and turned to run.

Time froze for everyone but Damian, Nate, and Vivian.

"Get the bottle, Viv. And for the love of the Goddess, don't drop it," her husband ordered.

Shaking off the oddity of movement when everyone around her was locked in place, she rushed to comply as her husband approached Morcant.

"Off with his head, Nate."

Just as Nate was poised to strike, time snapped back with a deafening pop.

Morcant disappeared.

"*Fuck!*"

They all felt the sting of Damian's blinding fury. It seared the skin without ever causing physical damage.

"Darling, you're hurting us," Vivian said, hoping to remind him how deadly his unleashed anger could be.

Stalking to her, he yanked the small jar from her hand and hauled her against him. Embracing her seemed to calm him, and because she needed the contact, too, she held on and didn't object. Despite their differences, he appeared to still care about her welfare, and for that, she was eternally grateful.

"What do you intend to do with that?" Vivian asked softly.

"I'd pour it down the drain, but it might rust the pipes."

She laughed. "I suppose we can't bury it in the backyard?"

"Actually, that's not a bad idea." Soleil approached and held out her hand. "Will you trust me to take care of it, Damian?"

Indecision was written on his breathtakingly handsome face, but it didn't detract from his good looks. Finally coming to a decision, he handed her sister the bottle.

"I'd suggest a volcano," Josie quipped.

Grinning, Soleil nodded. "I know exactly which one would work."

"Won't that produce a gas?" Alastair shared a concerned look with Nate. "I'm no scientist, but how do you plan to get away in time?"

"Throw and teleport?" Soleil shrugged.

A glittering light flooded the room and took the shape of a petite woman. In the next instant, the newcomer stood at the base of the stairs, a few steps below Nate.

"Evie!" Damian abandoned Vivian and rushed to greet her. "You should never have left the protective wards of Ravenswood! Where's my daughter?"

"I came for the poison, Damian. Give it to me so I may destroy it."

Right when Soleil would've handed it to her, Vivian stepped in her path.

"That's not Evie."

Damian reached the same conclusion, and he backed away with a nod to Nate. With one hefty swing and a pained frown, the Guardian decapitated Morcant.

"Clean up on aisle ten," Josie muttered.

After the body was removed, probably to be dumped in a volcano, and after Vivian assured herself Sabrina was all right, she joined Damian in the sitting room of Ravenswood.

He handed her a glass of wine and toasted her with his brandy.

Curling up on the sofa, she sipped her drink and watched as he settled on the opposite side of the couch. In the early years of their relationship, they would've cuddled, and the distance between them had never been more obvious. Sadness tugged at her heart, but she ignored it. Yes, they'd been through a traumatic event today, but that didn't mean their issues had miraculously been resolved. But oh, how nice it would've been if he'd have set aside his grievances and held her for a while.

"Thank you for everything you did for us today, Damian."

"Did you think I'd leave you to your fate, Vivian?"

She shrugged one shoulder.

When his brows shot up, she snorted. "Okay, maybe not, but you'd have been well within your rights."

His quicksilver grin took her out at the knees, and it was a damned good thing she was sitting down.

"It'll be a feather in my cap as far as the Witches' Council is concerned. Councilwoman Georgie Sipanil always believed Morcant had remained at large. He has a habit of staging his death, but turns up like a bad penny every decade or so despite claims of his demise."

"Unless Humpty Dumpty has a resurrection spell and a damned good friend who can put him back together, I don't think he'll turn up again."

"I'd have gone with a headless horseman comparison, myself."

Vivian laughed. "Yours seems much more accurate."

They drank in silence as they stared into the hearth. The snap and hiss of a fallen log was the only noise. The distance between them ate at her, and she longed to put to rights what had been broken. Only, she didn't know how.

A side glance at Damian showed a self-contained man whose thoughts remained locked in the privacy of his mind, never to be shared. Did he feel remorse for the actions he'd been forced to take? Likely not if it meant keeping their beloved daughter from harm.

"You can ask me anything, Viv," he said softly, keeping his focus on the flames.

The glow was reflected in his eyes and lent his visage a supernatural air.

"Does your job as Aether weigh you down?"

He did look up then. "At times." After finishing his brandy in one gulp, he carefully set the tumbler on the coffee table and shifted closer, facing her. "Do I wish I was mortal? No. I'd miss the convenience of magic." His lips curled into a half smile. "Do I sometimes wish I wasn't saddled with the responsibility of being an Aether? Yes. But it comes with the Dethridge name."

"I don't know if I want that for Sabrina," Vivian confessed. "The constant battle for supremacy. The fight to keep what's hers. The fight for her very life."

He watched her, waiting for her to continue.

"I fear for her, Damian. Every second of every day."

"You knew what it meant when you married me, Viv. That any child of mine had the potential to be the future Aether." Lacing his fingers through her hair, he tilted her head back. "I never made secret that marriage to me would be difficult or there would always be a threat. It's too late to turn back."

"Why? Why can't we bind her powers?" Leaning her face into his hand, she beseeched him. "Please, Damian. I know you have it in you to remove them. To give her a normal shot at life."

For one brief instant, she thought she'd swayed him, but his expression hardened, and he dropped his hand. "It's too late for that."

"It's not!"

"I can't win with you, can I?" Damian scoffed, rose to his feet, and crossed to the hearth. Resting a forearm on the head-height, twelve-inch-thick wooden mantle, he stared down into the crackling fire.

Charging after him, she gripped his wrist to gain his full attention. "What do you mean?"

"First, you think I'm a monster eager to steal my child's Goddess-given gifts, then I'm a monster for bringing her home to train her so she can protect herself. *Now,* I'm a monster for *not* removing her magic." Yanking away from her clutches, he cradled Vivian's face between his palms, gentle enough that she could escape if she chose. "What's it to be, my love? Pick one."

"It's not as cut and dry as all that. You know it's not."

"Isn't it? Why can't I simply be a man madly in love with his wife and child? One who's willing to give his life to keep them safe and make them happy?"

"Because you're so much more, Damian. It puts us at risk every single day."

He dropped his hands, and her heart plummeted to her stomach at the sight of his wounded expression.

"I see." Turning his back to her, he resumed his study of the flames. "You should go home, Vivian."

She hated the coolness in his tone. Hated the immediate distance he'd created. When she placed her palm on his back, he twisted away, as if her touch burned.

"Damian, please. Let's discuss this."

"What's to discuss? You want what I can't give you. Normalcy." With flat, expressionless eyes, he met her gaze. "Go, Vivian. Find your new normal. But my daughter stays here with me, where she is protected."

"I can't go. Not without her," she cried. "Please don't make me leave here without her."

"We're in a bit of a pickle, aren't we? She's not setting foot off these grounds, my dear. I'd offer for you to live here, but I don't trust you to not sneak away with her in the middle of the night—*again*."

"If I promise I won't?" she asked raggedly.

With a coldness of tone that made her heartsick, he said, "I wouldn't believe you."

CHAPTER 11

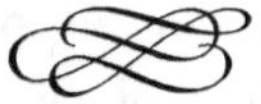

3 1/2 YEARS LATER

"You have to come up with a solution, Damian. She won't rest until she has a dog."

Damian Dethridge didn't respond to his wife's comment as he watched beyond the window, where their daughter Sabrina played with the fallen leaves. Using her natural-born abilities, she transformed the foliage colors from yellow, orange, and red into black and tan. With a trick their neighbor Mackenzie had shown her, Sabrina then gathered the leaves and formed them into the shape of puppies.

"They resemble deformed hellhounds more than puppies," he commented absently.

Vivian snorted a laugh. There was humor in the soulful depths of her eyes. "They do."

Damian and Viv shared an amused look, the first one in what felt like forever. Although Damian had unbent enough for her to move in with them, it was exceedingly difficult to find neutral ground when it came to their marriage. Theirs had become one of convenience, and Damian mourned the loss of what they'd once had. Only for Sabrina did they try. She needed her mother more than her father needed to be free of a wife who didn't love him.

75

Oh, but there had been one exquisite night after Vivian came back to the estate from some celebration or another, her face aglow with happiness and her inhibitions lowered from two glasses of honey mead. Due to his continued hopelessness regarding love, Damian had given in to his own urge to imbibe while she was gone. When she returned, he'd taken one look at the shining face she turned up to him and kissed her with pent-up passion from years' worth of denial and loneliness.

She'd led him to her room with no hesitation, and they'd conceived their son. That glorious event was never to be repeated, much to Damian's profound regret.

His gaze dropped to her expanding belly, and he desperately wanted to touch it. To feel the life growing there.

"How is Baby Nate this morning?" he gestured to her pregnancy bump with a warm smile.

She grimaced and wrapped her arms around the ever-growing mound. "He's abusing my bladder, the little devil. It wouldn't hurt my feelings if he made an appearance soon."

Damian chuckled and shifted closer. "May I?"

"Please do."

With one hand, he rubbed her lower back and placed the palm of his other over where he knew Nate's head was positioned.

"Give your mother a break, little one," he told his son. The pulse of energy he received in return made Damian chuckle. "Seems he's just as eager as you are to have him out of there. It won't be long, Viv."

"Thank you."

When she tenderly kissed his jaw, Damian closed his eyes and drew her close, resting his cheek against her silky white-blonde hair. Not caring if it was gratitude or her hormones urging her to touch him, he'd take whatever she offered. Goddess, he missed holding her and touching her the way he had when they were madly in love. Missed her willingness to touch him.

Sabrina's delighted squeal ruined the intimate moment, causing Vivian to back away, color high in her cheeks.

Wiping all emotion—primarily regret—off his face, he smiled and nodded toward the window. "Should we get her a puppy for real?"

"It's the only thing she truly wants for her birthday."

"Say goodbye to any peace and quiet for the foreseeable future," he said dryly.

Vivian laughed, and the sweet sound flooded his soul. "I think we did that when we created your female clone." Wrapping her arm through his, she laid her head on his shoulder as she observed Sabrina. "And Nate is going to be just as bad, I think."

"Thankfully, there are two of us. It evens the odds."

"Pfft. We can't keep up with the first one. What makes you believe we'll have anything under control with the second?"

"Valid point." Savoring the camaraderie between them, he didn't move right away.

"Oh!"

Vivian's squeak brought his head around a second before her water broke all over his leather shoes.

"Well, I suppose you're getting *your* wish, too," he said. "Our second beastie will be joining us for Sabrina's birthday celebration." Scooping Vivian up, he headed for the stairs, only pausing long enough to telepathically call Sabrina inside.

"But Papa!"

"Immediately, Beastie. Your brother is about to make an appearance."

The air around them contracted, and a small shower of twinkling lights heralded Sabrina's entrance.

"Nate?" Their daughter couldn't contain her excitement. "I've been waiting for him *forever!*"

Vivian snorted. "Not as long as I have."

"Beastie, I need you to call your aunts. Viv?"

Digging into his shirt pocket, she pulled out his smartphone. "You *do* know I'm not helpless, Damian. I can walk—oh!"

Patiently, he waited as she rode the contraction.

"You were saying?"

"Oh, shush." She handed Sabrina the phone. "Here, baby. Please tell them to hurry."

Waiting until their daughter was out of earshot, Damian asked, "How long have you been in labor, Viv? Why hide it?"

"Just a few hours. The contractions weren't bad, and I didn't want to worry you."

"Woman, I swear, you'd test the patience of a saint."

"You're up for the task." She surprised him when she laughed and patted his cheek.

"Between you and Beastie, I'm going to have a shorter-than-average life span."

Again, she laughed, but a painful groan followed on the heels of her merriment.

"Did you urge him along?" she gasped out.

"Not at all. I was hoping to put him to sleep to give you a few moments of peace," Damian replied.

"He's determined to come today, I think."

"Your sisters will be here soon. Do you want me to call anyone else?"

"No. But will you stay with me, Damian? Like you did with Sabrina?"

The vulnerability in Vivian's voice squeezed his heart. "Of course I will. Just you try to get rid of me, my love."

"Am I?"

Her uncertainty shone from her eyes, and for once, Damian dropped his impassive mask to show her the raw emotion always churning below the surface.

"Oh, Viv. It kills me that you even have to ask."

Her tears welled and spilled down her cheeks. Damian felt each and every one like acid droplets on his soul, and they burned like the dickens.

After he reached her bedroom, he set her on her feet and cradled her face between his palms. "I love you, Vivian Dethridge," he told her fiercely. "Never doubt it."

She simply nodded, and he wanted to beg her to tell him she felt the same, but it wasn't an ideal time. They had a baby to deliver. Still, when her eyes softened and she opened her mouth, he thought maybe she'd speak the words he'd longed to hear for over half a decade. Before she could utter a word, a commotion in the doorway distracted her.

"Viv!" Taryn charged into the room with Soleil on her heels. Josie was the only one of the three missing. "Sabrina said the baby's coming."

"Yep. Nate's decided today's the day."

The sisters were as different as night from day. Where Vivian resembled an ice princess, regal and cool, Soleil was shorter, rounder, and more earthy. Taryn was a mix of the two. Not as slim as Viv or as voluptuous as Soleil, but still curvy. If he looked at the three of them objectively, Taryn was probably the most beautiful of the four Stephens sisters.

"Where's Josie?" he asked.

"Manning the shop, if you can believe it," Taryn said with a small shake of her head.

"Tar, give her a break already." Soleil's tone was reproachful. "She's more than made up for her sins."

"She was in bed with the devil."

"For all your sakes, if I remember correctly," Damian said, siding with Soleil in regard to Josie. "She saw through Morcant's glamour and wanted to save you."

Taryn grimaced, nodded once, then took charge of the immediate situation and attempted to shoo him away.

Vivian reached for him when he would've backed up.

"You promised to stay," she said, desperation in her voice.

Raising her hand to his lips, he kissed her knuckles, then held their joined hands to his heart. "I always keep my word."

Five hours later, Vivian's heavenly cloud of hair was laid out on her down pillow, displayed in an arch around her head. If angels existed, she'd be their poster child. For a solid hour, Damian had watched her sleep as he held their son in his arms. Everyone in the house was downstairs except for him and Nate, who stared at him with large, myopic blue eyes.

"Welcome to the world, my beautiful boy," he said within the confines of his mind, knowing his telepathic link with his son was solid and unbreakable.

An open-mouthed, toothless smile was his answer. Already Nate was further along in his development than any other baby his age, with the exception of Sabrina. His Aether and witch DNA helped. At a point when words made sense to him, his son would speak to him the same way his sister had, and still did. But Nate understood intent right now, and his precious son recognized a father's love and pride.

"Damian."

He glanced up to find Vivian watching the two of them. Her expression unguarded. From early on, reading her mind had been impossible. Unlike most, his wife had the ability to hide what she didn't want him to know. He supposed it was for the best because a husband and wife should have some secrets from each other. If, as he suspected, she detested or feared him on occasion, he didn't want that positive confirmation of her feelings.

Rising to his feet, he crossed to her and settled Nate in her arms. Their son immediately turned his head toward her breast, insatiable in his hunger.

"With an appetite like his, he's going to be bigger and stronger than you," she said with a soft smile.

"Undoubtedly." Damian perched on the edge of the bed, one arm on either side of her waist as he gazed down at her. "How are you feeling? Do you need a healing boost?"

"I'm good. Your last one took away any lasting discomfort."

"Good."

"Thank you, Damian." She kissed Nate's downy head. "He's perfect."

"That was all you, my love. I owe you *my* thanks." He met her curious gaze with a small smile. "You returned here, provided Sabrina with the loving mother she deserves, gave me the gift of Nate." He swallowed hard. "I couldn't ask for more."

But he wanted to.

Wanted to ask her to love him forever as she'd once promised. He wouldn't. She needed to give of herself willingly. And if by the time the kids were grown Vivian still couldn't return his affections, he'd set her free, as *he* had promised when she returned to live with them.

Tears burned her eyes, and Damian felt the corresponding lump in his throat.

"So. About that puppy for Sabrina—"

"Nate needs one, too, Papa."

Hanging his head, Damian sighed heavily. "Of course you're eavesdropping, Beastie. It was too much to ask that you'd do as you were told and play in your room while your mother rests."

"Nate was calling me." Sabrina crossed the room and climbed up on the mattress, leaning against Damian to gaze down at her baby brother. "He's got a scrunchy face."

A bark of laughter escaped him, and Vivian joined in. When she had her giggles under control, she held one arm wide for Sabrina to curl against her side.

"You had a scrunchy face, too, baby girl. All infants do."

"All the girls will chase him when he is a grown-up," Sabrina predicted.

"I'm sure they will." Struggling not to laugh, Damian met Vivian's dancing eyes. "Let's get back to the puppy discussion."

"Nate needs one, too, Papa." Sabrina's expression was serious and lacking any guile for a change. "The hellhounds will keep us safe when the bad people come."

Heart thudding painfully in his chest, Damian forced himself to remain calm. Sabrina wouldn't be sharing this if it wasn't important, knowing his strict rule about revealing the future.

"Damian—"

He held up a hand to put a stop to Vivian's panicked questions and remained focused on their daughter. "What bad people, Beastie, and when?"

With a deep frown drawing her brows together, Sabrina shrugged one shoulder. "The Arcane Devourer."

A sickening dread soured Damian's stomach, and he fought like hell to rein in his fear.

Vivian sucked in a breath and shot him a terrified look. "But Nathanial killed him."

"Or who we thought was him. We had no proof the person posing as Evie and trying to retrieve the potion was Morcant," he concluded.

Sabrina nodded as if she understood the thread of their conversation. Likely she did with her heightened abilities.

"I don't know who his friends are, Papa, but one has a mark here." She drew a line down the length of her face from the edge of her temple to the corner of her mouth. "He's not very nice."

"And the others?" he asked with a calm he didn't feel, silently cursing the Fates for taking away his ability to see the future back when his mother was resurrected. "How many, and what do they look like?"

Sabrina relayed small details that Damian committed to memory. *No one* would harm his family while he still drew a breath.

With a show of nonchalance, he said, "But the puppies will help, huh? Any idea what kind of hellhounds we're talking about here? And why are we calling them that?"

Finally, a mischievous grin cracked Sabrina's face. "*You* are going to call them that, Papa. Uncle Baz knows what kind they are."

"Uh-huh." He chuckled and shook his head. "They wouldn't happen to be the new Rottweiler pups his pooch had a few weeks back, would they?"

Sabrina had gone over every day since Sebastian Drake's dog gave birth. Damian suspected that was what her black-and-tan leaf display was about earlier that day. His daughter had taken one look at those fluffy darlings and decided she wanted one for herself.

Eyes as wide and as innocent as his scheming daughter could manage, Sabrina said, "He said I had to ask you."

Giving no sign that he'd already intended to give in, he met Vivian's worried gaze. He winked, and his wife's relief was palpable.

Turning back to Sabrina, he said, "We'll talk to Baz tomorrow, my love. If they aren't all spoken for, we'll see about getting one for both of you, as a shared birthday present."

Launching herself at him, she hugged him around the neck, squealing her delight and possibly deafening him in the process. "Thank you, Papa! You're the best father in the whole wide world."

"Don't overplay your hand, you little minx."

She giggled and climbed from the bed, dutifully giving first him, then Vivian, and finally Nate a kiss on the cheek. "Seven-thirty tomorrow morning," she announced. "Any later, and Baz will give them all away."

With a face-splitting grin, she skipped from the room.

"Why do I feel like I just got played?" he murmured.

"Because she's one thousand percent your child," Vivian replied pertly. "Now, tell me what you intend to do to protect Nate."

"Talk to the Authority. They've been—pardon the expression—*hounding* me to head up their new task force. I suppose they'll get their wish in exchange for another Guardian to protect our children."

"Will it be dangerous? The job?"

Her worry warmed him. "Perhaps, but so far, there hasn't been born a standard witch or warlock who can defeat me, Viv. Rest easy."

CHAPTER 12

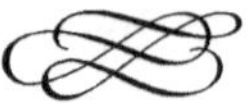

Sebastian greeted him with a handshake and a frown. "You're here early, Dethridge. What's up?"

Damian gestured to his daughter. "We are here to secure two of your new puppies."

"Ah." Baz's mouth twitched as he glanced down at Sabrina. "Looks like I owe you a free puppy."

"You made a side bet with her?" Damian scoffed. "Are you mad?"

With a grin, Sabrina charged toward the rear of the Drakes' home.

"Nah. It's not like I forgot the little sprite can predict the future. I simply had a hard time believing you'd welcome two pups, and not housebroken at that, into your pristine palace, old man."

Baz clapped him on the back, then followed Sabrina as Damian shook his head and trailed them. Before he could turn the corner, Mackenzie Thorne-Drake came down the terrace steps, holding her infant daughter, Delaney.

"Damian! Baz said you'd be here today to collect the pups. You'd have missed us in another half hour. We're heading out to Alastair's for a family celebration."

Ah, the reason for Sabrina picking this ungodly hour. Silently knocking over his king on the chessboard in his mind, he conceded the game to Beastie.

"Yes, well, Nate was born last night, and Sabrina assured me we're in need of two of your latest litter to keep her brother safe at some future date."

"Nate—oh!" She appeared taken aback. "Your visions haven't returned?"

"Not yet." He didn't want to tell her that he suspected the deities and the Authority were holding that particular gift of his hostage until he agreed to their job offer.

"Wait, what? Nate was born last night? Does Vivian need anything?"

"She's doing well, but you can take a few minutes to introduce Delaney to Nate if you'd like." According to a very recent prediction by Sabrina, the two children were bonded and would eventually be inseparable.

"No offense, but I'd better not. If they are truly going to bond, it's better to wait until we get back." She shrugged in her matter-of-fact way and tossed her brilliant red hair over her shoulder. "Neither of us needs to have inconsolable babies over the next few days."

"Truth. Are you intending to move in after you return, then?" he asked dryly.

She laughed, and the wind kicked up, causing the last of the autumn leaves to flitter down from their branches and settle on the ground around them. "We'll have to figure out a plan moving forward, or I suspect you'll be babysitting Delaney quite a bit in the future."

Mack was right to assume he'd never let his son off their property until Nate could protect himself. Sabrina had reached that stage, and still, it was difficult to have her out of his sight.

"I'm glad Sebastian found you, Mack," Damian said experiencing a bout of sentimentality. "You've healed the hole Vivian's defection left, and you've brought him the true love he didn't realize he was missing with her."

Her smile was pure sunshine. "Thank you, Damian. For every-thing you've done to help us get here."

Not long ago, the Enchantress had found a way to resurrect herself using Mackenzie's psychic abilities. Damian and Sabrina had both played a role in saving Mack and banishing the Darkness hounding them to the Netherworld. As a result, Mack and Sebastian had fallen in love, and the hatred Baz had felt for him was put to rest.

"You're the best thing that happened to all of us, Mack," he replied. "You helped my daughter come out of her shell, were instrumental in saving her life, and you've eased the bitterness your husband felt toward my family. It was a fortunate day when you set foot on this estate."

She laughed, and the beautiful sound of her joy carried through the barn, causing the birds overhead to pause their chatter and listen.

"None of us thought so at the time when your mother was freed from her tomb," Mack said pertly.

"True, but all's well that ends well, right?"

He grinned and heard her suck in a breath.

"Put that thing away, Aether," Baz growled. "I swear, you could seduce a snail from its shell."

"He should definitely come with a warning label." Mack's bright blue eyes were twinkling as she handed off Delaney to Sebastian, giving him a kiss on the lips. "But I'm yours, now and forever, babe."

Glancing down the aisleway to check Sabrina's whereabouts, she lowered her voice and said, "Let's get back to the business of this threat. What do you know?"

"There's not much to tell," Damian said. "Just this morning Sabrina told us we needed puppies to guard Nate and her from 'the bad men.' One of which has a scar from temple to jaw. Her descrip-tion of the villain's partners was vague. Other than to say one had scary yellow eyes, Beastie couldn't reveal any distinguishing information."

"But?" Mack asked, sensing correctly that he was holding back.

"But she said one of the men was Morgan Black. Also known as Morcant Thywyll. He's an Arcane Devourer."

"I don't even know what that is. Do you, Baz?"

Sebastian nodded. "Vaguely. Legend states they are magical individuals who gain power from feeding off another's energy."

"Energy vampires? That's a thing?"

Damian almost laughed. Probably would have if the situation wasn't so serious. "I think that's simplifying it, Mack, but yes. Morcant is the worst of his kind, but not the only one."

"Do you have a timeline?" Baz asked, shooting a frown down the aisle.

"No. I believe it's safe to assume the attack will be when the pups are big enough to defend my children." With a heavy sigh, Damian shook his head. "It never stops. However, I've been offered a position with the Authority, and I'm going to accept their deal."

"Damian, no!" Shaking her head vigorously, Mack said, "From what I understand, they require a lifetime commitment. Their contracts are written in blood, for fuck's sake!"

"What choice do I have? The Fates drive the Authority, and neither will relent. They've stolen my ability to predict the future, Mack. I need it to see the threat."

"You have Sabrina and me for that," she argued.

"And if I'm in a situation without either of you? It might mean my death."

She exchanged a worried look with her husband. "Baz? Want to weigh in here?"

"You've stated everything I would've, love. But Damian's a grown man, with centuries under his belt. It's doubtful he can be swayed by us."

Damian lifted his brows, and a wry smile curled his lips. "Way to make me sound like an old, stubborn fool."

"Well, if the shoe fits…"

"On that note, I'll collect my daughter and her hounds." He paused on his way to the back of the barn. "How long will you be gone? Do we need to care for your animals, or will Arabella and Gwennie be here?"

"My sister will be joining us, but Aunt Gwennie will stay behind. It's just for today, but if you could keep an eye out for her, I'd be grateful," Sebastian replied.

"Consider it done."

"Damian"—Mack placed a hand on his forearm—"please reconsider joining the Authority."

"Have you received a vision that would make it ill-advised?"

"No."

"Then I'll move forward until you do." He patted her hand like a kindly uncle. "I'll be in charge of a band of Sentinels, Mack. Hopefully, I'll inspire loyalty, and by extension, so will my children."

Damian left them to find Sabrina.

"This one is for Ronan, Papa. Her name is Buttercup."

Ronan.

Since the meeting of Ronan O'Connor and his daughter, the man had become one of Beastie's favorite people. He'd selflessly protected Sabrina when his cousins sought to murder her and consume her power for their own, causing himself untold pain in the process. Not only had he almost lost his life, but he *did* lose his magic for a time. Seeing him for the reluctant hero he was, the Goddess had promoted Ronan from renegade warlock to Guardian status, restoring what he lost and then some.

"I think you should ask Ronan before assuming."

"He needs her," Sabrina stubbornly insisted.

"I'll take your word for it, and that's something you'll need to work through with Ronan when the time comes. For now, point out the two you've chosen for Nate and yourself, and let's get back home."

Leaving Vivian and Nate for longer than necessary was causing him anxiety. Who the hell knew what dangers lurked in the shadows these days? It seemed he was in for more trials in the coming months.

It was time to secure his position with the Authority.

CHAPTER 13

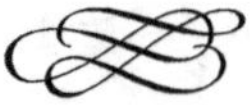

Yes, I'm continuing my time-honored Thorne Witches tradition in this spinoff series. So, this chapter has been omitted. Time for a bathroom break. Also, you may want to hydrate and stock up on munchies. This story is about to get REAL!

CHAPTER 14

Full of bitterness for having no choice but to accept the Authority's offer, Damian pasted on an aloof expression. He stood center stage in front of the U-shaped table where the thirteen council members watched him with varying degrees of curiosity from their raised platform.

He'd tried his damndest to get them to see reason over the last week, even going so far as to request an audience with the Fates, but they'd refused.

No one but him seemed to care that Morcant might still be alive or that Damian's children were his intended target at some later date. All they wanted was to have the Aether under their thumb.

He resented them all for forcing his hand, but he needed his full abilities without restrictions.

"Are you prepared to stand by your word and do your duty, Aether?"

Damian met the gaze of the smug-faced leader. "I am."

"You'll be contracted for life," another council member warned.

If he didn't know better, he'd almost believe the stately woman held compassion for his plight. But those belonging to the Authority were ruthless and controlling, without an ounce of empathy for others.

"I'm well aware of the conditions, Ms. Otherman," he replied coolly.

What he didn't say was that he intended to end his employment at his earliest opportunity. He'd grant them twenty years, and when his children were old enough to survive without him, he'd find a loophole. The Goddess Isis would assist him, he had no doubt. She'd been against the Authority's blackmailing scheme from the start. But if he couldn't trick his way out of his contract, he'd accept the penalty of death that went with breaking trust with the Authority.

"And you'll lead a team of Sentinels on missions of our choosing," the lead council added.

"You act as if I've forgotten the terms, Butthanger," Damian said, tone as dry as dirt.

"It's *Buttagier*," the man snapped.

"My bad."

Someone along the sweeping panel snickered, earning a dark look from Buttagier.

A buzzer sounded, and a glass panel on the floor in front of Damian slid to the side. From beneath the ground level, a desk-sized altar rose, and the stone it rested on locked in place of the previous panel.

"Step forward," Buttagier ordered.

Teeth gritted, Damian moved to take position behind the ceremonial table.

A female dressed in the long black robes of the Authority rose from her seat and crossed to him.

"This will require not only your signature but your blood to seal the deal, Aether." She lowered her voice for his hearing alone. "Do you understand what you are giving up, Damian?"

"Yes, Mattie." Had it not made her a target of Buttagier's ire, Damian would've smiled at her. Mathilda Price had been in his corner during negotiations. She'd tried to be the voice of reason and had gone toe-to-toe with the lead council to cut the terms of Damian's employment down. All she'd earned for her troubles was their displeasure.

"You'll be under *Butthanger's* thumb," she warned.

Lips twitching, he remained silent and nodded. Mattie hated the man as much as Damian did, and her slip almost sent him over the edge into laughter.

"Fine. When you read the contract, pay special attention to page seven. The loophole you need is written there." With her back to the council, she winked.

Not many people surprised him, and it took an effort to keep his jaw from sagging open. How she'd guessed what he intended was a mystery. One he'd solve in due time.

Mattie turned slightly and, raising her voice to include the others, said, "Very well, Aether. We shall proceed."

With great pomp, she withdrew a white quill and handed it to him. The tip wasn't a hardened shaft carved into a nib, as was the norm, but instead, it was metal with a razor-sharp point. Damian was expected to pierce his skin and sign his name in blood.

"Is this sanitary?" he quipped.

Biting her lip to keep a laugh at bay, Mattie darted a look toward the lead council. "Probably not, but you'll survive."

"True, but I'd like to keep all my fingers intact. I can't have them falling off from rot."

She did laugh then.

"Sign the bloody contract, Aether, and let's be done with it," Buttagier snapped from his perch.

To taunt him further, Damian slowly and continuously caressed the barbs of the feather, following the vane. "I'm going to want assurances that my blood cannot be removed from the parchment and that this lovely quill will be destroyed." He locked eyes with Buttagier and, in an arctic tone, said, "We can't have anyone attempt to manipulate me through dark blood magic, can we?"

Nothing had been proven, but there were rumors aplenty about the Authority and dark magic. Damian didn't intend that he should fall victim to another's foul play.

For the first time, the lead councilman lost his arrogance, and sweat beaded along his brow. He shot a glance to his left, down the length of the table. Councilwoman Otherman met Buttagier's gaze, and something unspoken passed between them.

Seemed a few others were in favor of Damian's request. Lifting his brows in challenge, he smiled. "That's not too much to ask, is it, Butt"—he paused deliberately—"agier?"

Resentment flared in the other man's eyes, but he gave an abrupt nod. "You may take or destroy the quill, as is your right to protect yourself. The contract will be secured in our vault system. None have access but those on this panel."

"Not good enough. I ask the contract be given to the Goddess Isis for safekeeping."

It didn't take a genius to recognize Buttagier wasn't thrilled with his demand, but Damian had his family to protect.

Councilwoman Otherman rose to her feet and slapped the wooden table in front of her. "Done."

After pausing to take a long look at her, Damian smiled at what he saw. "Exalted One, I almost didn't recognize you."

Isis shed her elderly glamour in an instant. Her long black hair was loosely braided and fell down her back. A gold circlet sat atop her glossy head. Eyes the color of amber topaz glowed with a goddess's knowledge and power. She had discarded the black robe of the council in favor of a sky-blue gossamer gown that enhanced her shapely body and was caught at the shoulder with a gold clip in the shape of the sun.

Isis sauntered down the steps of the dais and approached him. "Beloved."

Dropping to one knee, he lightly kissed the back of the hand she extended toward him.

"You may rise." She took the quill from him, casually examining the nib.

"Have you always been on the Authority's panel, or am I simply lucky?" he asked her.

"I have a vested interest in today's outcome." With a frown, she set the quill alight, then pinned Buttagier with a stare. "Did you know the nib contained a toxin, Councilman Butthanger?"

If the seriousness of her question hadn't struck Damian at the same time as her use of Buttagier's hated nickname, he'd have laughed. But as it was, he had to work not to freak the hell out. He'd been minutes, at most, away from pricking his finger to sign the contract.

Buttagier paled.

"N-no! I..." He rose and met Damian's angry glare with a sincerity that was difficult to ignore. "You have to believe that I would not condone anyone coming to harm under my reign as lead council."

Picking up the contract, Isis snapped her fingers, and the paper caught fire. When it would've reached her fingers, she dropped it on the marble floor to finish burning.

"The Aether is free of his promise to us," she proclaimed.

And immediately, Damian understood what she'd done. For him. For his family. By claiming there was a traitor in their midst who would seek to harm him, she'd set him free. The Authority wouldn't hold him to his promise, and they wouldn't send anyone else to threaten his children.

Relief swept through him, and the gratitude he felt at Isis's protective gesture nearly overwhelmed him.

"But we need him!" Buttagier protested.

Because he was a man of principle, Damian proposed a new deal.

One that was readily accepted.

For the next five years, he would consult on an as-needed basis. If required, he'd step in without objection. No contract. No blood oath. Merely a statement of intent to lead a team of Sentinels of his choosing, and they took him at his word.

CHAPTER 15

PRESENT DAY

"I want you to go with us, Papa."

Damian glanced up from his book and sighed. Sabrina was relentless in her desire to bring their family back together, unable to understand that once broken, some things could never be mended—even with the birth of a new child.

"Beastie, let it rest. I'm on babysitting duty tonight. Between your brother and those blasted hellhounds you talked me into, I'm chained to this house."

"No, Papa. You *promised*. Besides, Ronan and Dubheasa are going to watch Baby Nate."

Frowning, he closed his book and set it to the side. "I thought they were watching *you*."

"I told them you have to come," she replied in her bossier-every-day manner.

"When did yours become the ruling voice?" he grumbled good-naturedly. "Your mother and I should have some say in this house."

Left with no true objection if powerful Guardians intended to protect his son, Damian knew he'd lost the argument. Still, he couldn't let his daughter believe he'd give in so easily. As it was, she walked over him with steady frequency. Marshmallow fluff that he was, he always let her have her way.

"Papa! Come on!"

With a groan, he dropped his head back on the buttery leather chair. "You're killing me, child."

"Damian?" Vivian's soft inquiry brought his head around. There she stood, in the doorway, in a flowing white dress with flowers in her hair and a moonstone amulet falling into the shadowy valley between her full breasts.

Damian wanted nothing more than to scoop her up and teleport to his room, where he could rip that revealing gown from her luscious body, then make love to her until tomorrow, when the sun was high in the afternoon sky.

His fantasy died when she spoke again.

"My sisters will be here soon for the Beltane festivities tonight."

"I don't suppose I can skip it, then?" he asked, knowing full well he'd continue to be badgered by a pint-sized Tasmanian devil if he tried.

A soft smile graced Vivian's lovely visage, actually reaching her shining eyes. "I don't suppose you can. Come on. It'll be fun. Like old times."

His will was useless in the face of her sweet cajoling. "Can I just say, never once in all my years has anything associated with these blasted Beltane festivals actually added to my magic."

Viv's smile widened to an amused grin as she strolled across the room to join him. "Oh, I don't know. My sisters and I bathe in the Holy Well every year, and I think the healing waters help to keep us young and beautiful."

"That's genetics and witchcraft," he replied dryly.

"I seem to recall you didn't mind the results of the last festival we attended together," she said in a low voice.

Heat swept through him, and his entire body tightened at the memory of their shared night of lovemaking. Why was she so flirty tonight? If she had any idea of her effect on him, she didn't show it.

Although, if he thought back, Vivian had been different since the birth of Nate. More open.

Sabrina, in a dress that was a mini replica of her mother's but far less revealing, rushed over and tugged him out of his chair. "Where's your sense of adventure, Papa?"

"I'm over two hundred years old, Beastie. Any sense of adventure I ever had fizzled out eons ago."

She giggled as if he were the funniest of men and dragged him toward the terrace doors. "Mack and Baz are going with us, too."

"Safety in numbers, I suppose. Sebastian is sure to hate this as much as I do, so there's that to look forward to."

"Oh, hush, you." Vivian tucked her arm through his. "It's about time the witch community saw you as human instead of a mythical monster."

He frowned down at her. "People think I'm a monster?"

With a grimace, she patted his bicep. "Sorry, darling. I didn't mean it like that. I simply meant that very few people know the real you. Know that you're a kind man."

"I prefer it that way. It's safer. If they believe I'm a ruthless bastard, they'll leave us alone."

Pausing on the terrace, she shifted to stare up at him. As Vivian's curious gaze traveled over his face, Damian wondered what she saw. It was hell being unable to know her mind.

"Valid point." With a shrug and a light kiss on his cheek, she strutted away. The pronounced sway of her hips taunted him, tempting him to follow.

He did. Just like he always would.

As they reached the center of the lawn, the other Stephens sisters arrived.

It was hard to believe it had only been four years since he spied on them as they'd gathered, laughing and chatting in their excitement for the upcoming evening. Not much had changed. With the exception of the dresses, the sisters all looked exactly the same, right down to the glowing amulets they wore.

He caught Sabrina watching them with longing on her face.

When Vivian turned and held out her hand, the yearning shifted to joyfulness, and Damian released the breath he didn't know he was holding. It was difficult for an Aether to fit in. As an adult, he recognized why, but a child like Sabrina would never understand why she stood on the outs. Why everyone viewed her as something to fear.

Josie bent to hug her, straightening her crown of wildflowers. "Are you ready, small fry?"

Eyes shining, Sabrina nodded.

Glancing up at her sisters, a sly smile curled Josie's lips as they nodded.

"I think the vote is unanimous to make you this year's Stephens Beltane Princess. Are you up for the role of Grand Poobah?"

"What does the Grand Poobah do?" Sabrina asked warily, as if she feared she'd not do justice to the title.

Vivian's gaze locked with his over their daughter's crowned curls.

Just like when he first met her, his lungs ceased to draw a breath and his heart left his chest to return to her delicate hands to do with what she will.

He was such a sucker for love.

"Me, too."

Damian blinked. Had he actually heard her?

Frowning, he tested their connection.

"Can you read my mind, Viv?"

Her expression arrested, and she gasped, catching the attention of the others.

"You're like us now, Mama!" Sabrina cried her excitement. "You can hear Papa!"

"Remind me to find a way to block amorous thoughts from her," Damian said through his connection to his wife.

She laughed.

Never had there been a more lovely sound.

. . .

Vivian was surprised to hear her husband's voice inside her head—and oddly delighted. For too long, she'd gone not knowing how he felt about their situation, but tonight, something had shifted. Both in his expression and through this new connection.

"What do you suppose caused this?" she asked him.

Damian shrugged. "We shouldn't look a gift horse in the mouth. If those in charge are handing out presents like this one, we'll accept it, and happily."

"What's happening here?" Taryn asked, glancing between them. "Are you trying to say the two of you have telepathic abilities? If so, I'm going to be pissed I didn't gain any."

Josie laughed. "You're not married to the Aether, sister. Besides, it might be scary to be in someone else's head. Goddess knows I'd never want someone in mine."

"So, about that 'sucker for love' comment..."

Damian's unspoken words echoed inside her mind, and the sensation of "internal voices" was disconcerting. Her eyes locked with his.

"Are you, Viv?"

She nodded, unable to respond any other way.

His grin stunned her stupid, and she could only stare.

"Wow," Soleil whispered. "Just wow."

Vivian silently agreed. How could one man be so aesthetically perfect?

"We're going to wait over here." Taryn grabbed Soleil's arm and Sabrina's hand, then nodded to Josie. "By the maze, to give these two a minute to remember why they fell in love in the first place."

"They remember." Sabrina's voice, though young, held an age-old knowledge.

"Yes," Damian agreed, striding toward Vivian, where she stood frozen. He stroked her throat, and his gaze followed the trail of his fingertips as they wound up her neck, beyond the base of her skull, and into her mass of curls. Finally, he focused on her eyes. Heat burned in his. "Yes, I remember," he said softly.

Lowering his head, he kissed her, and Vivian was more than

ready. It seemed like forever since he'd touched her, but in reality, it had been sixteen months. Sixteen *long*-ass months.

Burning with want, she wrapped her arms around his neck and pressed her body to his. Had Ronan not interrupted, she'd have turned into a molten mess where she stood.

"Aye, it's good to see you're patchin' things up, to be sure." His humor-packed comment was spoken in his lilting Irish accent, and the suggestion of naughtiness he always seemed to convey caused Vivian's face to burn.

If anyone could rival Damian in looks, it was Ronan O'Connor. His wavy, white-blond hair fell to his shoulders, and although his face with its deliciously hard planes should've appeared more effeminate from the hairstyle, it didn't. Every part of him was beautifully sculpted. Somewhere along the way, Vivian had heard he was descended from Zeus, and she could damned well believe it.

"It's a start, yeah?" Ronan's girlfriend and fellow Guardian said from beside him. Dubheasa was the perfect foil for her mate. With her dark hair and challenging green eyes, it was easy to see why Ronan had fallen for her.

"Yes," Damian replied gruffly. He'd yet to turn his attention from Vivian, and she could feel the hypnotic pull to the far reaches of her toes. A warm smile curled his mouth, triggering a responding one from her.

With an attempt at collecting herself, she faced the Guardians. "Where's Nate?"

"Mack is settlin' Delaney in with him now. As soon as Baz comes down, we'll head up." Ronan nodded toward Damian. "We were after lettin' you know we'd arrived."

"I knew the moment you crossed the boundary to the property, but thank you." Surprising her, Damian clasped her hand. "We'll only be a phone call away. Please let us know if you need anything or if the babies become too much."

Sebastian and Mack stepped through the terrace doors. "All set?"

"Go, and don't be worryin' about your weens," Ronan ordered. "Sure, and we'll lay our lives down for them if we need to, yeah?"

Hugging him, Vivian said, "Thank you, Ronan. Your care of our children means the world to us."

A shot rang out, and from a short distance away, Josie cried out.

Damian and Ronan reacted instantly, throwing their arms up and encompassing both groups in protective bubbles.

"Get to my children! Now!" her husband ordered.

CHAPTER 16

"Go with them!" After urging Vivian toward Ronan and Dubheasa, Damian ran for his daughter. How the hell did neither of them see this coming? Where was their standard early warning system?

"Morcant," Josie gasped from where she'd fallen. "He's here. I feel him. He's tracked me here to you."

"How is that possible? He's supposed to be dead." Taryn looked up at Damian from beside her sister. "And why don't you seem as surprised as the rest of us?"

Ignoring her, he said, "Everyone remain calm. Remember, he thrives on chaos."

"He creates the chaos," Soleil muttered. She drew Josie's hands away from her belly to examine the wound, only to forcefully put them back and add the pressure of her own.

"How bad is it?" he asked.

"I'm not a doctor, but it doesn't look good to me, and Josie's growing paler by the second."

"I'll remove it. Let's teleport her to the dining room." Vivian's hand on his shoulder distracted him. "What are you doing here? I thought you were going with Ronan and Dubheasa."

She pointed to Sabrina, who had walked ten yards away to stare out over the tree line.

"What's she doing?" Vivian asked in a low voice.

"I'm not sure," he replied, equally as low. "Are you able to get your sisters safely inside?"

"Yes."

Damian approached Sabrina, following her sight line. "What do you see, my love?"

"They are testing your wards, Papa. But they won't get inside tonight."

"How did we never see this coming?"

"I did. Mama needs to let Aunt Josie's blood flow. You should tell her that."

His heart picked up its pace, but he regulated his breathing and focused on not giving his adrenaline the upper hand. Morcant didn't need the fuel.

"If her sister dies, I doubt your mother could forgive me."

"We need the Death Dealer. He can help."

Suppressing the urge to swear like a drunken sailor in a bar fight, Damian lifted Sabrina. "Is it safe to leave Morcant's crew out there?"

"Yes. They can do no more."

"Hold tight."

Closing his eyes, he visualized his study and sent out a magical feeler to make sure no one was in the room. When he was satisfied he wouldn't crash into anyone during the teleport, he allowed his cells to fire up. After they arrived, he set Sabrina on her feet. "Go tell your mother what you told me, Beastie. I'll call Trevor Blane."

"Okay." Acting as if it were another day in the park, Sabrina skipped away.

"Do you find it odd that your daughter has no fear in the middle of a crisis?"

Lifting a brow, he faced Sebastian. "At times. Where's Mack?"

"Upstairs."

"She had no inkling of tonight's events, either?"

"None. And she's disturbed by the fact." Baz twirled a hand around. "I'm assuming we're safe in this fortress of yours?"

"For tonight, according to Beastie. Who the hell knows about tomorrow." Lifting his phone, he waved it toward the sideboard. "Pour us a dram while I make this call, won't you?"

Trevor picked up on the second ring. "What's going on, man?"

"I need your help."

"With what?"

Damian sighed heavily as he accepted a glass of brandy from Sebastian. "An Arcane Devourer who refuses to stay dead."

"I'm not even sure what that is."

"Essentially an energy vampire who thrives off the chaos he creates. The bastard has nine lives, and it seems he's set his sights on my daughter. His goal is to live forever."

"Why the hell would he want to? Isn't one lifetime enough?"

With a short laugh, Damian said, "I tried to tell him that living this long has its disadvantages."

"So you want me to come there? Should I bring Simon?"

"Just you for now. Your brother can remain in the dark for a bit longer." Setting down his glass, he strode to his ceremony room and waved a hand to open the door. Once inside, he retrieved a spell. "I've got an incantation for you to get through my wards. When it arrives, commit it to memory and burn the paper. You'll have less than five minutes. Understood?"

"Yes."

As soon as he hung up, Damian snapped his fingers and woke the writing tools on his mother's old secretary. The pen scratched out the words needed to bypass his magical security system. Finally, it dropped to the polished wooden surface.

A wave of his hand dried the ink.

"Make a copy, then deliver yourself to Trevor Blane. The other is to be delivered to Alexander Castor," he instructed the parchment. "If you aren't destroyed within five minutes of receipt, self-destruct."

Both sets of instructions rolled themselves tightly and disappeared in a light puff of black smoke.

"That's Harry-Potter level, right there."

In his distraction over Morcant and getting his new Sentinels here, Damian had momentarily forgotten Sebastian. Nodding, he said, "I suppose it is."

"Does anyone really know what you're capable of, Dethridge?"

"It's doubtful."

"How do you suppose Morcant found your estate?"

"Josie. He arrived not long after her."

Dark brows to his hairline, Sebastian looked disconcerted. "They're in league together?"

"No. A magical marker in her bloodstream allows him to track her. I thought we'd taken care of it after the last incident, but it appears it still works." Expression grim, he shook his head. "Beastie said we need to let Josie bleed. I don't know what the hell that means."

"If she bleeds out, the tracker will too, correct?" Sebastian asked, looking thoughtful.

"In theory. Every drop of her blood would need to be removed. It could stop her heart."

"Sabrina wouldn't have suggested it if she hadn't seen a positive outcome, would she?"

"It could be as simple as Josie dying to protect us all. One never knows with my daughter. But death upsets her, so I'd say that isn't her goal."

The air around them contracted, and Sebastian straightened from the doorframe to face the room. Castor was the first to arrive, wearing a Hawaiian shirt, Bermuda shorts, and a lei around his neck. In his hand, he held an umbrella drink. His expression was so put out, Damian chuckled.

"You can't text like a normal human?" Alex snapped.

"I'm *not* a normal human."

His friend grunted. "Well, I've left my date for any predator to hit on. I hope you're happy."

"Please tell me she knows you're not returning anytime soon."

"I'm not a total asshole. I gave her a credit card with your name on it and told her to live it up."

Sebastian barked a laugh as Damian shook his head. Wry amusement curled his lips. Alex would never change.

Next to arrive was Trevor.

"What's he doing here?" Alex nodded toward him. "No offense, but Death Dealers make me nervous as fuck."

"Look at you, learning modern slang. One wouldn't think a warlock of your years would be so hip," Trevor retorted.

Ice-blue eyes narrowed, Castor smiled, and the shark-like grin would've given anyone shivers. "A warlock of my years knows how to—"

Damian held up a hand. "Enough, gentlemen. We have bigger fish to fry."

With one last warning look at Trevor, Alex gave Damian his full attention. "What's going on, Dethridge?"

"Do you remember Morcant Thywyll?"

"The Arcane Dickweed?"

"That would be him."

"What about him? Didn't you off him a decade or so ago?"

"Yes. Also a few years back. Apparently, it wasn't him. Or if it was, he's returned from the dead. Again." Damian crossed to the sideboard to refill his glass and pour one for Trevor. "I'd offer you a brandy, Castor, but it seems you're happy with your fru-fru drink."

Alex took a slurping sip to show he was unfazed by the dig against his manhood. "Who doesn't love a strawberry daiquiri?"

Hard-pressed not to laugh, Damian gestured to the dining area. "I'm afraid time is of the essence. Josie's been shot, and we need to let her die. But—"

Unfortunately, his wife had rushed into the room on the tail end of his comment.

She paled.

· · ·

"What?"

Vivian couldn't believe what she'd heard, and she stared at Damian, wondering how he could be so damned calm when her sister lay dying.

"Damian?"

Shaking his head, he swore softly and strode to her. Placing the tumbler in her hand, he ordered her to drink up. "You misheard, Viv."

"I don't think so. You said, 'We need to let her die,' as I walked into the room." She downed the brandy with a gasp and shoved the glass back at him. "Why?"

"I was about to add that we would immediately revive her, but you distracted me."

"He said, 'but,'" Alexander Castor said with a wave of a fruity cocktail. "I heard him."

She noted Trevor Blane's presence in addition to Sebastian's. It was the latter she focused on. "You never lie to me. Tell me what's happening."

"I'm highly offended you believe I do," Damian said dryly.

"Hush, you. I'm talking to Baz."

"Your daughter told your husband that you needed to let Josie bleed out. He's currently trying to find a work-around to save your sister but drain her of her blood at the same time."

Vivian's knees grew weak. As usual, Damian anticipated her reaction and provided a steadying hand. "Taryn's been in there, trying to ease Josie's pain, all the while waiting for you to remove the bullet, Damian. Now you're saying we're supposed to let her die?"

"We'll figure this out in just another minute, Viv. Trust me to take care of it."

The sincerity in his eyes came through their link, causing her nerves to settle.

"Where's Sabrina?" she asked.

Her blood ran cold at his forbidding expression.

"What do you mean? She was supposed to tell you about Josie.

Did she?"

"No."

"Beastie!" Damian roared, abandoning their group to run for the stairs. Halfway there, he halted and spun toward the French doors. "No!"

In a flash, he was gone, and all Vivian's anxiety came rushing back. Sebastian snagged her wrist, effectively stopping her in her tracks when she would've charged after her husband.

"Baz—"

"Trust him to find her, Viv."

She did—for all of two heartbeats. "Go after him. Find my daughter!"

Before she finished speaking, Trevor and Alexander were out the doors, hot on Damian's heels.

Terrified Sabrina had gone to confront Morcant, Vivian began to shake.

"It's okay, Viv," Sebastian said softly as he drew her into his arms. "Damian won't let anything happen to her."

"She's been a target since she came into her powers, Baz. Morcant, the Darkness fueling the Enchantress, Ronan's cousins. And now, Morcant again. I'm afraid she's never going to be safe."

"Sabrina is a clever lass. Like her mother." He drew away and lifted her chin to meet his confident gaze. "Trust her to know what she's doing."

"She's a child!"

"She's a hundred-year-old woman in a pint-sized body," Ronan said as he joined them. "Are ya after tellin' me where she's gone, or do I need to be scrying for the wee wild beastie?"

"I don't know," Vivian admitted. "Damian teleported with Trevor and Castor on his heels."

"My uncle Alex shouldn't be hard to find." Closing his eyes, Ronan said, "Blood of my blood, draw me to thee."

He was gone in a flash.

"Vivian! We're losing her!" Taryn hollered from the hallway. "Hurry!"

CHAPTER 17

Damian found his daughter hiding in the maze with the puppies curled up in her lap.

"What the hell are you—"

"Shhhh, Papa!" She pointed to the sleeping pups. "The opposite of fear is hope and love."

It took him a moment to digest her comment, but when he did, he shook his head. "You clever, clever girl."

"If fear feeds him, hope and love make him weak, right?"

"You're ever hopeful, and you love your hellhounds," he concluded.

She grinned, and her already adorable features transformed, making her prettiness more pronounced. One day, she'd be a great beauty, rivaling his mother. Damian tried not to let his mind wander that far ahead or worry about what those types of looks could attract. Sabrina was smart, with the ability to see through to the heart of a person's true nature.

He turned as Castor shouted his name.

"In here, Alex," he called back.

Sitting next to her, Damian wrapped an arm around her shoulders and rested his cheek on the crown of her head. "I can't leave you out here by yourself, Beastie. We have to save Josie."

"Ronan can sit here with me, Papa." She pointed to her protector when he arrived.

"What about Nate and Delaney? Should they be left alone?"

"Dubheasa's with them," Ronan said. "Have ya seen me Dove's fierceness? She'll not allow harm to come to anyone."

"I don't like having her outside the house. It makes me itchy," Damian admitted.

When Castor bent to pet a dog, Sabrina lifted the one she'd named Willow and deposited her into his arms. "They need proper training, Uncle Alex. Papa says so."

"Are you saying I'm supposed to train it?" he asked with a disbelieving laugh.

"No, silly. You're supposed to bring her to Aunt Josie to hold. She needs to think happy thoughts."

As a whole, their confusion showed.

Sabrina sighed like they were all the veriest of dimwits. "Josie needs to not think bad thoughts, or you won't be able to get rid of Morcant's tracker. Uncle Alex is cute, and so is the puppy."

Ronan laughed and slapped Castor on the back. "Did ya hear her, then? She thinks you're grand."

"If you weren't my nephew, I'd send you to hades." Despite his surly reply, Alex cuddled the pup under his chin as he rose. "I guess I'll see you inside."

"Rumor has it you specifically requested me. What's to be my role in all this, kid?" Trevor asked. His arms were crossed, and he stood a good fifteen feet away as if he were afraid to ruin the enchanting scene of a girl and her pups.

"Hi, Mr. Blane."

He smiled. "Hi, Sabrina. What's the plan to save your aunt? I know you have one."

"You can bring her back."

Frowning, he sought confirmation from Damian. "Not after she dies, I can't. Once she's gone, that's it for me."

"You *can!*" Sabrina insisted.

"Beastie." Touching her cheek, Damian guided her head up so she could look at him. "That's not within his power. He can heal, take a life, or obliterate a soul, but he can't revive someone after death."

"Yes, he can."

"I'm sorry, but I don't know how," Trevor confessed.

Dumping the second puppy in Ronan's lap, she climbed to her feet and crossed to the Death Dealer. Gesturing for him to lean down, she waited until his face was level with hers, then placed two fingers on each of his temples. "Learn."

The magical shock wave sent Trevor to his knees with a cry, and when he gripped her wrists with the intent to shove her away, Damian jumped to his feet. Before he could intervene, the entire incident was over, and Sabrina was patting Trevor's shoulder.

"Now you know, Mr. Blane," she said simply, ignoring the fact the man was sweating profusely and looked like she'd taken a sledgehammer to his head.

"I have aspirin in the house," Damian told him, trying to hold back his black humor and not laugh. He knew very well what an infusion of Sabrina's knowledge felt like when imparted out of the blue.

"I think if you unleash that kid of yours on your enemies, she can take them out in one fell swoop," Trevor replied as he flopped down on his back and flung an arm over his eyes. "Christ! That hurt."

"I've been the recipient before, so I know exactly what you're feeling." Damian nudged him with the tip of his shoe and held out a hand when he had the Death Dealer's attention. "It's time to go back inside. Josie is suffering, and I can feel her pain from here. Which means Morcant can, too, if he's still close."

After casting one last glance at Ronan to ensure he'd guard Sabrina with his life, Damian touched Trevor's shoulder and teleported back to the house.

Josie was dying.

She felt the coldness taking over as the blood flowed from her wound.

And not a single damned soul intended to save her.

Not the blond-haired angel with the puppy, not her sisters, and certainly not that devil, Damian.

She appealed to the angel. "Please. Help… me."

"I will," he assured her. "We all will. For now, take comfort in holding Willow, and think happy thoughts."

"Like Peter Pan or… some shit?" she ground out between gritted teeth as another excruciating wave hit her abdomen. "Aren't we a little… old for fairy… tales?"

"Why do people insist on calling me old?" the angel muttered.

"Castor, when I tell you, stop time for everyone but you, Blane, and me," Damian said from the other side of her, where his hands hovered over her wound. "Josie, I'm going to remove the bullet from your abdomen. For that, I need to put you into a deep sleep."

She looked at her sisters, who both appeared fretful.

Yeah, she was dying.

"Wait!" She hugged the puppy to her chest and prayed she didn't hurt it as she fought against the next stabbing pain. "Viv, if I don't make it—"

The silent tears rolling down her sister's face lent to her tragic air. "Don't say that, Josie. You're going to be fine."

"But if I don't—"

The angel placed a finger over her lips, and when she met his ice-blue eyes, her heart stuttered.

"None of that, gorgeous," he told her. "Happy thoughts, remember? You don't want to give that fucker Morcant the upper hand, do you?"

Where she found the strength to smile, she'd never know, but she managed to, albeit only slightly. "Never."

"That's my girl. I knew you were a fighter the second I saw you."

Her scoff ended in a groan as the next wave hit.

"Castor, leave off flirting, and let's get on with this."

"You're always determined to spoil my fun, Dethridge," Castor replied with a wink at Josie. "Hang in there, gorgeous. Only dream pleasant dreams. If you want to fantasize about me, I'll allow it."

He was outrageous, and yet Josie appreciated his ridiculous humor. It was the only reason—other than the fact she was dying—that she didn't roll her eyes at the absurdity of it all.

A kiss before dying would've been nice, though.

His naughty grin flashed. "A kiss before dying, huh?"

She frowned, certain she hadn't said it aloud.

"It's no trial on my part," Castor assured her.

Just as Josie was poised to comment, he swooped in and kissed her.

Open-mouthed.

With tongue.

Holy shit on a shingle!

Her angel kissed like a wicked-ass demon, and he tasted like a dream. Strawberry daiquiri. Her favorite.

"Castor!"

The Aether pulled Josie back from the brink of heaven with his barked reprimand.

Not bothering to look at him, Castor shrugged. "Take that with you into your dream state, gorgeous. Think happy thoughts, yeah?"

For a brief second, she thought she detected an underlying Irish accent when he spoke, but she must've imagined it. Prior to his last comment, he'd sounded as American as she did.

Damian shifted and placed the palm of his left hand over her forehead. "Sleep."

"What the fuck, Castor?" Damian muttered as he prepared to remove the bullet and repair Josie's intestines.

Alex shrugged. "You told me to distract her. That's what I was doing."

"Think the date you left with Dethridge's credit card is going to appreciate the fact you were making out with another woman less than a half hour after leaving her to fend for herself?" Trevor asked, smirking.

"You're really starting to annoy me, Blane."

"Focus, fellas. That's my sister on the table."

"Viv, I need you and Taryn to stop stressing. If I can feel it, it's possible Morcant can, too." Damian gave her a confident smile he didn't quite feel. "We're going to save your sister. I need you to believe that."

With a deep, cleansing breath and a clasp of Taryn's hand, Vivian nodded and gave him a tight smile in return.

"Here's the plan, fellas. First, I'll remove the bullet. Next, Castor will stop time for everyone but the three of us. During that short span, I'm going to remove all her blood and place it in a cylinder. While it's contained, Trevor will need to find every single bit of magic and obliterate it. I'll do the same to her cells. Lastly, we'll restore the blood to her body."

Vivian gasped his name.

He ignored her.

"We have a small window. Less than a minute after I repair her body. Got it?"

"What's he saying, Viv?" Taryn demanded. "Damian? Will Josie be powerless?"

"This is about saving her damned life," he snapped. "We'll worry about the rest later."

Duly reprimanded, she dropped her gaze to Josie and nodded.

Satisfied there would be no further questions or interruptions, Damian began the painstaking process of locating the bullet. His hand was an inch from the lead when a warning ricocheted through his mind.

He withdrew and swore savagely under his breath.

"Morcant is far more clever than I gave him credit for. Apparently he foresaw I'd try to heal her, and he's spelled the blasted thing against me. I could counteract it, but it would take precious time we don't have." Glancing at Castor, Damian said, "He wouldn't have anticipated you. Only a handful of us are aware you exist." Knowing Alexander preferred not to get messy if he could avoid it, Damian grinned evilly. "I hope you're not squeamish."

"It isn't like I've not seen blood in my lifetime." With a sour look, Castor asked, "What do I need to do?"

Under Damian's instruction, he stuck his hand in the body cavity and removed the damaged part of the bowel.

"I'm not going to lose a finger, am I, Dethridge?" he asked, somewhat seriously for him.

After a pause to play out the scene in his mind and a check for any indication the surgery would go south, Damian shook his head. "No. You're good to go."

The bullet clinked as Castor dropped it in a ramekin dish Vivian had set aside.

"I don't know what healthy intestines should look like, Damian. How do you want me to repair it?"

"I can do that. Suspend time while Blane and I do the rest."

Fifty-nine seconds later, Josie's blood was restored and her body was knitting together.

Time snapped back with a resounding pop.

"Good work, fellas. Let's get cleaned up, and I'll wake Josie." Damian met Taryn's worried gaze. "I'll restore what she's lost. You have my word."

CHAPTER 18

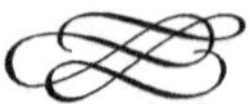

*D*amian was in the middle of scrubbing his hands when he recalled what Sabrina had said to the Death Dealer.

"You can bring her back."

His blood ran cold.

Bellowing Trevor's name, Damian ran for the guest room where they'd put Josie to rest. With the others hot on his heels, he burst into her room. Her skin had begun to gray, similar to Morcant's sickly pallor when he'd taken the Stephens family hostage.

Touching his fingers to her neck, Damian felt for a pulse.

Nothing.

"Fuck."

Placing his palm over her heart, he visualized a beating heart. All he knew about CPR was that he had to keep the blood flowing to the vital organs.

"What did Sabrina tell you to do, Blane?"

"I need you to channel electricity for me. She said it will pass through me to Josie."

"Let's do it." Damian told the others to clear the room. "I can't risk hitting any of you."

"Do you need me, Dethridge?" Castor asked with a worried look down at Josie.

"I don't think so. Please take the pup and check on Beastie."

After everyone had left. Damian made short work of pulling the electrical molecules from the air around them. "Tell me when, Blane."

Positioning himself with one hand flat over Josie's forehead and one on her chest, Trevor visibly prepared himself and blew out a breath of air. His unease was palpable.

"Are you positive Beastie told you this was the way?" Damian was skeptical of the process. "The wattage could fry your circuits for good."

"Do you trust your kid, Aether?"

Did he? Yes. Despite her young age, she'd never failed to come up with a workable solution to a problem. Pride for her clever brain flowed through him.

"I do. Ready?"

"Hit me."

The bolt slammed into Trevor at roughly two million miles per hour and charged him with approximately one billion volts. His body jerked, but impossibly, he maintained his stance as he manipulated the energy to do whatever he needed it to.

As if coming up from a deep dive, Trevor and Josie gasped simultaneously, natural color returning to her cheeks. For a split second, the Death Dealer's face assumed Josie's sickly gray pallor before returning to normal.

Having expected it, Damian caught Trevor as his knees buckled, and eased him to the floor.

"I've got you, Blane. Take it easy," he said soothingly.

"I'm good, Aether. How's Josie?"

A glance showed her sitting up and feeling her stomach for the wound. "I'd say healed."

"What happened?" Her amber gaze met his, and her unguarded expression was one of confusion.

"Mr. Blane brought you back from the brink of death." There

was no need to scare her with the entire truth, so he held back that particular tidbit of information. Damian perched on the edge of the mattress and clasped her hand. "How do you feel, my dear? Any pain?"

"I'm achy. Muscles, bones… hell, even my teeth." She grimaced. "Did you happen to get the number of the truck that hit me?"

He snorted in the face of her dark humor. "It was going too fast for me to see a plate."

"Isn't that always my luck?" Groaning, she flopped back on the pillows. "I had the strangest dream. I was floating over my body, then I could see Morcant…" She shuddered. "Holy hellfire, he's an ugly sonofabitch. Creepy as fuck."

"You saw him? Where?"

"The northern boundary of Ravenswood, I think. There was an estate to the left, at the top of a hill." Frowning, Josie met his steady gaze. "They were discussing it and pointing, but I couldn't make out what they were saying. One of the men began walking in that direction, but Morcant struck him down."

"Killed him?"

"No. Gashed his face, though." She gestured along her cheek. "Pretty horrific cut, if you ask me."

In a sharper-than-intended tone, he asked, "Where did they go? To the other estate?"

"No. Morcant wouldn't take his eyes off the maze."

"All right. Rest now."

Josie gripped his wrist as he stood. "It wasn't a dream, was it, Damian?"

"I don't believe so, no."

"Was I dead?"

Pressing his lips in a tight line, he nodded. "But you're back with us, and you have my daughter and the Death Dealer to thank."

"What happened to the angel?"

Lifting his brows in question, he smiled when she flushed.

"Castor, I think you called him."

"The man is no angel, my dear. Closer to a wily devil, in my opinion."

"Ouch, Dethridge. That stung." Castor sauntered over to the bed and clapped him on the back. "Don't think I don't know that you purposely said it to hurt my feelings. You felt me behind you, didn't you?"

"You're a pain in my ass most days, Alex. How could I not feel the irritating prickle of your presence?" Damian replied dryly.

"You love me. Don't deny it," Alex said with the confidence of a best friend.

They shared a grin.

"I'm going to leave Josie in your questionably capable hands." Damian crossed to Trevor and offered help up. "Try not to seduce her, Alex. She's still recovering from surgery."

"I'm not an animal."

"Debatable."

Castor's hearty laugh rang out, causing Damian to smile. It was impossible not to like the man, which was probably why they were as close as brothers.

"How's my daughter?"

"Happily talking Ronan's ear off. That man has the patience of a fucking saint."

"Careful. That's my child you're insulting." But Damian wasn't offended. Beastie could chat a person into a coma.

"Go save my nephew," Castor said good-naturedly. "Also, you might want to deposit a few mil in his bank account for going above and beyond in his babysitting duty."

Damian stopped short of leaving and looked over his shoulder. Frowning, he asked, "Is he hurting for funds?"

"Not really. I just know you're a fucking billionaire who can spare the change."

With a wry shake of his head, Damian escorted the Death Dealer out the door. But not before he heard Castor take up the flirting mantle.

"I don't know why Damian is being a tight ass about our new

relationship," Alex told Josie. "It isn't like I didn't have my hand all up in you less than a half hour ago."

She choked out a laugh.

With a chuckle of his own, Damian left them.

"How is she?" Vivian asked her husband as soon as he appeared downstairs.

"Good." He cupped her cheek and brushed a thumb across her lips. Leaning down, he bussed a light, lingering kiss across her mouth. "Better than good, Viv. She's alive and, unless I miss my guess, flirting with Alex."

"There are worse men to flirt with, I suppose," she replied, wrapping her arms around Damian's waist. "Thank you, darling."

"You're welcome." His tone was warm, his voice husky. "I have to go see Ronan and Beastie to figure out the next step with Morcant. Hopefully, she can tell me how to send that bastard to hell once and for all."

"It won't be soon, unless the future drastically altered today." Vivian sighed as she released Damian. "Remember what she told us the day Nate was born? The hellhounds would protect them."

"Christ! You're right. Although, technically, they did protect us today."

"True."

He scrubbed a hand up and down his face, and it occurred to her that he looked more human at that moment than she'd remembered seeing him in recent days. The strain of the situation was reflected in the tightness around his eyes and mouth. Still, he was gorgeous, and she had the urge to sigh like a girl with her first crush.

His eyes crinkled at the corners as he smiled. "Gorgeous, huh?"

"Oh! I forgot our new connection."

Turning serious, he stroked her jaw. "Does it bother you, Viv? I can see what I can do to sever it if it does."

Searching her feelings on the matter, she decided it didn't.

"Maybe it was given to us for a reason. Should we ask the Goddess?"

"I don't see the point. If Isis had anything to impart, she'd be here." As if he couldn't help himself, he kissed her again. "I need to go."

"I'll prepare a feast for everyone. I imagine we'll be hunkered down here for a while."

"Thank you, my love."

As he strode off, Vivian couldn't help but compare his fluid, graceful movement to a jungle cat. Damian had a barely suppressed energy about him, as if at any moment, without warning, he could strike.

Dangerous.

And sleek.

And beautiful.

And sexy.

"And yours."

She meeped when his voice reverberated in her mind.

When he reached the French doors, he glanced over his shoulder and winked.

"And mine," she murmured aloud.

After he left, she shoved aside her obsessive thoughts and sought her sisters to help clean the dining room and set the table for the others.

She felt it was her job to make things as normal as possible in the midst of the madness. If she could help everyone retain a calm demeanor, then they could keep the life-giving negativity from Morcant's hands. Anything she could do to support Damian and Sabrina in this endeavor, she would. Even if it meant clubbing her own sisters over the head to keep them from becoming hysterical at every turn.

Not that they were inclined to. Josie was fiery, not stupid. Her emotional plea earlier had been understandable. Especially because she'd believed she might be dying.

Taryn wasn't prone to strong feelings in general. Not unless they had to do with a sister stealing her boyfriend, as Josie had done with Morgan/Morcant. They all knew it was good riddance, and Taryn was learning to live and let live. Her main point of contention was that Josie hadn't told them the truth from the start.

Taryn wasn't wrong.

Neither was Josie.

Since none of them could see through Morcant's glamour, she did the only thing she could to keep them all safe. Betrayed trust and all.

Leaving her younger sisters to set the table, Vivian went upstairs to check on Josie before the scheduled feeding for Nate.

As she peeked inside the door to the guest room, she noticed her sister dozing and Alexander Castor watching her from a comfy chair in the corner. Unnoticed, Vivian witnessed his melancholy expression.

He's lonely.

Deep inside her mind, she heard Damian reply, *"I believe so, yes."*

"Stay out of my head, stalker. It's creepy."

His chuckle made her grin.

Castor glanced up, and a warm smile curled his lips. "Viv."

"Hey, Alex." She crossed to the end of the bed and looked down at her sister. "How is she?"

"Right as rain. No need to stress it."

A pang struck her heart. "I had no idea Morcant had his claws so deep in her. I feel like a horrible person for not seeing it."

"People show you what they want you to see," Alex replied simply. "Some have more to hide than others."

Facing him, she cocked her head and studied him, with his suddenly blasé attitude. "Like you?"

"Among others. Your husband comes to mind, though."

Vivian smiled, although she didn't exactly think his comment was amusing. "Yes. Damian is the king of secrets.

Lifting his cool eyes to hers, he nodded. "But he's a good man, Viv. The best, really. Never forget it, okay?"

"I'll try not to," she replied softly.

"It's harder to see when you're in it, but your husband would move mountains for you and your children. He'd kill for you without a moment's regret."

"I know that."

"If you do, then what's the problem?"

"I'm not sure he's forgiven me for leaving or for the years he missed with Sabrina."

"If he didn't forgive you, you wouldn't be here. He wouldn't let someone close to him if he didn't trust them."

"You think?"

"I *know*." Castor rose and claimed the spot next to her. Gripping the brass bars of the footer, he shrugged. "Damian saved me when I was a lost teenager. He took me in when I had nobody to give a shit one way or the other." Meeting her gaze, expression stark, Alex shook his head. "Did he ever tell you that I'd tried to rob him and Alastair after I ran away from home? No?" A wry smile curled his lips. "I was a cocky shit back then."

"You still are," Vivian said with a light laugh.

"True." He nodded his acknowledgment. "Your husband could've punished me, but he formed a pact with Al. Their goal was to teach me right from wrong. They trained me to be a formidable man who'll never be victimized again."

Her heart went out to the scrawny teenage boy who felt the need to escape his awful family. "Your brother, Loman, did a number on you, didn't he?"

"And Ronan, too." Alex swallowed hard. "I'm just sorry I wasn't there for him like Damian was for me."

"He turned out all right."

"It's truly a miracle, yeah." In his deep emotional state, Castor forgot himself, and Vivian could hear a hint of Irish accent.

"I'm glad Damian helped you." She placed a hand on his forearm. "And I imagine, deep down, you still feel undeserving, but that's not true. You *do* deserve good things, Alex."

His mouth twisted in a slight grimace before he smoothed his features. "All I'm saying is that an unforgiving asshole doesn't do what Damian did for me. If you ask him, he'll tell you he forgave you a long time ago, Viv."

Tears burned her eyes, threatening to spill, and she blinked to gain control.

A thoughtful light filled Alex's eyes. "Ah."

"What?"

"You don't forgive yourself."

CHAPTER 19

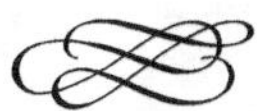

*W*as it true? Was Vivian the problem? Was her inability to forgive herself for separating father and daughter during Sabrina's formative years keeping her at a distance?

Maybe.

Probably.

Yes.

Vivian shook her head as she held Nate tighter to her.

He didn't protest her firm hold and, instead, raised his arm, flattening his tiny hand over her heart. Calmness settled over her. An odd sense of rightness. Had her son done that?

As she stared down into his wide, baby-blue eyes, she thought perhaps he had. Offering her index finger, she smiled as he gripped it and a second warm pulse was transferred from him to her.

"You're going to be as strong as your papa, aren't you, my little man?"

He gave her a toothless grin as he released her nipple.

Vivian shifted him to her shoulder and covered her breast, then proceeded to burp him. Sensing she was no longer alone, she sought the source.

Damian lounged in the door opening, his arms crossed and an indulgent smile on his perfect face.

How had she gotten so lucky to gain the attention and affection of the Aether? He was so dynamic and important, yet he held no artifice or conceit. His every action was thought out, as if he weighed the consequences of every possibility before making a single move.

Deliberate.

Damian was *always* deliberate.

What would it be like if he wasn't? She couldn't recall him ever simply letting go. Not even during lovemaking. The one place he was free to be himself had been her bed, and yet he hadn't been. Looking back, it seemed a sad way to live.

"What has you thinking so hard, my love?"

She smiled in the face of his curiosity. "You don't know? Can't read my mind?"

"I could, but you called me a creeper earlier."

"A stalker, and I said it was creepy that you could."

"Right, so I decided I won't." He straightened from the wall and strolled across to them. Holding out his arms, he asked, "May I?"

"Of course. He's your son." After handing Nate off, she stood. "Here, take a seat."

"I'm too wound up to sit." Rocking the baby, Damian approached the window and looked out over the estate. "I can still feel him out there. Like a buzzing in my mind."

"I'm assuming you mean Morcant."

"Yes."

"But he can't get through the wards?"

"No. Nor the extra barrier I've added to encase the property."

"You're still worried, aren't you?"

"I'm trying not to be. It's imperative we set aside negative emotions."

"Is that possible? People have negative thoughts every day."

He turned and raised a brow.

"Am I too fat? Am I pretty enough? Am I interesting?" She

paused and smiled softly, feeling the old insecurities rise up. "Does my husband love me as much as I love him? Does he forgive me for being foolish and leaving when I should've faced my fears and stayed?"

"The first three questions should never plague you, my love." Damian's expression softened as he gazed at her. "And as for the last two. *More*, and of course he does."

"Really?"

His look turned thoughtful as he contemplated a response.

"Please give me the unvarnished truth, Damian. No matter how badly you think I'll take it."

"I was trying to understand why you didn't believe me the first time I said it."

"Because it feels like an unforgivable offense. I believed another's lies when I should've taken you at face value. You never gave me a reason to assume you'd hurt Sabrina."

"And?"

"And because you missed three years of your daughter's life," she said raggedly.

"Do you think I need to constantly berate or torment you when you do enough of that yourself, Viv?" he asked gently.

"Probably not," she admitted with a watery smile.

Walking to the crib, he eased Nate onto the mattress and covered him up. When he straightened, he strode to her, stopping short of touching. "Your fears weren't truly yours, my love. They were the manifestation of another's magical trickery. You're not to blame for running. You never were."

Vivian flung herself into his waiting embrace and let her silent tears flow.

"I'm sorry, Damian. So sorry," she whispered fiercely.

"Shhh. You're back where you belong, and moving ahead, we're going to be stronger than ever."

"Yes."

Drawing back, he tilted her chin up and gave her a butterfly-soft kiss on the lips. "I can't tell you how happy that makes me."

"Me, too."

The skin bracketing his eyes crinkled as he grinned, and those same eyes were lit with mischievousness, reminding Vivian of Sabrina when she was in a particularly playful mood.

"Can I tell you a secret?"

She nodded.

"I scryed every damned day. I may not have been there, but I saw Sabrina's key moments. I also witnessed your love for her."

Laughing, Vivian rested her forehead against his chest. "Why doesn't that surprise me?"

"Don't stress those wasted moments. Yes, it was painful not to be there, but in the entire scheme of things, that time is a mere droplet in a bucket of water."

Because Aethers live for centuries.

"Yes," he replied to her internalized realization. "Can I tell you another secret?"

She lifted her head to meet his burning gaze.

Her mouth went dry.

"I spied on *you*, too, Viv. I couldn't go a day without seeing you and making sure you were happy."

"Oh, Damian."

"Were you happy, love?"

"No. Not without you."

Standing here in front of her husband, she felt like a teenager again—nervous and excited all at once. His calm, adoring eyes never left hers, yet she sensed his wariness beneath the surface. It was as if he worried she might suddenly reject him, and that human quality only made her love him more. Really, what woman in her right mind would ever say no to him?

She had, yes.

However she'd been under the magical influence of others, and it could be argued she wasn't in her right mind at all.

Reaching out, she clasped his hand and led him down the hallway to her room, the one they'd shared when they were first married. When they reached the bed, she stopped, unsure how to proceed. Was she supposed to be the aggressor? Did she offer up control to him? Would she appear like a silly twit after all this time?

Damian shifted closer, wrapping one arm around her waist and the other across her upper chest. Drawing her back against him, he said, "I've missed you. Missed this. Us. So damned much."

She could feel the warmth of his body against her own, and a shiver ran down her spine.

"I've missed you, too," she replied, her voice barely above a whisper. "This. Us. More than I can ever say."

Without another word, Damian turned her toward him. Cradling her face, he covered her mouth with his, sliding his tongue between her parted lips. His kiss was the perfect blend of gentle and fierce. Almost worshipful as it went on.

She fell into the act, kissing him back like there might be no more tomorrows for either of them. With the threat of Morcant, there might not be, and Vivian would be damned if she wasted one more second on insecurity or regret. Making love with Damian was the balm to her wounded heart. Wounds she'd inflicted upon her own person. But she required *him* to make her whole again.

Picking up on her need, he returned her passion with urgency and assuredness. As if once he recognized she wanted him as much, if not more, than he wanted her, his uncertainty dissolved into determination.

With every move, every touch, every sweep of his tongue across hers, he drugged her, drawing her further under his seductive spell like he had every other time before. If sex had a poster child, it would be her husband.

Her husband.

Hers.

Vivian smiled against his mouth, and he inched away with a questioning look. Shaking her head, unable to explain her possessiveness and pride, she unbuttoned his shirt and eased it down his sinewy arms. Her eyes devoured his beautifully sculpted chest, and she let her hands wander over his golden skin.

"I don't believe I've ever felt as objectified." Laughter was evident just beneath the surface.

"I'm calling bull. Every woman who's ever encountered you has totally objectified you."

Damian surprised her when he grew serious. "I've never wanted that. It's important you know."

"I do. I trust you, darling. Always and forever moving forward."

A dark scowl hijacked his features, and he halted the exploration of her hands. "You think I was unfaithful in the past?"

"No." Running her fingers up his chest, she wove them into his thick hair and drew his head down. "Never. You're too honorable. I should've said I've always trusted you and I always will. But we both know there was a time I let Josie sway me. Moving forward, *you* are the one I'll believe above all others."

Mollified, he replaced her palms flat against his pecs. "Carry on."

Laughingly, she did.

Leaning in, Vivian licked the tight bud of his nipple. His hands came up, and he threaded his fingers through her hair, holding her in place. Another lick elicited his soft moan, and latching on, she suckled his nipple, toying with the tip.

"Mmm. I think we should lie down before my knees give out like an overwrought debutant," he said in a deep, raspy voice.

His was akin to the voice of a god, with the barest hint of a British inflection leftover from his childhood, and the sound shot a thrill through her. It was as hypnotic as the rest of him.

"Don't use words like overwrought or debutant unless you care to give away your ag—"

"Don't you dare say *age*, wench!"

"Wench went out about a hundred years ago, too," she informed him pertly.

"Don't say I didn't warn you," he growled.

Her clothes were gone in a snap, and his lips and hands were everywhere at once, but nothing felt rushed. He caressed her as he'd done a thousand times, hitting all her erogenous zones without fail. Stimulating her and driving her into a frenzy over and over again.

As the fire within her grew, she cried out, pressing up against him and begging for mercy.

Their eyes met and held.

The fierce longing in his gaze was her undoing.

There was no play, no teasing after that.

Only raw need.

Vivian wrapped her hand around his hard length and glided the tip of his penis along her swollen, wet flesh. "Please, darling. Now."

He stole her breath with his first thrust, pulsing magic through their connection and causing her to cry out. Gripping his hair, she turned her head slightly to whisper into the shell of his ear.

"I love you, Damian."

His body tensed, and the burning desire in his smoldering dark gaze made her catch her breath in anticipation. Never breaking eye contact, he eased out only to thrust back, time and time again, vigorously driving them toward the brink. Chant-like, his name fell from her lips between pants, and when she came, she buried her mouth against the hollow of his throat to muffle a scream. His cry of release followed on the heels of hers.

Rolling to the side, he pulled her against him.

"I love you, too, Viv," he murmured, sounding half asleep.

With a sigh of contentment, she snuggled closer and closed her eyes.

This was where she belonged.

Forever and always.

CHAPTER 20

"We should find Beastie." Damian yawned and scratched his chest. "Ronan will require a break by now."

The picture of a satisfied lover, Vivian lay facedown with her crossed arms pillowing her head. She didn't bother opening her eyes when she replied, "Surely he's ushered her off to bed. It's past midnight, and he can't have that much fortitude."

Chuckling, he leaned over and nuzzled her silky-smooth throat, breathing in the faint smell of gardenias. She'd once told him it was her favorite flower, and her sister Soleil did her damndest to keep one alive during their harsh Northeast winters. Earth witches were nothing if not dedicated.

"Rest, my love. I'll go check on them. If he's torn his hair out from the stress, you'll cry to see it."

"He *is* the perfect eye candy. I'm not about to deny it."

"This is only a suggestion, but perhaps you should refrain from thinking about 'eye candy' when you're in bed with your husband. It's not a well-known fact, but he's jealous to the extreme and likely to uglify the handsome Guardian in his rage."

When Vivian tucked her face to hide her grin, an easy peace

132

settled in Damian's chest. This was the way marriage should be. He drew the sheet down and feathered kisses along the exposed skin of her back, taking great satisfaction when she shivered her pleasure. She was highly responsive to the slightest stimulation, and he loved how his overtures brought out her wild side.

"I suppose you'll have to keep me occupied with other things," she murmured huskily.

"Mmm. Yes. I suppose I will." As he started to draw the bedding down farther, a surge of childlike energy hit him, and he sat up. "Beastie's almost to our door."

Visualizing pajama bottoms and a t-shirt, Damian snapped his fingers. Vivian, too, managed to clothe herself an instant before the door burst open.

"We need to remember to engage the lock," she murmured as she shifted to a sitting position.

As if she suspected they were hiding something from her, Sabrina paused overly long in the doorway and gave them a suspicious look. Whatever her curious mind came up with was satisfying enough, and she ran to dive into Damian's waiting embrace.

"Are you and Mama all better?"

"I didn't know we were sick," he replied dryly.

With an exaggerated eye roll, she bumped her bony shoulder into his chest. "You're silly, Papa."

Sharing a glance and a grin, Damian and Vivian nodded in unison.

"I think we're all better," Vivian said softly, never taking her eyes from his.

Feeling lighter than he'd been in recent years, he laughed. "Indeed."

"I'm going to check on Nate." Vivian leaned in and kissed first Sabrina, then him. "Whatever she's plotting, don't cave. It's past her bedtime."

After his wife left, Damian could better feel his daughter's insecurity. "What has you troubled, Beastie?"

"Can I sleep in here with you and Mama tonight?" Sabrina's

question came out of the blue and surprised him with its hesitant quality.

"Why would you want to?"

With a half-hearted shrug, she focused on her sparkling pink socks.

A sickening dread began to build, and Damian frowned as he hugged her. "I think you need to tell me what it is you've seen, my love."

"I'm not ready to go with Morcant yet."

Rarely could people shock him, but his daughter managed it quite frequently of late. It took a solid minute for him to form words.

"Morcant will never get you. *Ever.*"

When she looked up, the sadness in her almond-shaped eyes gutted him.

"Tell me," he demanded.

"He will take me away, and you will find me."

"No. No." Damian shook his head so hard. "No one will *ever* take you away from me again. Understood?"

Her silence said it all. She'd seen her own kidnapping and that her own father—the mightiest warlock on the planet—could do nothing to stop it. Never in all his life had Damian felt the urge to vomit as he did then. Sweat broke out on his upper lip and lower back, and his skin felt clammy.

"Beastie," he whispered raggedly. "Please tell me you see an alternate future. *Please.*"

Why the hell hadn't he gotten a vision of the upcoming event now that his abilities had returned in full? Had Morcant developed the power to block him? Highly unlikely, which meant the Authority or the Fates had a plan for Damian's daughter and knew he'd rebel.

She swallowed hard, shaking her head.

"Then I'm not letting you out of my sight."

"It will be worse if you don't," she said in a small voice.

"How long?"

"Tomorrow."

"No, how long will it take me to tear the world apart to find you?"

"Not long, Papa. I swear."

She was hiding something. As someone who'd always told her never to reveal what she knew, to keep from affecting future outcomes, he couldn't insist she tell him. But as the father of a future missing child, he wanted all the details.

"Promise me that, no matter what, you'll remain positive, Beastie. You can't give him your power."

"I promise."

"And you'll stay alive, no matter what it takes. No matter the cost."

"I…" Her lips compressed, and unshed tears made her dark eyes large pools of bleakness.

"I'm not letting you go until you tell me you'll survive this, Sabrina Dethridge." He pressed his forehead to hers. "You're my heart, and it won't beat without you, child."

"But what about Mama? You and Nate can't live without her either," she said brokenly.

Never in his life had Damian been so overcome with emotion that he couldn't speak. There were no words to assure Sabrina that Vivian would gladly sacrifice her own life for her children, just as he would. True, he might never love again, but he would eventually come to accept the loss if it meant Sabrina and Nate would live a full life.

When he managed to unlock himself from the shock chaining him in place, he shifted to sit her on the mattress and knelt before her so they were eye level.

"No parent wants to outlive their children, Beastie. The hurt is too great. Neither your mother nor I could handle it if something happened to either you or your brother. Do you understand?"

Compressing her lips, she shook her head.

"No, you don't understand, or no, you don't believe we'll go mad without you in our lives?"

Her gaze focused on something behind him, and rather than turn, Damian allowed his senses to seek what was there.

Vivian.

How much had she heard?

"All of it," she said hoarsely. "I'll kill Morcant myself before he touches one hair on your head, Sabrina Evelyn Dethridge. And you'd better damned well believe it."

Shooting off the bed and darting past him, his daughter launched herself at Vivian. "I'm sorry, Mama. I'm sorry," she sobbed.

The sight of them blurred.

Swiping a hand across his eyes, Damian was startled to see moisture.

Vivian clutched her distraught daughter and turned her terrified gaze to Damian. The sight of his tears stunned her speechless. In the confines of her mind, she tried to build a wall to block out her fear from Sabrina.

Directing the question to her formidable husband, she asked, *"What do we do?"*

He shook his head, apparently at a loss, like her.

After conjuring tissues, Vivian shifted and knelt in front of Sabrina. She dabbed her daughter's tear-swollen eyes and smoothed the hair back from her hot forehead.

"We're going to get through this, my darling girl. I promise you, we will."

There was zero hope in Sabrina's tortured expression. "I don't want you to die, Mama."

"Listen to me. Your father is correct. If it comes down to you or me, let me be the one." Unable to stop herself, Vivian dragged her daughter back into her arms and pressed a cheek to Sabrina's silky black hair. "I mean it. You are meant for great things, and your papa needs you. Nate needs you to guide him and be the best big sister imaginable."

Joining them, Damian wrapped them both within the circle of his arms.

"I need you both," he said, and there was no compromise in his tone. If it was up to him—and Vivian prayed it was—they'd all survive Morcant's malevolent machinations.

"I think it's time to gather your new Sentinel team, Damian," Vivian said in a low voice. "It's time to wipe Morcant from the face of this earth for good."

"Consider it done."

The sharp click of the door marked his exit.

Vivian guided Sabrina to the nearby chaise. After fluffing pillows and urging her daughter to lie down, she drew a blanket up to her slender shoulders and sat on the floor next to her.

"Can you tell me every scenario available to us? And before you tell me that your papa says you're not supposed to, know that I don't care about Damian's rule this time. I need to be able to come up with the best solution."

"Morcant wants to keep me sad, Mama. He wants to kill you and Papa and Baby Nate."

"I understand that. So, his plan is to what… spread the grief apart? Take us out one at a time to keep you mourning?"

"Yes, but he can't. Not after you."

Vivian sucked in a breath so hard she coughed. Could her Oracle daughter make her death any plainer?

Fuck.

"If he can't, then what?"

"He will kill me, too."

"I see. But not if Damian finds you first, right? Is that a possibility?"

Nodding, Sabrina blinked heavily, as if her emotional outburst had exhausted her and she was fighting sleep.

Jumping to her feet, Vivian ran to the en suite bathroom and found a pair of scissors. After snipping a long strand of her hair, she returned to Sabrina and did the same. Clearing her mind, she centered herself and cast a small protective circle around the chaise. As she wove the locks together, she called on the Goddess Isis.

"Goddess, hear my plea.
Assist me in this time of need.
Through these locks, bind my daughter's tumultuous emotions to me, so she feels naught and Morcant Thywyll cannot feed.

Suppress my pain, worry, and fear
in this, our time of strife
to keep all feeling from him
and to protect blood of my blood for life."

The impact of Sabrina's unimaginable power hit Vivian like a freight train and knocked her flat on her back. Grunting, she held onto the bracelet of hair she'd created as her daughter's fear and insecurities latched onto her. Like wild animals, the heightened emotions clawed at Vivian's soul, doing their best to shred and consume it.

As suddenly as the magic hit her, it was gone. In its place was an odd sense of detachment.

Cocking her head, she looked at Sabrina, who stared back, wide-eyed.

"Too much?"

With a shake of her head, her daughter promptly closed her eyes and drifted off to sleep.

"It felt like it was too much," Viv murmured.

After snuffing out the candle and closing the circle, she turned around and froze.

"Damian."

"It was a clever idea, Viv. However, you've made a grave error."

"Why?"

"When you die, it breaks the spell."

Fuck.

CHAPTER 21

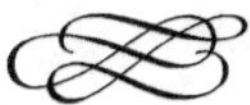

amian shook his head as he entered the bedroom. "Not to bring up a touchy subject, but I'd have thought you'd remember that from the previous binding spell you cast on her, Viv."

"I wasn't thinking. Merely reacting."

"Yes. You tend to do that," he replied dryly, smiling when she narrowed her eyes at him. "Are you completely emotionless?"

"No. Just the negative stuff." With a sigh, she glanced back at Sabrina. "When Morcant kills me, he'll still have the upper hand. How do we maintain the spell?"

"We add to it. A transference."

She lifted a blond brow and handed him the bracelet. "Using this?"

"Yes."

Twirling a finger through a small section of hair at the back of his head, Damian fed the strand, urging it to grow. When it was approximately the length of the bracelet, he held out a hand for Vivian's scissors.

After snipping his hair, he pressed it to the other two locks, fusing them together until it was impossible to tell one color from another. Encasing the entire thing in platinum, he slipped it on his wrist.

"I'll consume any darker responses either of you should experience. Should anything happen to either of you..." The bleak image forced him to catch his breath. Swallowing hard, he continued. "Should anything happen to either of you, the other will not be able to grieve unless I destroy this bangle."

"Good. But Sabrina brought up a secondary problem. What's to stop Morcant from killing her to gain her power if he can't drain it through her emotions?"

"She's too strong. When she wakes in the morning, I'll make her practice a protection spell. She already knows the basics. It's the same one I used for the property, but on a smaller scale. She can encase herself in a bubble until we get to her."

Nodding, Vivian strode for the door.

"Where are you going?"

"To bring Nate in here. I'll watch over them throughout the night, and you'll take the morning shift."

"In case I never told you, you're one badass Mama Bear, my love."

A delighted smile curled her lips. Probably because the word badass came out of a two-hundred-year-old man.

"Never doubt it, darling."

When he was alone, Damian casually waved a hand and made the bed. He climbed onto the mattress, sitting with his back to the headboard and crossing his legs at the ankles. Left with a private moment to himself, he played out all the possible options in his mind as he watched his daughter sleep. He couldn't contrive a sure-fire plan to capture Morcant without using Sabrina as bait.

It was no surprise when Ronan and Castor sought him out.

"Vivian sent us here to ya. She informed us of the wee beastie's prediction." Ronan crossed to the chaise and tugged the blanket up higher to tuck around Sabrina's neck. "Did she give ya a time frame, then?"

"Tomorrow."

"The hell you say!" Alex looked shell-shocked. "We're all here, Dethridge. He can't get in."

"She knows something she's not saying," Damian replied grimly, never removing his gaze from his daughter's slight form. Tilting his head back, he banged it once on the wall. "I'm all-powerful, and yet, apparently, I'm helpless against this new threat."

"We can only assume your wards will fail and Morcant will sneak in. It's his only option."

"Or someone will be sneakin' out," Ronan mused.

Alex shook his head. "No. That child is too intelligent to cause her own demise. What would be the point?"

"We need to find out what the authority knows—"

Paling, Castor collapsed.

With a colorful curse, Ronan dropped to his knees beside his uncle and felt for a pulse as Damian came off the bed.

"Is he alive?"

"Aye, but his feckin' heart's galloping away with him."

Placing his palm flat on Alex's forehead, Damian attempted to meld his mind with his friend. All he got for his troubles was a wicked-sharp pain to his frontal lobe.

"Jaysus! And where did *you* come from while your body's layin' here, man?"

Castor, not the one on the rug, strode over to them. With his stubbled jaw and mussed hair, he looked more haggard than Damian ever remembered seeing him.

"Alex?"

"I thought it was worth popping back in time."

"What the fuck is going on?"

"Morcant. He goes on a Dethridge killing spree in the not-so-distant future. The slaughter starts tomorrow, if I'm not mistaken."

Slaughter? Damian's stomach dropped before he got control of himself. Castor had a tendency to exaggerate, though why he would choose a term like slaughter if it didn't apply was questionable.

"How?"

"Your wards fail. Someone at the Authority is working against you, taking your abilities as they see fit. All in the name of the Fates."

Cold dread filled Damian. Unknown enemies were the worst. One never saw the attack coming.

Unless they were Sabrina.

"Sure, and let me get this straight." Ronan ran a hand through the hair Vivian admired. "There's a bastard wantin' to strike at the Aether, and he keeps encouraging a feckin' Arcane Devourer to do it?"

"That's it in a nutshell."

"Do you know who?" Damian asked future-Castor thoughtfully. If he could find them, he could end this madness immediately.

"No."

"Wonderful. For all we know, it might be one of the Sentinels I've brought into my home to protect Sabrina."

"If it is, I can't say which one," Alex replied. "But for sure, someone is working to bring down your wards."

"I see." Damian rose and shook Castor's hand. "Thank you for risking yourself to return. Go. I'll clean up this mess."

"Take care, and don't go after your daughter alone. You have friends, Dethridge."

As Alex positioned himself to leave, Damian halted him with a touch on his arm. "Wait! Am I alive in this future reality you're from, and how distant are we talking?"

Expression grim, Castor nodded. "Yes, and perhaps a week. Most of us are running on little sleep, and the days are blending together."

"This bracelet"—he lifted his arm to show Castor—"is it on my wrist then?"

"I can't remember seeing it, but I wasn't looking."

"Thank you, Alex."

With a nod and shower of lights, he was gone. A mere second later, his present counterpart groaned and sat up, holding his head like he'd been on an all-night bender and was suffering the hangover.

"What the fuck happened to me?" he groaned.

"You did, my friend. Or rather, your future self."

"Next time, tell that fucker off for me."

Damian squatted. "Alex."

"What?"

"This is me, telling you off as per your request."

"Very funny. Send me the Death Dealer. Maybe he can put me out of my misery once and for all."

"Whine, whine, whine," Damian mocked before shifting to all-business mode. There was no time to spare. "You told me someone is working from the inside to hurt me." He checked his watch. "We have the six hours until sunup to discover who."

"No bleedin' pressure, to be sure," Ronan quipped, following it with a heavy sigh. "Yeah, and all we know is that your betrayer isn't in this room. Nor is it me Dove or your Vivian. Who else is there?"

"Viv's sisters, but I can't see any of them helping Morcant, and none of them work for the Authority." Damian began to pace. "I'd stake my life on the fact Blane is trustworthy, too."

Alex agreed. "He's come through for us whenever we needed it."

"Yes." Addressing Ronan, Damian asked, "What do you think?"

"Sure, and I wouldn't be casting my suspicions in that direction."

"Okay, so who did you bring in tonight, Dethridge?"

"My entire future team. Ten of us in all. That includes the two of you, Trevor Blane, Fintan Sullivan, and Narissa Sullivan. I've a magical call out to summon Draven Masters, Creed Caldwell, Jordan Brothers, and the Wraith."

"The Wraith? Dude's a myth, Damian. I wouldn't expect him to show."

"The *dude* is a dud*ette*, and she'll be here." Sensing the new presence, Damian paused his pacing and glanced out the window into the darkness. "Kassiani is a friend, and I'm betting she'll be here."

"Why have I never heard of her?" Castor asked.

The question was legitimate. As one of his two best friends, he knew a great deal about Damian.

"You were in hiding for fifty years, Alex. Until recently, everyone believed you'd died. Me included. I met Kass not long after you disappeared."

"Yeah, and now you've got me curious, to be sure." Ronan dropped into a chair and propped his feet up on the ottoman. "Sounds like a grand tale that needs tellin' one day."

With a shake of his head, Damian turned away from the window and crossed to the bench at the foot of the bed. Hiking up his pants leg, he belatedly realized he was wearing his pajamas from when Sabrina rushed in earlier. He heaved a regretful sigh for the sleep he was going to lose and snapped his fingers, changing into slacks and a button-down shirt.

"She's a magical bounty hunter by birth. Only a handful of people know of her existence. I made her acquaintance when I hired her to look for you, Alex. I believe you're the only one who managed to evade her."

"I'm honored."

"I wouldn't be if I were you, Traveler," a heavily pitch-accented voice replied.

As one, they all faced the window.

Casually sitting on the ledge, dressed in head-to-toe black and looking like a pint-sized ninja, was the Wraith. A touch of her hand to her ear unhooked the gauzy veil covering her nose and mouth.

"Hello, Kass," Damian said warmly. "Good of you to finally join us. How long have you been listening?"

"Since the present Traveler dropped to the floor." Soundlessly, she hopped off the ledge and, with a flick of her finger, shut the casement window behind her. "You might've told me what he was when you first sent me after him," she said sourly, though her put-upon tone didn't match the sparkle in her hazel eyes.

Grinning, he clasped her hand and kissed her smooth cheek. "It would've given you an advantage, my dear. I wanted to make your hunt challenging."

"Pfft." Her eyes lit on Ronan and widened marginally. "I don't know for certain, but I can *sense* what he is. A Guardian, no?"

Giving her a roguish grin, Ronan nodded. "Aye."

For a brief instant, her eyes darkened. "Draven is dead?"

"No. He's expected shortly." Damian moved to the chaise. "Ronan was specifically assigned as a Guardian by the Goddesses Anu and Isis. He's been gifted powers to protect my daughter, Sabrina."

Surprise flared in her eyes, and she lightly stepped around Ronan.

"She is a tiny replica of you, Aether." Her tone sounded wistful, and he couldn't discount the longing rolling off her. After a soft smile, unusual for her, she turned away from Sabrina and gave the men in the room an encompassing glance. "Enough of this. Why have you called me here? It's not for the Traveler."

"Would you believe I'm calling in my marker?"

"After forty years of silence? No, but I will help you all the sam—ah! The child's mother." Kassiani's expression was one of surprise as Vivian entered the room with Nate in her arms. "Two children? You've been busy, Aether."

He laughed. "Come, Kass. I'd like you to meet my wife."

CHAPTER 22

"You're hosting team meetings in our bedroom now, darling?" Vivian asked Damian as she joined the others.

Damian shot her a wry look. "Not intentionally. They all felt the need to seek me out."

"How many more are we expecting?"

"In here, none. In the living room, five for sure, possibly two more. We can adjourn downstairs, but we'll take the children with us."

"Of course." There was no way in hell she was leaving Sabrina alone now that she knew they were preparing for the battle of their lives.

Ronan stood and scooped up Sabrina, who burrowed closer to him and smiled in her sleep. "I've got the wee wild beastie. Lead the way."

When they were downstairs in the main living area, he shooed the newcomers, Fintan and Narissa, off the comfy sofa in the corner, then settled his charge and tucked the blanket around her. Formidable Guardian that he was, Ronan perched on the arm of the couch and crossed his arms.

No one was harming her daughter on his watch.

Vivian touched his shoulder to express her gratitude, and he nodded to show he understood.

Sitting so she could keep an eye on Sabrina, she placed her sleeping son beside her and laid out pillows around him to keep him from rolling. When Vivian was done, she glanced up to find Kassiani watching her.

"You're welcome to hold him," Vivian said softly after seeing the fleeting longing on the woman's face. "Nate loves the attention."

"I thank you, but no. Perhaps after our business is settled."

"The offer stands."

"What about me?" Castor asked, dropping down on the opposite side of Nate. "Can't I hold my godson?"

"Who made you his godfather?" Damian asked with a short laugh.

"Are you saying I'm not? Who is? I'll fight them for the right."

Vivian half suspected he was serious as he gazed down at Nate with adoration. "It's good to know that if anything ever happens to Damian or myself, we have a line of friends willing to care for our children."

"Which brings us to this meeting," her husband said, and there was no denying the grimness in his tone. "Future Castor paid us a visit earlier. For those who don't know, Morcant Thywyll is back and going by the name of Morgan Black. He's determined to destroy my family and gain an endless battery source in the process."

Narissa uncrossed her legs and leaned forward.

"Battery source?" she asked. Her accent was Deep South, as if she were born and raised in Georgia or South Carolina. At any moment, one would expect her to say, *"Bless your heart!"* Mixed with her large, challenging aquamarine eyes, her endless waves of blonde hair, and a stripperific body with its form-fitting clothes, the effect was pure femme fatale Georgia peach.

"Sabrina." Damian gave each person a lengthy look, as if sizing them up. "Castor said we have a traitor in our midst."

The news didn't surprise Vivian as much as she suspected it might have had she been in possession of all her emotions. However, knowing the truth, she studied everyone with new eyes. They all appeared either surprised or outraged as they viewed each other with suspicion.

"For what it's worth, I don't think it's anyone here," she said, gaining everyone's attention. "With the exception of Kassiani, I've known all of you for a while, and you've had Damian's back at every turn. Whenever he's called, you all have come running."

Moving to stand behind her, Damian laid his hands on Vivian's shoulders. "I'm in agreement. Based on Castor's information, I get the impression the source is higher up."

"Sure, and my money's on the Authority or the Fates," Ronan added. "They both love to fuck with the lives of others, as if we're nothing more than pawns in their feckin' chess match."

"Aye." Fintan nodded, and as much as he resembled his cousin Narissa with his lion-mane coloring and light eyes, he was the opposite of her in many ways. His Irish accent and gruff, single-syllable replies being the primary ones. "So what's yer plan, Aether?"

"I don't have one. *Yet.* That's why I'm turning to all of you for help." He moved to the center of their circle. "Please assist me in keeping my children safe."

Narissa met Fintan's hard stare and nodded once. Facing Damian, she said, "We're in, sugar."

Ronan and Alex were already a sure thing, but they verbally pledged their allegiance.

"Okay. That leaves Creed, Masters, Brothers, and Blane," Damian said with a satisfied smile.

"I'm in," Trevor said, entering the room. With a thumb gesture to the hall, he shrugged. "I heard the bulk of it as I was arriving. You know Simon would also be on board, Dethridge. My family owes you a debt."

"I'm not calling in debts, Blane. Anyone on this team should be here because they want to be. Not because they have to."

"Fair enough. But I feel confident in saying that you've earned the respect of everyone present. My brother and I included. We'd be honored to stand by you."

"Thank you."

A knock at the terrace doors caught their attention, and Damian went to welcome the last of his invitees.

The only person Vivian recognized was Draven Masters, the reluctant Guardian who had gone AWOL for a good number of years. His magic was likely the only one there that might rival Damian's, and it pulsed off him like an angry beacon.

With his rugged, unshaven jaw and sharp features, he appeared more world-weary than most people of her acquaintance. His whiskey-colored eyes were flat, too, as if he'd seen too much of life and it had left him cold. The deep laugh lines engraved in his skin suggested that, for a time, he'd been happy. Although attractive, he didn't use a glamour to hide his age or boost his looks the way a standard witch or warlock might. Here was a man who didn't give two shits what anyone thought of him.

After shaking her husband's hand, Draven produced a poker chip and traveled it across his knuckles, causing it to disappear at his pinky, then reappear at his thumb to start the motion all over again. The gesture seemed more absent-minded and habitual than deliberate.

As if he sensed Vivian's regard, his eyes found hers, and he nodded politely.

She returned the gesture before shifting her attention to the man on his left.

Fit was the only way to describe him. Not bulky in stature, but muscled nonetheless, he didn't appear to possess a spare ounce of fat. That lack lent his face a chiseled quality, as if he were made of stone. Like Draven, his eyes held no joy, and he looked around him with disinterest—*until* his gaze landed on Narissa.

The man's expression sharpened, and anger was obvious in the tightening of his mouth, as if he struggled not to swear up a storm. There was history between the two. Vivian would stake her life on it.

Running a shaking hand through his chestnut hair, he returned his attention to Damian. "Why am I here, Dethridge?"

"Creed. Please, come in and have a seat. We've much to discuss."

With a glance around and a purposeful avoidance of Narissa this time, Creed shook his head. "It appears you've gathered the Authority's mindless minions. I'm not one of them."

"You do my friends a disservice, Caldwell. They are all free thinkers here by choice." Damian's tone had cooled considerably, but he made his next offer, nonetheless. "I can have you reinstated or leave you to your fate. The choice is yours. However, I hope you'll consider joining my team after what you learn."

With a reluctant nod, Creed entered farther into the room. "Where's the booze?"

Vivian pointed. "Sideboard. Help yourself," she said with a smirk, knowing full well he intended to.

Draven followed him, which left only one newcomer Vivian didn't know.

"Jordan, thank you for answering the call." Damian gestured to the room. "Please, have a seat."

Jordan Brothers appeared fresher and less disillusioned than his two companions. Similarly built to Draven, he was lanky, with a youthful face and kind eyes that searched out and cataloged information in the environment surrounding him. Vivian noticed he missed nothing as he took in the room as a whole, and his attention was eventually caught by the wall of books behind Ronan.

Rather than sitting, he went to explore.

Damian's lips twisted in an amused smile as he shut and locked the doors.

Within five minutes, the three men were caught up to speed, and Vivian was absolutely positive Narissa and Creed had been lovers at one point in time. The air around them sparked with unspoken emotion and an attraction he didn't want to acknowledge. Though she tried to hide it, Narissa seemed hurt by his coldness.

"Don't try to figure it out, *cher*. Not unless you like soap operas, that is." The gruff Cajun voice startled her. Vivian hadn't been aware of Draven moving next to her.

"Perhaps it's the mystery behind the emotion that I find interesting," she replied in a low tone.

His chuckle was deep and sexy as hell, drawing the attention of the other women and a narrow-eyed look from Damian.

No need to be jealous, darling, she telepathically relayed to him.

I'm secure enough, he replied with a smirky half smile.

"Ah, true mates," Draven said, nodding his dark-blond head.

"How can you tell?" she asked.

"The conversation you're holdin' in your mind with the Aether."

"You can hear that?"

"No, but I can feel the buzz of the energy transferrin' back and forth." With a shrug, Draven downed his drink and set the glass to the side. "I doubt anyone else can."

"Interesting," she murmured. There was much she didn't know about the people who were labeled Sentinels. "This telepathy thing is new to me."

His sharp look caused her nerve endings to tingle.

"What?"

"No one can block the Aether from their thoughts if he wants in, *cher*," Draven said simply. "How you've been able to do it is a complete mystery, no?"

"I suppose it is," she agreed with a curious glance at her husband.

Had he been giving her privacy all this time to only now start spying on her thoughts, when he was worried someone was working against him?

Disappointment flashed on Damian's face as he watched her from afar.

No. Their connection was new to him, too. Despite whatever was at play here, they'd developed a new tool that could be useful moving forward, and Vivian didn't intend to look a gift horse in the mouth. They needed any advantage when it came to fighting their enemies.

Damian nodded and turned to answer a question being posed to him.

CHAPTER 23

*V*ivian cornered him after their visitors dispersed. "Damian, how is any of this going to help?"

"We have a team in place now, Viv. One with members who have been through wars and fought with honor. They've been overlooked or discounted by the Authority because of their rebellious natures, but each and every one is the best at what they do."

"But how does it defeat Morcant? How does it stop our daughter from falling into his clutches and that fucker from hurting our family?"

"I'm not sure that it does. However, the more firepower we have, the better. They are wise and battle-scarred. They won't give in to despair or fear easily, and Morcant won't be able to use negative emotions against them to gain the advantage."

With his arm around his wife's waist, Damian led Vivian over to the sofa where Sabrina slept.

"She's going to do something to cause all of it, isn't she?" Vivian asked fatalistically.

"I believe so," he replied in a low, solemn tone. "Only she can see the outcome, and if it means putting herself in danger, she'll do it to protect those she loves. It's her greatest strength and our greatest weakness."

"She's worried Morcant will kill me, Damian." Turning to him, she cradled his face between her palms. "Promise me, when it comes down to her or me, you'll do what is necessary and let me go. Promise you won't let her mourn or blame herself for the final outcome, and you won't do it either."

"Viv—"

She kissed him and stole his wits. Drawing back, she locked gazes with him, and in her eyes, he could see acceptance of what was to come. "Promise."

"For her, yes. For me, no." Wrapping his arms around her, he drew her in tight against him. "I'll never forgive myself if anything happens to either of you, and if you go, I'll mourn you forever, my love."

Her heavy sigh spoke to the heart of him. They both had strong thoughts about what was to come.

"Who do you suppose the Authority member is? The one working against you? I can't imagine it's the Fates, unless they've decided to create a new line of Aethers."

Her question was thought-provoking. Was it possible the higher-ups wanted him gone because he wasn't as easy to control as they wished?

With a buss to Vivian's temple, he moved away and squatted next to Sabrina. Stroking her hair back from her brow, he called her name. Though her lashes fluttered, she didn't wake.

"Rise and shine, Beastie," he urged gently, giving her an added boost to clear her mind. "We have things to discuss."

She shifted to a sitting position and rubbed her eyes. "Is it time to go with him?"

"No. It never will be, either. I wish to discuss alternate timelines."

"Uncle Alex was here from the future?"

"He was." Damian rose, then sat next to her, gesturing for Vivian to do the same. "He told us a few disturbing things, and I'd like you to clarify something for your mother and me. Can you do that?"

Sabrina nodded.

"Morcant has someone powerful backing his agenda. Do you know who?"

"No, Papa."

"Is that the truth, darling girl, or is it what you want us to believe?" Vivian asked.

"It's the truth. I can't see it in here." With her finger, Sabrina tapped the place between her eyes and frowned. "I don't know why."

"I suspect I do." Whoever was behind the Dethridge family takedown would've anticipated the need to block Sabrina from seeing them. Damian shared a frustrated glance with his wife, then addressed his daughter. "You intend to sneak out and give yourself up to Morcant, don't you? You believe by doing that, you can save Nate and me, is that correct?"

"Mama, too, if she stays away from him."

Wrapping an arm around Sabrina's thin shoulders, Vivian kissed the top of her head. The poignant picture was one he'd hold onto forever.

"I'm never not going to try to find and save you," Vivian told her. "You're my child first and the Oracle second. The first is what's important to me."

"Nate needs you, Mama."

"So you've said, but so do you. I intend to be here for both of you until the day I can't."

"Castor believes our wards will fail, Beastie. Do they fail, or do you lower them?" Damian asked her.

"Fail. But I'll put them back, Papa. I swear."

She appeared so earnest in her desire to protect them that Damian's heart ached. No child should have to carry the weight of responsibility his daughter did. Perhaps Vivian had been correct when she tried to bind Sabrina's powers years ago. Didn't she deserve to have a childhood like any other kid?

"Because I can't?" he asked gently.

She nodded.

"So someone is playing fast and loose with my abilities." Tipping her chin up, he considered his next question. "When am I to confront the Authority about this? Now or after?"

"After. They won't interfere when you come for me."

"Then why all of this in the first place? What's the point?" he mused aloud.

Feeling an unfamiliar presence behind him, Damian rose, prepared to blast the newcomer to hell. Although he didn't drop his arms, he did relax when he saw Draven Masters pouring himself another drink.

"I thought you'd gone, Masters."

"Just to test the wards at the edge of your property, friend." After a single gulp to empty the glass, he set it on the sideboard and faced them. "They're faulty at times, but there's a pattern. If Morcant or his cronies are paying attention, they'll feel it. If not, he'll continue to believe he's locked out."

"How frequent are the glitches?"

"Every five seconds at thirty-foot intervals."

"Can you reinforce it, Masters?"

"I tried. It seems whoever is fighting to bring yours down has already blocked my ability to create a new one." His whiskey-colored eyes were truthful and shockingly concerned when they locked on him. "You've got a helluva high-powered enemy, Aether. Especially if they can neutralize me. No one's done that in eighty years or more, I believe."

"You *know* that was me. It was never made secret." Dropping his arms to his sides, Damian moved closer. Should he find a way to put the Guardian's loyalty to the test? Was his troubled look all an act, and did the man actually have it out for him? "Are you carrying a grudge after all this time, Masters?"

A self-deprecating smile curled Draven's lips. "No, *cher*. I was out of control when my wife died, and your interference saved me. You should've let the chips fall where they landed, though."

"Why? Because you believed you had nothing left to contribute? Because you still do?" So much wasted talent. Damian barely managed to refrain from shaking his head at the frustration of it all.

"You're wrong, Draven. You were impressive then, and you're impressive now. I want you on my side for the fight to come."

"I'm as useless as a pair of deuces in a royal flush. Especially if they can take my powers so easily, and you know it."

"I can help you, Mr. Masters," Sabrina said as she joined them. Stepping close to Draven, she smiled up at him. "They can't take your magic if I seal it."

Seal it?

"Do you mean steal, Beastie?"

"No, Papa. *Seal.*"

After sharing a confused look with the Guardian, Damian approached and lifted her into his arms so they were level. "Explain, please."

"Guardians are made, not born like us. Their magic can be taken away by a god or goddess or you."

"Any of us can remove magic at any time to maintain balance, my love. You know that."

"Yes, Papa, but not if it's sealed to him."

"Are you saying it can never be undone?"

She beamed as if he were the brightest student. "Like I did with Liz. Remember?"

A few years back, when the Thorne witches had suffered an attack, an enemy of theirs had found a way to suppress the entire family's magical abilities. Because Liz Thorne had helped his daughter fight off the encroaching Darkness, Sabrina had restored her power and sealed it so it could never be removed again.

"I do, but this is different. Draven is not an average witch, Beastie."

"I know. That's why you need to help me."

"Thank you for the offer, *ma petite amie*, but I'm not deservin' of such a gift." With a magician's flourish, Draven produced a gold coin from behind Sabrina's ear and handed it to her. "I'm not to be trusted with that much power."

She laughed in the face of his honesty. "Yes, you are, Mr. Masters. You're a nice man."

Dark-blond brows spiking, he looked at Damian. "Do you want to tell her of the destruction, or should I?"

"She already knows, Masters. She's an Oracle."

Frowning, Draven nodded slowly as if processing the information.

"I killed a man, *cher*," he finally said to Sabrina. "That doesn't make me a nice man."

"Please put me down, Papa."

After Damian complied, she gestured for Draven to come down to her level. Dropping to one knee, he cocked his head and watched her curiously.

"We are *not* the sum total of our past deeds, Draven Masters," she intoned as if the words came from another. "Our core actions drive us, but we are more if allowed to be."

A chill swept Damian, and the hair on the back of his neck lifted. He'd heard those words before—from his Enchantress mother when he was only a year younger than his daughter. Right before his mother went insane.

"Why did you say that? Where did you hear it?" he asked sharply.

With a heavy blink, Sabrina shook her head. "Grandma Isolde said it to you. But it's true, isn't it?"

"To a degree, I suppose it is." He grudgingly nodded, not wanting her to imitate his mother in any way. It wasn't that he hadn't adored her, but two centuries later, he still felt the raw sting from her decisions.

"Then Mr. Masters can have his magic sealed. He's a good man," Sabrina replied with a stubborn angle of her chin.

As he weighed her words with what he knew of the Guardian, Damian came to the conclusion that his daughter would always do what she believed best, regardless of his counsel. He only hoped the Authority and the Fates didn't see it as her overstepping. Perhaps their vision of the future didn't include a young girl running about willy-nilly, gifting supreme power without their consent.

"We should seek permission, Beastie."

"Isis said it's okay, Papa."

"When exactly did she say that?" he demanded.

"Here." She tapped her temple. "Just now."

Throwing up his hands, Damian left them to pour a brandy. In one gulp, he downed it, swallowed against the burn, and prepared another. This one he sipped as he contemplated his Oracle offspring and her direct connection to the deities.

"Okay." He faced child and Guardian. "Do what you will, Beastie. But make sure Draven is on board with whatever you and Isis have planned." He touched a fingertip to her nose. "It wouldn't hurt if you gave your mother and I a heads up now and again."

She grinned and reached for Draven's hand. "You need to sit down for this, Mr. Masters. It hurts a little bit."

Damian snorted. "She means lie down, and it's going to hurt like the very devil."

CHAPTER 24

"*D*id your daughter put bad gris-gris on me, Aether?" Draven asked as he pressed his sleeve to his forehead to mop up his sweat. "I swear, I feel like the two of you burned the devil from my damned soul."

Damian smiled his commiseration and opened his mouth to respond, but Ronan replied for him.

"Aye, and she likely did." Ronan handed Draven a glass of iced water and a pint. "Hydrate, man. Ya may be after something a might stronger, but I'll be advisin' against it, to be sure. If ya mix whiskey with that buzz you're feeling, you'll be too pissed to function."

"If I wasn't already friends with Fintan, I'd require a translator." After consuming the water, Draven set the glass aside and picked up the pint. "Thanks for your kindness, O'Connor."

Ronan grinned as he strode away.

"How did he know?" Draven asked, nodding toward the retreating Irishman.

"He's had his abilities removed and restored so many times, he's an old hand at it."

Glass paused halfway to his mouth, the Guardian slowly turned to look at him. "Ya think maybe that's why people are inclined to take you out? It's been a while, but what I remember of the Author-ity, they don't like others playin' fast and loose with magic."

"Doubtful. It's always been in the line of service to bring down evildoers."

Alastair Thorne arrived, coffee mug in hand. With a toast for them, he settled down at the far end of the dining room table and conjured a newspaper. Pausing to fold the top down, his gaze searched the table. "No scones? What's the point of stopping by for breakfast if you don't supply the necessities?"

Typical Alastair. Filling his stomach always came first.

"Conjure your own, you bloody mooch," Damian retorted. "Can't you see I'm playing nursemaid here?"

Masters snorted into his Guinness. "Your life is far too exciting for the likes of me, friend."

"You've no idea."

"Why are you out of sorts, Dethridge?" Alastair asked as he sipped his coffee. "And what's with all the firepower hanging about?"

"You don't want to know. It's a nightmare in the making."

"So Castor wasn't being dramatic when he called me to say Morcant intends to wreak havoc?"

As clever and willing as Alastair was, when it came down to it, he was no match for Morcant and would likely wind up a victim of that sonofabitch like countless others before. However, Castor had a terrible tendency to entice others in to what he deemed was an exciting fight.

With an irritated sigh and a shake of his head, Damian rose to his feet and shoved the chair under the table. "He's a pain-in-the-ass drama queen and shouldn't have involved you, Al."

"We're in agreement on the first, but total disagreement on the second." Folding the paper in half, then half again, he casually set it aside and tugged his shirt cuffs below his suit jacket sleeves, playing with the link at his left wrist. "I'm hurt you didn't seek my help right away. I thought we were friends."

"We are."

"Friends don't exclude friends from all the fun." Standing, Alastair took one last sip of his coffee, then placed the mug on the table and lifted a dark-blond brow. "Who are we smiting today?"

Regardless of how serious a situation was, Alastair's dry wit always tickled Damian's funny bone. Very little affected Al unless it was a direct threat to his family or person.

"Nathanial would be thrilled with how much you love trouble."

"I learned from the best," his friend replied.

His cocky grin was the spitting image of his great-grandfather's, and bittersweet memories flooded Damian. Christ, he missed Nate so goddamned much it hurt. It was hard to believe he and Evie had moved on to the Otherworld for good.

Pulling himself back from his side trip to the past, Damian asked, "How much do you know?"

"The whole of it." All humor left Alastair as he met Damian's tired, gritty eyes. "You haven't slept. Why don't you nap for a few hours? Alex, Ronan, and I can keep watch over your family. I can call in my son-in-law if the need arises."

"I'm not sure I'd be able to sleep, knowing my wife and daughter are in danger, Al. I wish I had a clue what the hell was going on and why the Authority is allowing Morcant to target us."

"Have you summoned the Goddess?"

"No. I haven't dared to leave here."

With a decisive nod, Alastair strode toward the terrace doors. "I'll go see what she knows, if anything."

"For a man without a designation, he's fearless," Draven observed.

"Yes. He's also come up against Morcant in the past and lived to tell the tale." With a frown, Damian considered how long Draven had been alive. "It seems odd you've not run up against him. Morcant seeks out the powerful to steal their magic."

"We've met in passing. But for an Arcane Devourer to feed, the energy must be negative. I feel nothing most days." Shrugging, Draven finished off his pint.

"What do you know of him?"

"The man's relentless in his quest for more. Energy, status, power. Once he targets some poor fool, they're as good as dead." His wise eyes locked with Damian's. "But my money's on you, friend. I'm betting Morcant bit off more than he can chew this time around."

"Here's hoping." With a healthy sigh for the trials ahead, Damian gathered the glasses and mug. "You should go rest, Masters. Third floor, first door on the right. The bed has fresh linens."

"Are you certain you don't want me to remain on guard?"

"It'll take you a good hour to feel a hundred percent. I'll call if I need you before then."

Left alone, Damian walked to the kitchen, checking for anything out of place. He was startled to see Vivian's sisters at the prep table.

"Ladies."

Taryn's smile was strained, but Soleil was as open and refreshing as always. "Hi, Damian. We were about to start breakfast. Any requests?"

Glancing down, he noticed blueberries in whatever batter she was mixing. "It looks like you have my favorite covered, and I'm sure it's going to be delicious. Thank you."

She beamed under his praise, lighting her round face. Fuller-figured than her siblings, Soleil had a Rubenesque quality. He remembered a time when she would've been the woman men sought for her voluptuousness and unintentional bawdy laugh. Today's men were fools to overlook her beauty.

"I'll leave you to it." He turned to go.

"Damian?"

"Yes?"

Color crept up her neck, and she lowered her gaze to the work-table. "Um, who is... er, um..." She cleared her throat and tried again. "Who is the man you call Blane?"

Although they were surrounded by trouble, love was in the air. Damian curbed his amusement at her embarrassed stammer, not wanting to make her feel bad for her obvious interest. "He's a Sentinel for the Authority. One in a family of Death Dealers."

"What is that?"

Catching a brief glimpse of her future, he shook his head and smiled. "I'll explain in due time. If you don't mind, I'd like to look in on Sabrina and Viv."

"Oh! Yes. Of course. I didn't mean to bother you," she gushed.

Always the protective sister, Taryn wrapped an arm around Soleil's shoulders. "He's not bothered, Lei. He's just distracted."

Blush deepening, Soleil nodded. "I get that. I just… yeah, sorry."

"Not at all, my dear. I'm happy to answer all your questions when circumstances aren't as dire as these."

"Thank you."

He faced away before smiling. When Morcant was defeated, Soleil and Trevor needed a formal introduction. Two more polar opposites didn't exist, and it would be interesting to see how things played out.

Damian stopped short outside the door to the kitchen and chuckled. Was he assuming Alastair's matchmaking mantle now? Perhaps.

Sabrina selected a colored pencil from the craft carousel and started shading the image she'd drawn. When it was time, her father would need the picture she'd created to find her, or her mother, should things go differently than she expected.

Sometimes that happened. No future was absolute, but as the Oracle, she could see every possibility. It wasn't a gift she would've asked for, given a choice, but it made her feel better knowing. She hated surprises.

Pausing to watch her mother blow kisses on Baby Nate's belly, Sabrina smiled and tried to memorize the moment. If she could recall it when she needed, she might not be as scared. And she *would* be, because Mama's spell to remove her emotions hadn't worked on her. The Aether power in her blood had slapped back and pushed her mother to the ground.

Yes, she did have Sabrina's hair—or Papa did—but other than to lend strength to the original enchantment surrounding Mama, it was useless. If her mother sacrificed for her, which she hoped would *never* happen, Mama wouldn't feel the fear or pain. If Sabrina was the one to die, Mama wouldn't know grief until Papa took his revenge on Morcant and eventually broke the bracelet.

"What are you thinking about so hard, darling girl?" Mama asked as she bundled Nate in his blanket.

"You."

"Me?" Frowning, Mama crossed the room. Sabrina had just enough time to wave her hand and make her drawing look like the garden outside the window.

"What a beautiful picture! How did I not know you had an artist's talent?"

Sabrina leaned into her mother's hug and stared down at the real drawing she'd created.

A warehouse in America.

She couldn't say for certain what the address was, but Papa would remember it from past business dealings. At least, she hoped he would.

"Mama?"

"Mm?" Her mother's hand felt comforting as she smoothed the hair down Sabrina's back.

"Does Papa remember everything from when he was alive to now?"

"I'm not sure. Most things, I imagine."

"What about a hundred and fifty-three years ago?"

Vivian laughed. "*That's* specific. You'd have to ask him. I don't know what he recalls."

"Okay."

"Why is it so important?" Mama's hand had stilled as soon as she realized it was. "Sabrina?"

"He'll find us there if he remembers."

"And if he doesn't?"

Sabrina shrugged and put the pencil back in the carousel before selecting another. "I think he will. Most of the visions are the same."

"Most? You see alternate endings to Morcant's plans?"

Nodding, she worked on the sign overhanging the warehouse door. Not as it currently was, but as it appeared in the past when her father had frequented the place.

"What are you truly drawing? And before you lie to me, you should know nothing is appearing where you're coloring," Vivian said dryly.

"Crud," she muttered. Papa's bark of laughter drifted to her from the doorway, and she looked up to meet his indulgent gaze.

How had she ever feared him?

He was the best father in the world. Sometimes, when she recalled how Aunt Josie had lied to break up her family, Sabrina got mad, and she was forced to remember it wasn't Aunt Josie's fault.

It was Morcant's.

She desperately wanted Papa to kill him for good this time around.

"Let her keep her secrets, Viv." Taking Nate from Mama, he breathed in the baby scent of him and brushed a finger across Nate's chubby cheek. "She'll tell us when she's ready."

"You do realize you're giving her permission to lie to us, right?"

When Papa turned his considering expression on her, Sabrina shook her head. "I won't lie."

He raised a brow. "But you won't always tell the truth, either, you miscreant."

Because he was right, she gave him a sickly grin.

His mouth pressed tightly together like it always did when he tried not to laugh at her, and Sabrina smiled for real. It took a lot to make Papa angry, and he was never harsh when she crossed the line. He'd understand this time, too.

"What do you remember of your past, Damian?" Mama asked him with her hands on her hips.

"Every detail."

"Good." Taking Nate back, she kissed Papa on the mouth. "I think your fabulous photographic memory is going to come in handy when your daughter decides to share whatever she's drawing."

After he watched Mama walk away, Papa frowned down at the paper. "Why are you sketching an old warehouse?"

Crud.

CHAPTER 25

Forty minutes later, Damian returned from conferring with Alex, Trevor, and Ronan to find Sabrina missing. With a sense of foreboding, he stalked to the desk and discovered her note.

Dear Papa,

Please don't be mad. It is always this way in my head. I'll stay positive. I promise.
Baby Nate needs Mama, so don't tell her where I am.
Also, when I told Grandpa Nate that you needed to cloak and take the long sword from your special room, it was the wrong time. But you need them soon.
You said you remember everything, but don't forget me, Papa.
They'll try to make you, but don't, okay? I love you.

Love,
Beastie

Damian's heart seized, and the pain was excruciating. Suddenly, his breathing required a concerted effort, and hyperventilation was causing lightheadedness.

"Oh, Beastie. What did you do?" he whispered achingly. A sound at the door caught his attention, and he turned in time to see Vivian looking wildly around the room.

"Where is she, Damian? Where's Sabrina?"

Unable to speak, he held the paper up and helplessly watched Vivian pale. The bracelet on his wrist burned his skin from the strength of her fear, and belatedly, he realized he couldn't feel Sabrina through the link. They'd never truly bound her stronger emotions! She was in deeper trouble than she anticipated.

"I was only gone a minute," Vivian croaked disbelievingly. "A single fucking minute to give Nate to Dubheasa. How? How the hell did he take her in that time? Why didn't we feel the wards drop?"

Hissing from the pain of the continual burn, he met her halfway and dragged her into his embrace. "I need you to calm down, Viv. We'll find her. Believe it."

Pushing him back, she shoved her platinum hair back from her flushed cheeks. "I know that. I do," she insisted when he frowned. "But I'm livid, and I don't want that monster anywhere near my baby girl."

"It's too late for that," he replied grimly, scrubbing his face with his hands. Goddess he was exhausted, and sleep was not in his immediate future.

She gripped his seared wrist. "Jesus, Damian! Is that from the bracelet?"

"Yes, but never mind that now."

"How is that possible?" she asked, ignoring his comment.

"Your fear is great. It's transitioning to the bracelet."

"Adding to hers! No wonder…" She trailed off as he shook his head. "What?"

"You weren't able to bind hers, Viv. I don't feel her through this damned thing at all."

Her hand flew to her mouth, and Damian got another jolt to the wrist. He wasn't able to prevent his wince.

"Oh, fuck! I'm sorry, darling." Closing her lids, she slowly inhaled and exhaled as if to center herself. When she was done, she opened her eyes. "Better?"

He nodded and handed her the note. Returning to the desk, he tore it apart, looking for the picture Sabrina had drawn earlier. When he couldn't find it, he grabbed a charcoal pencil and a blank page, then recreated what he remembered of her drawing.

"It's the wharf in New York," he said. Looking up, he realized he was speaking to an empty room. Having been to the city countless times, Vivian must've recognized the surrounding scenery and foolishly went to Sabrina's aid. *"Fuck!"*

Suppressing the urge to rush after her, he raced for the stairs, bellowing loud enough to shake the entire house.

At his wrist, the metal bangle glowed red and cooked the skin beneath it.

"I can take it," he reminded himself. "For them. I can take it."

But Vivian's fear and pain began to override his ability to remain calm. Through his blood connection to Sabrina, he felt her horror surge and die, with a suddenness that robbed him of breath. Searching their blood bond for any small sign she was alive, he came up empty. No pain, no life, no emotions at all.

Fueled by his outrage, immediate hatred, and a driving need for revenge, Damian's cells ramped up, and the Aether magic became a living, breathing thing all on its own. Rumbling started, growing stronger with each passing second. The reverberating sound of tumbling trees and stone walls added to the rattling earthquake his tumultuous emotions caused.

Draven Masters skidded to a halt at the top of the stairs as Damian hopped down the last few steps to the landing two floors below.

"Dethridge! Stop this right now, or you'll kill us all."

"Sod off!" The forcefulness of Damian's retort blew Masters back three feet, and a look of wariness crossed the other man's face.

From where his blinding rage came, Damian couldn't say. Perhaps it was the years of complaint-free service he'd provided to the deities, or maybe it was caused by the more recent betrayal of the Authority and Fates. But without a doubt, his sudden terror for his wife and daughter topped the list of things triggering his uncontrollable fury.

An electrical bolt struck him center mass, sending him crashing through the railing and onto the four-foot-wide wooden foyer table. He barely registered the cut from the broken crystal vase as he rolled to his feet and glared up at Draven.

"You're a fool if you believe you can stop me. I'll kill you if you try, Masters," Damian snarled.

The air crackled between them, and the Guardian shifted as if uncomfortable in his skin. Likely he was. Aether energy was substantial.

"I'm not trying to stop you, friend. I'm trying to get you to calm the fuck down so you don't get your family killed."

His family.

Like a bucket of ice water, Draven's words had the effect of shocking Damian out of his heightened state. Sucking air between his teeth, he held his breath and calmed his mind. If his wife and child were still alive, they needed him to stay focused.

When he opened his eyes, he saw his friends gathered around them.

"Beastie's gone, and Viv went after her," he said as calmly as he could. Still, there was a hoarseness to his voice.

"We'll find them, Damian," Alex said, infusing confidence into his tone that didn't match the concern in his pale eyes.

Alastair pushed aside the others to grip Damian's arm. Placing his palm over the wound, he knitted the skin closed, then handed Damian a handkerchief. "Get every last bit of blood up, and burn that thing."

Wise instructions. One drop of Aether blood was a weapon in his enemies' hands.

As soon as Damian had wiped the crystal clean, Alastair fused the broken shards together, righted the table, and conjured fresh flowers for the vase.

"Really, Al?" Alex said incredulously. "Interior decorating at a time like this?"

"Bugger off. We can easily set the estate back in order as we plot Morcant's demise."

Alastair reached to straighten the tie he wasn't wearing and frowned his irritation.

"What do you need us to do, Dethridge?" Trevor asked gently as if he feared another earthquake-inducing reaction.

The moment the Death Dealer caught his attention, Damian knew the plan.

"How comfortable are you wielding a sword, Blane?"

Casting a wary glance around the group, Trevor shrugged. "I've never had much interest in cosplay, but I'm game."

"Someday, you'll have to tell me what cosplay is, but for now, I need you to go with Alastair and get the broadsword from my ceremony room."

Once they were off, he conjured fire, applied it to the handkerchief, and dropped it on the marble floor. To Draven, he said, "Get Fintan here and summon Kass. They need to stake out a warehouse in New York. It was once attached to the Wayfarer Inn before the inn burned down."

"When was that?"

"A little over a hundred years ago."

"Shouldn't be too hard to find." With a small salute, the Guardian shimmered away.

Damian faced Castor. "Take your nephew and reinforce the estate wards, please."

"Be back in a jiff."

"And me?"

Josie peered down at Damian from the landing.

"Your magic hasn't been restored, and I'm afraid I don't have the time to do it properly."

"Understood." She gestured toward her sisters. "They can scry to make sure no one crossed the border of your land while you were throwing your tantrum."

Acknowledging the suggestion and her accuracy of his earlier reaction, he said, "Thank you."

"Vivian." Morcant inhaled deeply, ready to consume her worry for her daughter. He frowned when he didn't receive the angsty response he'd expected.

Her arms were bent behind her back, and she was suspended between the two men who served him, showing no fear.

Why?

Slowly, keeping his thoughtful gaze on her until the last possible second, he turned his head toward her child, trying to discover the reason she wasn't concerned. It made no sense. No mere witch could hide their deeper emotions in a setting like this. Not with their child in a cage.

Granted, Sabrina Dethridge was no ordinary child.

She'd appeared by the property line of the estate and informed them she would meet them outside this building. Before anyone could react, she was gone.

For the first ten minutes, they'd suspected a setup, but when the Aether didn't arrive to beat down their door, they realized the girl was calling the shots.

Again, *why?* Why would the Aether allow his daughter to act as bait?

"What is she?" he asked Vivian.

"An innocent child," the woman snapped.

A hint of her anger surfaced, but was immediately whisked away before Morcant could feed. What the devil was happening? Was the mother charmed in some way? Was she the only living human able to deflect his power?

The Aether could if he concentrated. As his mate, was she gifted the same ability? What did that mean for their child? Could she continually resist him with her glittering protective bubble?

There was only one way to find out.

Vivian Dethridge must die.

"Kill her," he ordered.

From her place in the far corner of her prison, Sabrina lifted her head and met her mother's steady gaze, then she stood and moved toward them.

"Tell him, Mama. Tell him what I do."

"No."

Unease teased his mind.

"What is it she does, Vivian?" he asked coolly, trying to appear unaffected.

"Tell him I can see the future and all the horrible ways he can die." The child's mouth curled into a mocking smile when she looked at him. "The way you will *all* die if you hurt my mama."

"You can't predict the future. Josephine would've told me if you could." The lying jade!

"Papa will be cross. But Nate will be madder."

"Who is Nate?"

"Hush now, darling," Vivian scolded gently. "Don't give him any ammunition."

"Who is Nate?"

Mother and child were as dissimilar in coloring as two individuals could be, and yet they offered up the same stubborn expression. Neither would speak.

He'd had enough of their games.

Nodding to Black, he said, "Do it."

A stinging slap knocked him off his feet, and he belatedly registered Black and Carl had fared the same. Vivian was the only one left standing, but she'd realize her helplessness soon enough. The few precious moments she paused to consider the C4 on the cell door were all Morcant needed to gain the upper hand.

Her neck snapped with surprisingly little effort. Tossing her to the floor like yesterday's garbage, he pointed to Sabrina. "You're next."

CHAPTER 26

In Sabrina's bedroom, Damian searched for the object she valued most by running his hand along her collectibles and feeling for heat.

"What are you doing?" Trevor asked after finding him.

"I need something of Sabrina's to locate her. Normally, our connection would do it, but if Morcant is cloaking her with the help of the Authority or higher..." Damian let his answer trail off. There was no need to rehash the who or why. His daughter was being held captive by an Arcane Devourer with abilities to rival the Aether's own. He had little hope Sabrina could maintain the force-field spell he'd taught her.

"Energy can be transferred to beloved objects through deep emotion, causing a heat spike by at least five degrees," he explained. "Everything not possessing sentimental value is usually the same temperature as the air surrounding it."

"Interesting." Moving farther into the room, Trevor made a study of the place. "Can I help?"

"Yes. Start at the bookshelf on the far—ah! I found it." Folded inside a tiny sparkling Unicorn t-shirt, Damian found a spatula.

He smiled sadly as he recalled the morning after he'd brought her home. She'd refused to change from those clothes even after spilling maple syrup on the top. It took Nathanial an hour to convince her the new one he'd conjured for her was just as good as the old one. Both shirts rested on the shelf by her bed. Yet it appeared the silicone utensil was her prized possession. The very one Damian had used to flip the pancakes that morning.

"You surprised me, Beastie," he said aloud, as if she were with him. "I'd have thought you'd keep the one your Grandpa Nate used."

Spatula obtained, he gestured to Trevor. "We're done here."

Perhaps the man was too polite to ask, but that didn't stop him from looking askew at the item in Damian's hand.

"Okay. What's our next step?"

A baby's agonized scream echoed from down the hall, and Damian bolted. The distraught cries that followed caused his ears to ring as he accepted Nate from Dubheasa and cradled his son to his chest. The second they touched, Damian had a clear vision of Vivian's sightless eyes and lifeless body on the warehouse floor.

Nate was inconsolable at the broken connection with his mother, and Damian, as heartbroken as his son, understood better what Sabrina had meant when she said Nate needed his mother. Theirs was an otherworldly bond, similar to the one Damian shared with Beastie.

Shifting his son, he placed him back in Dubheasa's waiting arms and stroked Nate's brow with his thumb, casting a slumbering enchantment over him. "Sleep peacefully, my sweet boy. When you wake, your mother will be well."

Goddess, he prayed it was so. When two souls were linked, like his children to their select parent, the loss was unimaginable.

"Thank you for watching over him, Dubheasa. Just a little longer now."

Her emerald eyes were intent as she looked at him. "My family will gladly help for all you've done for us, Damian. You know that, yeah?"

"I do. I just don't know what more can be done at the moment."

Though appreciative of her offer, he didn't know how to tell her that, despite the great power the O'Malleys recently had returned to them, they were still novices with hot tempers, and they were no match for Morcant.

After joining Trevor in the hall, Damian paused and called to Dubheasa across the short distance.

"If anything should happen to me, if I don't return for him, you'll need to take him to the Goddess to break his bonds and bind his power."

"Sure, and why would that need to happen?"

"Because it means my wife and daughter are dead and Morcant has won. Nate will be his next target. And the bond, well, you saw how he reacted just now to Viv"—he swallowed hard—"to Viv's death."

Both Dubheasa and Trevor sucked in an audible breath.

Damian nodded bleakly. "I'm going to fetch my family, but before I do, I'll sign over everything to you and Ronan as a contingency. Please always protect my son."

Tears brimming, she choked out a "yes."

"That's all I can ask. Thank you."

"You're the reason we're alive, Damian. You don't ever need to ask. We'll be here for him."

He smiled his genuine affection for her. "You're not enslaved to me, my dear. Saving you was not for gain. It was because you're my friends."

"Taking care of your children is our honor, man, because we're *your* friends," Ronan said from behind him. "I'll be going with ya to get the wee wild beastie back."

"You should stay with your mate. If Morcant wins this round, she may need the backup."

Ronan's light-blue eyes locked on Dubheasa. "It's your call, me love."

"There's wisdom in his words, but I don't see how Morcant can win with so many of you to take the fecker down."

A wicked grin nearly split Ronan's face in two. "Sure, and he'll surrender all on his own if he learns he's to facedown you, Dove. A more fierce opponent never lived."

"Go on with you, you eejit."

"You sound more like your sister, Bridget, every day," Ronan quipped. Striding across the room, he swept her in a dip, baby and all, then planted a loud smacking kiss on her laughing mouth before uprighting her. "Sure, and that should be keeping ya 'til I return."

A sweeping sadness, not his own, settled in Damian's heart, and he shifted to face Trevor. "Are you upset she picked Ronan over you?"

"No. I didn't have time to fall into feelings," he replied with a humorless chuckle. "But at odd moments, I feel the sting of loneliness. Unfortunately, what I am doesn't allow for long term without consequences for a lover."

"Your brother, Simon, found love."

"That's my point. His wife contracted cancer because of him. If you didn't step in, Evelyn would've eventually gone the same way as his first wife."

"I'd offer to step in for you, but we both know I might not be around by the time you form a relationship." Damian clasped a hand on Trevor's shoulder. "But I promise you, Blane. If I am, I'll infuse the healing magic into your mate's DNA."

Lips twisted in a semblance of a smile, Trevor nodded. "How about we get through today first? If we want to revive Vivian, we don't have much time left."

***

Sabrina kept her eyes squeezed shut and concentrated on the memories of Papa laughing with Grandpa Nate as they made pancakes for the contest she was to judge. Her father hadn't been scary after that day. Within a short time, he'd become her adoring Papa, and nothing she did was bad to him. Most times, he laughed behind his hand when Mama scolded her for being naughty.

Remembering when he would sneak her chocolate cake after

Mama said no, Sabrina smiled and hugged the feeling close to her. Anything to block the image of her dead mother.

For a second, her mood shifted, but she righted it again. If she gave in to the sadness trying to overwhelm her, Morcant would break her protective bubble and get her. She wasn't beyond feeling satisfaction that he'd burned himself when he shoved her into the cell earlier.

"When your father comes, he'll die just like your mother, girl," Morcant's partner jeered, hoping to pierce her emotional shell.

Lifting her lids, she focused on his cruel beady eyes. "You're going to burn when Papa comes. Like the witches of Salem."

When wariness crossed his features, she smiled cheerfully. "You are going to scream and scream and scream, but no sound will come from your throat. No one will hear you in your last minutes."

"Shut your mouth, bitch, or I'll shut it for you."

"You can try." Sabrina laughed, hoping she sounded exactly like the Enchantress when she had terrorized the witch community.

Fear filled his face, and he glanced over his shoulder to see where his friends were.

"They can't help you, Ernie."

"Why do you keep calling me Ernie? My name is Carl," he practically shouted.

She cocked her head and smirked, knowing it was driving him crazy that she wouldn't say. The second she'd seen him, she almost laughed. With his orange spray tan, bulbous nose, and spiked black hair, the man resembled the puppet from a popular children's show.

His skin darkened with his anger, and Sabrina began to sing the Rubber Duck song to annoy him further.

"I hope Morcant sucks your magic dry, girl. When he does, I'll teach you respect."

"One has to earn respect, Carl," Morcant stated succinctly. Stepping from the shadows, he approached the bars. "Go."

After Carl scurried away, Morcant spoke to her. "Your resistance is impressive, but you'll soon grow tired, and when you do, I'll feed off the untethered emotions of your dreams."

"You won't live that long." Grinning was harder in the face of his confidence, but Sabrina managed it.

His anger made his eyes smaller, but he didn't reply. Instead, he pointed to her mother's body on the floor just outside the cell wall. Sabrina knew if she looked, she'd be unable to block out the sight, and he'd gain the upper hand. Shutting her eyes, she hummed a cheerful tune Grandma Evie had taught her. Once again, she recalled the pancake contest and how Grandpa Nate had winked at her as he magically altered Papa's pancakes to taste bad, behind his back. Papa, not to be outdone, undid the damage and had altered Grandpa Nate's.

"You're both cheating!" she'd cried out.

"Of course we are, honey," Grandpa Nate said. *"Where's the fun in an honest contest?"*

Papa had burst out laughing, so hard, that he doubled over and wiped tears from his eyes.

"I'll win in the end, child," Morcant promised from far outside her memories.

And he would if Papa didn't find her soon.

CHAPTER 27

$\mathcal{A}$ pressing urgency consumed Damian as he awaited Draven's return. If he didn't get to his daughter soon, he'd go completely mad. To distract himself, he poured three drinks and handed one to Alastair and the other to Ronan.

"You never told me what Isis said, Al. Should I be concerned?" he asked.

"There wasn't much she could say that we didn't already know. Someone in the Authority is tampering with your magic. But whoever it is, they aren't sanctioned by the Authority council members."

"Did you ask if the Fates are involved?"

"I did. She couldn't say with any certainty."

Damian rolled his eye as he sipped his brandy.

"She would've, if she had the answers, Dethridge. I'm positive of it," Alastair said gently. "She adores Sabrina and wouldn't see her hurt."

Nodding absently, Damian sauntered to the French doors and stared out over his gardens. "I lived for almost two hundred years without realizing what was missing from my life. With the birth of my daughter…" A pain squeezed his heart, and he pressed his palm to his chest. This was what it must be like for mortals dealing with heart attacks. "She's everything, Al," he said hoarsely. "My child is everything I live for. I'd give myself up to Morcant if she could go free."

"It's sorry I am for failin' ya both," Ronan said heavily. The weight of his guilt caused his shoulders to sag.

"You didn't." Damian turned and cast him a tight smile. "It takes an entire village to keep up with Beastie. Especially when she devises her own plans, like today."

"Have you been able to locate her?" Castor asked, entering the room and crossing to the sideboard to fix himself a drink.

"Yes and no." Damian moved to join him and held out his glass for a refill. "We know she's in an old warehouse in New York. Fintan messaged to say they were converted years ago, as we expected." After another sip of brandy, he sighed. "Scrying only shows her in a cell, and Viv…"

Goddess! He still couldn't believe his wife was gone. If he thought about it at all, his grief would explode and he'd be in a world of hurt. Yes, they'd been separated for a time, and yes, they'd had a rocky marriage in the interim, but she'd been safe. He'd watched over her and Sabrina, prepared to do whatever was necessary to keep them that way.

"I don't see how a modernized building could resemble a cavern with cages." Alastair distracted Damian from his morose thoughts with his comment.

"Sounds more like a dungeon," Castor said as he lifted his glass to his mouth.

"Good Christ! Of *course!*" Wrapping an arm around Alex's neck, Damian dragged him forward for a loud, smacking kiss on the head. "You brilliant man." Facing the others, he grinned. "She's in the tunnels *below* the building."

Alastair rose and tugged at his cuffs. "Let's go bring her home."

"We need Blane. He should be wrapping up his ceremony."

"What the feck is he doin' that's taking so bloody long, then?"

Ronan shoved off the wall he'd been holding up and set his empty tumbler on a side table.

"Infusing Stephan's sword with Death Dealer magic." Damian smiled his lethal intent. "No matter who wields it, Morcant and his cronies won't be keeping their heads this time. There will be no substitutes in his place."

"How can you be sure he doesn't already have decoys in place?"

Alastair jumped in to reply to Castor's question. "Empathic abilities only work from a short distance. He'd need to be close to Sabrina to drink in her emotions." Addressing Damian, he asked, "How do you want to play this?"

"I'll go in alone—"

"Fuck no!" A violent sneeze bent Alastair double, and Damian fisted his hand to stop the plague of locusts his friend's swearing triggered. Only Alastair and his three children suffered this curse, and he'd never say what he did to deserve it. However, Damian assumed it had something to do with his sneaking into the Otherworld and escaping again without express permission from the Goddess.

"I appreciate your concern, my friend, but had you let me finish, I wouldn't have to fend off insects."

The temptation to tell him to go to hell was written all over Alastair's face.

Castor barked a hard laugh, and it earned him the middle finger from Al.

"I took future-Castor's warning to heart," Damian assured them. "And as I was saying, I'll go in alone, and the rest of our team will come in through a portal. It's my fondest wish that we'll get the jump on them." The tension in his neck and shoulders was building to an uncomfortable level, and Damian stretched to relieve the ache. "Alastair, with permission from Isis, will you summon Nathanial one last time? We'll need him to join the fight. Beastie predicted it years ago."

"Him or me?" Alastair shrugged when Damian frowned. "You've

said it yourself; our resemblance is uncanny. Is it possible Sabrina got us mixed up in her vision? Your mother did once."

He was referring to the time when Isolde knew the Darkness was about to consume her completely. Triggered by a vision, she'd used the last of her free will to write a spell that she'd accidentally sent forward in time. Alastair received what was actually meant for Nathanial.

"Are you okay with dirtying your pristine suit?" Damian asked with raised brows. "For all we know, Morcant's blood might have a similar effect as battery acid and eat through your fine duds."

"Stuff it, Dethridge. It isn't as if we don't shop the same tailor."

A humorless smile kicked up Damian's lips. "Let's try it. What do we have to lose?"

"Our lives, but who's really going to care at this point?"

"Sure, and ya need to be speakin' for yourself, yeah? My Dove would throw herself off Moher in her grief, she would." Ronan scowled when they laughed. "Feck all the way off, the lot of ya!"

"Where's Mack?" Alastair asked. "I know your ability to see the outcome is on the blink, Dethridge, but is it possible she can tell us something?"

"She's in the guest wing with Delaney, Sebastian, and his family. It's a smart idea to consult her. Thank you."

"I'll go. Gather your Sentinels and finalize your plan of action. It wouldn't hurt to have a way to cloak our less-than-positive thoughts from Morcant if you can come up with a way."

The suggestion brought to mind the bracelet Vivian had created, and Damian experienced a eureka moment. "You're scary brilliant at times, Al."

"I don't know what I said to deserve high praise, but I'll take it." With a tug of his cuffs, he teleported away.

"I'd like to know why he deserves such a compliment, myself." Castor's brows shot up. "I mean, we all know I'm the brains of the operation."

"All right, Brains, help me mass-produce ten rings." He smiled when Sabrina's earnest face came to mind. "Make that ten and a child-size one, just like ours."

Castor lifted his hand to examine his signet ring with the tanzanite crest. "How will that stop our worry? Do we plan to have telepathic counseling sessions?"

"Arse," Ronan muttered even as he chuckled.

"My wife cast a spell earlier this morning. It bound her negative feelings with mine in the form of this bracelet." Damian removed it from his wrist and dispassionately noted his blistered skin. When had that happened? A zing shot through the metal to his fingers, and he jerked.

Hope bubbled up. His thoughts were controlled. That meant either Vivian was still around, or she'd managed to capture some of Sabrina's more powerful emotions. Because it made him feel closer to them, he slipped the bangle back on.

"So the rings we create will suppress our fears?"

Damian nodded. "That's the hope. In addition, I'd like to build in a coms system, like you, Al, and I have."

"We'll need Alastair for that one, Dethridge. I don't remember what he came up with."

"I do, but yes. You make the bases, I'll obtain the stones, and Alastair can enchant them." Tossing his cellphone to Ronan, he said, "The numbers for the Sentinels are listed. Bring them here. I'll be no more than ten minutes." As he shifted to go, he paused and turned back. "Please ask them, O'Connor. No one should feel obligated for this mission. It could cost them their lives. That includes you."

Ronan's thoughtful frown softened, and deep respect heavily entwined with caring shone in his silvery eyes. "You were my family when no one else cared to be, Damian. You, Viv, your boy, and the wee wild beastie hold the place in me heart next to Dubheasa." He shrugged matter-of-factly. "I could never stay behind when one of mine is in trouble, all the same."

In an act foreign to him, Damian hugged Ronan. Words would never be enough to express his gratitude, and by the looks of it, they weren't needed. They shared an understanding. Each would fight to the death for the welfare of the other and the loved ones they shared.

"Five minutes," he reminded him gruffly. With a nod toward Castor, who was serious for once, Damian strode out the door to the flat expanse of land east of his home.

Opening the gate to the serene garden that had once housed his mother's tomb and the deadly roses that strove to feed her the magic she'd been long denied, he grimaced.

Nostalgia for the young boy he'd been rose up inside him.

Once, he'd been a toddler, loved by his mother and father. They'd been like any normal family for the first five years of his life. Until his mother consumed the Darkness infecting his father, believing she could save them. Had she known it would backfire? That she'd never be able to contain it when she drew it from Father's rapidly deteriorating body? Perhaps. As arrogant as Aethers could be, she'd likely assumed she could control it.

She couldn't.

Her overconfident choice had shaped his entire life.

Damian swore he'd never be spontaneous. Would never rush into a situation without thinking through every possible escape. But here he was, ready to rush after his wife and child without any true idea of the outcome.

There were those who knew, though.

At the center of the clearing, he stretched out his arm, palm outward and parallel to his body, then rotated in a complete three-hundred-and-sixty-degree circle as he called up the standing stones. The ground rumbled as the dirt parted, and the columns rose to tower over him like giant tombstones with jagged tops. For the most part, they blocked out the sun, but rays filtered between the pillars and touched on him where he stood. The warmth felt like a blessing from the Goddess.

Each stone was roughly fifteen feet high and five and a half feet in width. If one strained, they could make out symbols etched into the hard surfaces. There were fourteen formations in total, and the number was as significant as the need for seven witches of a coven to resurrect them. But Damian was no ordinary witch. His was the power of a hundred combined.

"Exalted One, I call on you now. Please come."

He'd only spare Isis four minutes. If she didn't show up, he'd collect the tanzanite he needed and return home. Delay any longer, and Sabrina was likely lost to him forever.

The Goddess arrived in one.

Today, she wore a shimmering white dress secured by tiger's eye scarabs at the shoulders. In her hand, she held eleven tanzanite stones sized perfectly for the rings Alexander was forming.

"Beloved."

"My Queen." Dropping to his knees, Damian bowed his head in deference to her status.

"I believe you need these, yes?"

She sauntered over and poured her offering into his hands.

"Someone's been spying," he quipped.

Her merry laughter floated on the wind. "How am I expected to ignore my favorites, my child?"

"I'm glad you're not. I need your help."

"My hands are tied, Aether. From those higher than me."

Scoffing, he stood and gazed down into her cautious amber eyes. "I've always done as you asked. Do me the honor of not lying to me."

"You think me untruthful?"

"I think you crafty, but not without artifice," he replied in a hard tone. She might smite him, but he was done playing games. "My daughter's life is at stake, and barring that, her psyche could be shattered if she bore witness to her mother's death."

Unimaginably, Isis remained calm in the face of his boiling temper. "Vivian hasn't crossed the plane to the Otherworld, Damian. You still have time."

Eyes closed in relief, he nodded. Lifting his lids, he locked gazes with her, seeking the truth. "And my daughter? I can't feel her."

"She's alive and encased in a protective shell of her making." A wicked smile curled her lips. "I may have given her an added boost when she conjured the shield."

Relief profound, he nodded, blinking in rapid succession to dispel the unexpected tears filling his eyes.

"Thank you." His voice was gravely but packed with gratitude.

"Your daughter is like none I've ever seen, Beloved. In her blood is the culmination of all her ancestors' power before her. Your mother's and yours, as well. When you die, she'll be stronger still. Do you understand what I'm saying to you, Damian?"

"Yes and no."

She held a finger to her lips, then gestured him closer.

Touching his temples, she drove him to his knees. It was as if she'd impaled his brain with a white-hot poker, and he gritted his teeth in soundless agony. One by one, images rolled through his mind as if they were a movie reel. Snippets of conversation wove together. Some of the Authority in heated arguments, others of the Fates debating the merits of stripping the Dethridge line of their power.

None had ever seen a witch will their power into being with a simple wish.

There were those who argued in Sabrina's favor, Isis among them. But the bottom line was grim. The majority feared a tiny girl who possessed the ability to effortlessly kill them if she chose. Sabrina was in peril because grown men and women were terrified of her. Damian was, too, because those same people feared his retaliation should they harm a single hair on his daughter's head.

Morcant had indeed died the day Nathanial cut off his head. But he'd been revived by the Authority to destroy a peaceful family.

Little did they know, they'd woken the sleeping beast within Damian. Had they come to him and expressed their concerns, he'd have found a way to lessen Sabrina's power. Now, he'd channel her gifts to use with his own. Those who opposed him, who had voted to sacrifice his family, would one day pay.

"You understand what you must do?" Isis asked him solemnly.

"I do."

CHAPTER 28

"If any of you have reservations about helping, now is the time to voice them." Damian checked the clock on the wall behind his mahogany desk. "In ten minutes, I'll take whoever is willing and retrieve my family from Morcant."

When he arrived home a quarter of an hour ago, he'd found everyone in attendance: the Death Dealer, the Seer, the Traveler, the Siren, the Healer, both Guardians, and the Wraith. In addition to them, Alastair Thorne, Mackenzie Thorne-Drake, and Creed Caldwell were present. Drawing on all the cumulative power available between them, their group soundproofed and cloaked the room from prying eyes.

"If you're in, take a ring and wear it at all times. There will be no spoken communication from this moment on." He spared the time to look each of them in the eye. "If you're out, no hard feelings, but your memory of this meeting will be wiped for group safety. I'd also encourage you to stay away from the Authority for the foreseeable future."

One by one, every member of his rag-tag team of Sentinels slipped on the signet ring, expressing no reluctance to do Damian's bidding.

"Thank you," he mentally projected. *"A few of you will be familiar with how telepathy works. For others, it will seem strange at first. All you need do is think of the person you wish to speak with and play the thought in your mind. Please, one at a time, try it now."*

He conversed with each and had them practice with one another.

"We're at the seven-minute mark. Split into your teams."

Mack, Ronan, Creed, and Jordan formed the first team. Fintan, Kass, Trevor, and Draven made up the second. Alastair, Narissa, Castor, and Damian were the final four.

"Each grouping has a Seer and someone with the power of a Guardian or stronger. Ronan, Draven, and Castor can manipulate time. Stay close to them unless I tell you otherwise. They, and only they, have the ability to reverse time to save your ass, should the need arise." Pointing at those able to predict the future, he said, *"Mack, Fintan, and I are to be consulted before any move is made. There will be no reckless stunts. My daughter's life is at stake, and I'll decimate the soul of anyone who jeopardizes her welfare. Am I clear?"*

As one, they nodded.

"Good."

"Damian?" Mack's face was without her standard smile. *"What about those left behind?"*

He grinned and pointed toward the hall.

Nathanial and Evie, in their corporeal forms, waved.

"They're on loan from the Goddess." Crossing to Mackenzie, he gently squeezed her black-clad shoulder. Inspired by Kass's ninja-like outfit, Mack had created something similar. *"They're here to protect our babies, Mack. Nothing will happen to Delaney or Nate. I have guarantees."*

The room was brighter when her sunny smile flashed. *"Then let's go kick some bad-guy ass!"*

"If we teleport as one giant group, we'll be a large blip on the Authority's radar despite the cloaking. My recommendation would be to space it out and go one at a time," Creed suggested.

Damian nodded his acknowledgment and pointed to Trevor.

"You after me. We'll alternate one from every team at one-minute intervals. We won't—"

"Damian, if I may?"

He raised a brow in Kass's direction as she sauntered into the center of the crowd. *"I've had experience dealing with slipping under everyone's noses. The key is to divert the teleport. Go to a location, but before you land, change directions a time or two. If anyone is tracking you, it leaves your signature in the first one or two locations."*

"A decoy landing. Clever, cher." Draven nodded his approval.

"What about cellphones? Do we leave them behind to prevent tracing?" Jordan asked, holding his up.

Alastair shook his head. *"No need. My security staff can scramble the signal. No one outside of us will be able latch onto it. I've been doing it for years."*

"Security team?" Kass frowned as she looked toward the windows as if disturbed she'd missed them.

"They are working remotely," Damian replied, smiling as her features smoothed. *"They're a backup. With their military training, they are likely the only ones capable of rescuing us should we fail."*

"We won't fail," Fintan growled.

"You know this?"

He shook his head with a slight, one-shouldered shrug. *"Feel it."*

"Sure, and any other questions, or is this feckin' gabfest over?" Ronan demanded. *"My skin's getting itchy to retrieve the wee wild beastie."*

"No more than mine." Damian swirled a finger in the air as a signal to get moving. *"I'll see you there."*

He didn't bother to conceal his destination. No one in their right mind would believe he wasn't going directly to his daughter's prison. Taking his time, he strolled around the building, testing for strengths and weaknesses. As soon as Trevor arrived, Damian uncloaked himself and entered.

Not bothered if Morcant knew he was present, Damian strode to the building's reception desk and smiled when the middle-aged female behind the counter sucked in her breath. A check of her name tag gave him the ammunition he needed to charm her. So much for not doing as his Enchantress mother had done. If seduction meant saving his family, he'd fuck the entire United States and then some.

Leaning his elbows on the counter, he slowly ran his eyes down the length of her uniformed body, then met her startled gaze with a wide, appreciative grin. "Mona. What a perfect name for such a lovely woman."

Her skin took on a ripe cherry-colored hue, and her mouth dropped open.

Castor's voice sounded in his mind. *"Like taking candy from a baby, Dethridge."*

"Stuff it, Alex. I'm working here."

"Should've let me do it."

Damian hoped his irritation didn't show. "Mona, I need a favor. Do you think you could help me?"

She nodded emphatically, and he had the desire to laugh as the bulk of his arriving team snorted and the women outright chortled. The receptionist neither heard nor saw their approach.

"Excellent." Weaving in an enchantment to scramble her reasoning, Damian hoped to avert her concern. A stranger seeking the subterranean passage beneath this particular high-end apartment complex was suspect. "I'm looking for an access door to the tunnels beneath this building. Would you happen to know where it is?"

Shaking her head, she appeared ready to cry. Her shame at disappointing him was great.

"That's all right. But perhaps you could point me to someone who might know?"

"N-no one is h-here, sir." She gulped and squared her shoulders. In a firmer voice, she said, "The m-maintenance m-men are off this weekend."

"Fuck."

Alastair's savage curse amused him to the degree he smiled wider.

"I see." Taking one of her hands between his, he filled her with a sense of peace and joy. Widening his eyes, he locked onto hers and spoke in a soothing, hypnotic tone. "Mona, you won't question why I'm searching the first floor of this building. If anyone asks, you hardly saw me at all, other than to deliver flowers to one of your residents. Do you understand?"

With a blank stare, she nodded.

"Perfect. Should anyone come, please direct them away from the area I'm occupying. Can you do that for me, my dear?"

Again, she nodded.

"Thank you." He released her and moved two steps away before another thought occurred to him. "Mona? Have you seen a trio of men hanging about recently? One may have had a scar down the side of his face, here." Damian ran a finger from temple to jaw.

Frowning as if struggling to remember, she finally nodded. "Not three. Just that one. He was hard to miss."

"Do you recall what he was after?"

"He asked me about vacant apartments on the ground floor. He signed a lease for 1C."

"I believe I found what I'm seeking. Thank you, Mona. You've been a great help to me." Removing five-thousand dollars from his coat pocket, he folded it and pressed it into her hands. "You should go buy yourself something nice. Immediately."

Standing, she removed her headphones, grabbed her purse, and left.

"What are you going to do when someone enters the building and she's left the lobby unmanned, Dethridge?" Creed asked with a cynical-sounding chuckle.

"No one will leave their apartments. Your team will see to that with an enchantment." As Damian turned toward the hallway, he said, *"Be sure to add in a contingency should this place catch fire and innocents need to get out."*

Addressing Alastair, he said, *"I'm going to need your guys to alter the security footage so she's not seen leaving. I'd dislike it if she lost her job from our interference. Please make that call.*

"Narissa?"

The Siren lifted her brows in question.

"Please stand guard at the front door and distract anyone wishing to enter." Damian then directed Kass toward the exterior windows of the building. *"1C should be on the west side. Find an escape route, should we need it."*

It was do-or-die time.

Preferably Morcant would be the one dying.

"Castor, you're with me. Masters, take the rest of your team and find another way into that fucking tunnel."

Striding toward the hallway with Alex cloaked beside him, Damian clenched his jaw and forced himself to keep his hands relaxed by his sides. He'd be damned if he gave in to the stomach-churning fear that they were too late.

Five feet from the door, he felt her, and he was dizzy with relief. *"She's below us."*

Castor halted and looked down at the floor as if he could see to the tunnels below.

Putting a hand on his arm to gain his attention, Damian inhaled deeply.

"Alex, if things go south, don't try to reset time for me. Get my daughter out of here. Have the Sentinels help you guard her until Isis wraps her in magic to hide her." Squeezing the forearm under his palm, he asked, *"Will you do that for me? Please?"*

"Christ, Dethridge, shouldn't this be a request for Ronan? You can't ask me to leave you behind. I don't know if I can do that."

Damian stared at Alex until the moment became uncomfortable for both of them.

"Fuck. Fine. I'll leave you here to rot and abscond with your child so she can flit about unsupervised. There. Are you happy now?"

If the situation hadn't been so serious, Damian would've taken delight in Castor's pique. As it was, he nodded. *"Thank you."* To the others, he said, *"You heard him, gang. Make sure he keeps his promise."*

"I hate you," Alex muttered.

"No, you don't. Not even a little bit," Alastair said as he joined them. *"You're just annoyed you'll have to take responsibility for something."*

"I'm going to teach her to be a pickpocket and appreciate umbrella drinks. See if I don't."

Ignoring them, Damian lifted his hands and conjured hurricane-force winds to blow the door from its hinges. "Honey, I'm home!"

"Look at him, being all Jack Nicholson and shit."

Alastair chuckled.

"He's missing the axe." He removed his suit jacket and hung it on the doorknob of the apartment opposite 1C. *"I'm ready."*

"Is this how you three always conduct a mission?" Creed snapped through their link.

Mackenzie's winsome laugh floated through the connection. *"Always. Alastair doesn't do stodgy or predictable."*

"Exactly right, child. Where's the fun in that?"

CHAPTER 29

Roach-like, the two henchmen scurried to hide from Damian, but he held up a hand and smiled. His jovial appearance confused them into freezing.

"I'm not here for you, fellas. You're free to go."

They shared a wary look.

"If you fear me, you feed Morcant, and we can't have that, can we?" Damian said cheerfully. "I want that bastard to starve."

Only the one with the angry yellow eyes looked like he'd object. The other darted for the exit as fast as his skinny legs could carry him.

"When he gets outside, kill him," Damian ordered the others with no change of his expression.

"What's your name?" he asked Yellow Eyes. Not that he cared, but he needed to get a feel for the man's intentions. Keeping him talking would do that.

"Morgan Black," came the surly reply.

"Seriously? Morcant borrowed your name when he went after the Stephens sisters?" With a harsh laugh, Damian shook his head. "You do realize, had all that gone sideways, you'd be a hunted man right now, yes?"

Black cast a frowning glance at the trapdoor ten feet away.

"Well, now I know where he's holding my daughter. Open it, please."

"Wait, what? No." The man backed away, visibly worried.

Damian sighed. Fisting his hand, he broke the man's neck.

"Hopefully, his unease didn't reach Morcant," he said aloud, not caring if anyone responded. Closing his eyes, Damian felt for booby traps.

"Don't," he warned Alex when he would've reached for the handle. *"It's spelled from the underside. Morcant put explosives in place after these two left the tunnel."*

"How do we get down there?"

"We mine our way down, Castor." After Alastair delivered that juicy tidbit, he began to roll up his sleeves, much to their amusement. He paused on the second sleeve. *"Why the stunned disbelief?"*

"I don't think we've ever seen your forearms before," Damian replied with a shake of his head. *"You've got muscles. Will wonders never cease?"*

"Don't flirt with me now, Aether. You've had your chance."

If he'd taken his eyes out and threw them like dice, Damian couldn't have rolled them any harder.

Grinning, Alastair said, *"I've been known to get dirty."*

"We know, Al. You've got children." Castor slapped him on the back with a wicked laugh, then turned to Damian, as serious as a nun in church. *"Where do we dig?"*

"Front-left corner of the room. Anywhere else might detonate the bomb."

"Should we use a different room in the apartment? Or start a second tunnel down?"

"Not a bad idea, Alex. I'll let you start there. Closest to where I felt her before we walked in." Damian examined his options. It was possible he could create a bubble to contain the explosion, but he risked a cave-in. Why had Morcant done that? Was it to kill Sabrina because he couldn't get to her? Remove Damian from the game?

"Beastie," he said aloud. "If you're here, speak to me."

"Papa?" Similar to radios of old, static came through their mental connection, and he was left to assume it was due to her protection spell. She didn't sound terrified, which was comforting, but she also didn't seem like herself.

"I'm coming to get you, my love. Never doubt it."

"I don't."

"Good."

"Mama—"

"I can't think about her right now. We both know what happens if I get distracted."

Silence greeted him, and Damian fought the clawing sense of panic. His or hers or perhaps someone else's, he couldn't say.

"Al?"

"I feel it, too."

"Who?"

"Don't know, but it feels familiar."

"Keep drilling."

Alastair nodded once and went back to work. After acquiring tap water, he tossed the liquid in the air, then harnessing his elemental power, swirled the water faster than the human eye could detect the movement. Adding pressure, he created a magical water jet that cut straight through the marble tile and was currently working through the subfloor and concrete.

"Roll call. I want everyone attached to this mission to check in, please."

They all did, with the exception of Narissa.

"Fintan? Mack? Any visions or idea of Narissa's whereabouts?"

Both answered to the negative.

"Beastie, is the Siren with Morcant?"

"No, Papa. Just me. He's walking around outside the cage, and he keeps looking up."

"Can you hear Alex or Alastair drilling?"

She paused a long moment, then replied, *"No. But there is scratching on the other side of the wall."*

"Can you sense the—"

Draven cut in. *"It's me, cher. We're almost through."*

"How do we get there, Masters?"

"The alley between the buildings. Kass discovered a basement apartment for the live-in maintenance worker. There's a trapdoor in the main bedroom."

"How hard was it to find and open? Do you think that's Morcant's escape hatch?" Damian asked him.

"It blended with the floorboards, and there was dust in the cracks. And yeah, that could be spelled to conceal the openin', but I didn't feel a magical signature."

"Fair enough. I would also assume if you're having to break through the wall, he's not using that tunnel."

"What do you want us to do once we're through, friend?"

Damian considered his options.

"Sabrina first. Get her out." He paused to swallow down the encroaching grief. *"She may be resistant without her mother, but let her know I won't leave Viv."*

Even in his head, his voice sounded gruff with emotion. Closing his eyes, he pictured his wedding day. Recalled how stunning Vivian had been when she walked down the aisle to where he anxiously waited. Her beaming smile had quieted all his concerns, and he became lost in the beauty of that memory.

Alastair touched his shoulder, returning Damian from the past. *"Better?"*

"Yeah. Thank you."

Draven spoke up and said what Damian could hear most of the Sentinels thinking. *"You shouldn't go down there, cher."*

"Because?"

"Your reaction when Vivian left the house to chase your daughter. Here's the thing, friend. If you see what you don't want to, you could cause a collapse."

Scrubbing a hand over his face, Damian contemplated what the Guardian had said. Yes, he *had* gone off the rails, but there were no surprises awaiting him. He now knew what to expect.

"I'm going in," he said simply. "Anyone afraid to follow me, stay behind. No one will think less of you for seeing to your own safety first."

"Speak for yourself, Dethridge. I'll think less of them," Castor quipped. "A whole helluva lot less."

"He's not wrong, Alex. You saw what I did. My rage could kill you all."

"I'll take my chances. I'm sure my date in the islands, whatshername, has moved on by now. I've nothing left to live for anyway."

Alastair's amused snort traveled through their telepathic link. "Well, whoever is going, let's do this. It's breakfast soon at Thorne Manor, and my niece makes the most divine cinnamon rolls. Your daughter's favorite, next to your pancakes, if I'm not mistaken, Dethridge. We'll let her have first pick."

Unable to speak his undying gratitude to his best friend, he pulled Alastair into an iron-tight embrace. When Damian released him, they shared a moment of understanding. "Then we should get going. I know how cranky you get when you haven't eaten."

"It's better for us if he hasn't." Castor grinned. "He'll mow down anyone in his path, Morcant included, to get to the table." Holding up his hands as if to ward off an attack by Alastair, he said, "Just a warning for others not to get in your way, Al. They're taking their life in their hands."

"Didn't you say I get to wield Stephan's sword, Dethridge?" Alastair asked with an arched brow.

Castor laughed.

"You two stay here and finish boring the hole," Damian told them. "You'll know when to come through. For the love of the Goddess, avoid triggering that bloody bomb, or we won't need to worry about my temper causing a cave-in."

After sending out a feeler to the alley and detecting no movement, Damian teleported. "Al, have your team check for cameras out here and scramble or delete footage of our magic."

"They're already on it."

Within two minutes, Damian had joined the others at the wall. "Beastie? Can you hear me, my love?"

"Yes, Daddy."

He held up a hand, halting all movement. Blanking his mind, he removed his ring, held it up, and gestured for the others to do the same. Once their mental connection was broken, he conjured paper and pencil. After writing the message, he gave it to Draven to pass along.

"My daughter doesn't call me 'Daddy.' It's always been 'Papa.' Morcant has likely tapped into our connection and is trying to sound like her, or Sabrina is trying to warn us."

They each nodded their understanding, and he returned pencil to paper. "Someone take these notes to Alastair and Castor. Let them know we are about to put on the performance of a lifetime."

Putting his ring back on, he nodded for the others to do the same.

"Are you all right, Beastie? Can you tell me where Morcant is?"

"He left, Daddy."

Which meant the bastard was close at hand. Gesturing to Fintan, he once again removed the physical link to allow them to communicate and jotted his instructions.

"Get Mack down here, Draven. I need to use the collective gift of the Seers."

Expression neutral, which hopefully meant his thoughts were too, the Guardian rushed topside.

"You good with this?" He flashed the note to Fintan and received a sharp nod in return.

Putting his ring on his pinky, he allowed his thoughts to flow. None negative, but enough that, should Morcant be listening in, he'd know Damian was making preparations to rescue Sabrina. Only, he wouldn't be privy what those were.

It took another excruciatingly long three minutes, but Draven finally reappeared with Mack in tow.

"Narissa?" he asked aloud.

She nodded. "She's fine."

"How's your acting?" he wrote the question and showed it to Trevor, who leveled his hand and shifted it from side to side in a so-

so gesture. "Good enough. I need you to converse with Beastie as if you're me. Do you think you can manage it?"

With a nod, Trevor started a dialogue with Sabrina, leading her to talk about made-up memories and assuring her he'd take her home soon. His ability to mimic Damian was uncanny and uncomfortable.

For the final time, he indicated Fintan and Mack should remove their tanzanite jewelry as he was in the process of doing.

"Follow me," Damian mouthed.

Leading them to the maintenance apartment, he waved his hand and stacked all the furniture in the corner of the minuscule room. The other two, understanding exactly what he needed, went to work. With her index finger, Mack drew protection sigils in the air as Fintan cast the circle. Damian conjured candles and gave them to the others. As soon as the pentagram was complete and the wicks lit, they sat.

"I need clarity. The three of us combined can overcome any restrictions the Authority and Fates deemed necessary to place on me. Are you prepared to help me?"

Mack smiled. "Whatever it takes."

Her willingness to trust him in all things was heartwarming. Beyond familial bonds, his affection for her grew deeper, morphing into lasting friendship. Whatever and whenever she needed, he'd be there to return the favor. To repay her for the help in saving his family.

Sensing this, her grin grew wider.

"Fintan?"

"Aye."

Concise and to the point. Damian could appreciate the efficient manner in which the Seer lived. Fintan, too, would benefit from this gift of trust.

They all joined hands, and the punch of power was heady, giving Damian a better understanding of exactly why the Darkness had hungered for more and more. Of why his mother gave into its allure.

Shaking off the temptation to draw their abilities in and keep them, he merged his with theirs and fed it through the circle.

Mack's expression arrested in her awe, and Fintan rocked back, barely managing to maintain his grip.

When they shared one collective thought, they began to delve into what awaited them on the other side of that cell wall.

CHAPTER 30

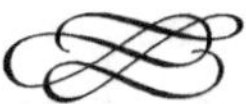

Watching Morcant warily, Sabrina waited for Trevor to finish his mental dialogue. She'd laughed aloud a time or two at the wildly funny memories—all fake—that the Death Dealer had created. In a flash, she saw his life, and she smiled at how successful he'd become as an author. In a flourishing garden, he'd write books for young adults, keeping future generations entertained and begging for more.

With a secretive smile she knew would drive Morcant crazy, she listened to Trevor.

Inside the cell with her, the Arcane Devourer shifted closer, testing the sturdiness of the bubble she'd conjured. His sour expression gave her a little thrill. As strong as he was from the power he'd amassed over the last day, he was still no match for her. But he could be soon.

Papa had made a mistake by not clearing the building. Although his team had provided a sense of security to the residents, none of them would know those same people were being fed horrific images and tortured by Morcant. Convinced death and destruction awaited them if they left their homes, most of the occupants huddled inside their living rooms or bedrooms. Those non-magical mortals were his main energy source, and they were giving him the strength to piggyback the telepathic lines her father had created with the Sentinels.

A buzzing began, as if the fluorescent light above her was about to fizzle out.

With a dark frown, Morcant glanced at the ceiling.

"Beastie?" Papa's voice cut across Trevor's, the buzzing, and the ever-shifting visions of today's outcome.

She didn't answer him. Didn't have to, because she knew he could see her in his mind. Her smile widened and had the bonus effect of making Morcant nervous. The man had no idea what she was hearing.

"That's my girl," Papa said approvingly. *"Why did you call me Daddy instead of Papa? Was that a warning?"*

She nodded and pointed at Morcant, then to the roof of the tunnel, lined with gray clay-like blocks. Earlier, she'd heard the real Morgan Black call those soft bricks C-4 as he removed the wrappers and inserted the black and red wires. He'd said it was enough to take down a city block.

"Stop pointing, girl," Morcant snapped.

Channeling her grandmother's taunting laugh, Sabrina extended a finger in his direction.

"Are you prepared to die, Morcant Thywyll?" she asked in a deep voice, pretending to be the Ghost of Christmas Past, like in movie versions of her favorite Charles Dickens book. "Repent now, or burn in hell."

She only had a general idea of what repent meant, but it sounded good, and it caused his skin to pale more than it already was. Deathly pale, she'd heard it said.

Papa's chuckle filled her mind, along with Mack's light laugh. Sabrina thought she'd heard Fintan snort, too.

"Keep it up, my diabolical darling. Your distraction is pure brilliance."

After she threw around a few more dire predictions, she crossed her arms smugly.

"Nicely done," Papa told her approvingly. *"Are you able to maintain your protection spell a while longer, or are you growing tired?"*

To show she could, she added a ton of glitter to the dome. Her father's bark of laughter made her happy.

"Good. In case I've never verbalized it, I'm extremely proud of you, Beastie. A parent couldn't hope for a more clever or resourceful child than you."

His voice sounded raspy in her mind, as if he had something in his throat, and she understood it as love because she felt the same way. *"Papa? Thank you for coming to get me."*

"As if I'd ever leave you in Morcant's clutches!"

She smiled. *"I meant from Mama's old house. The day you and Grandpa Nate made me pancakes."*

"My deepest regret was ever letting you go in the first place." The buzzing stopped for a few heartbeats, but when it started again, Papa said, *"I'm sending Mack to warn the others about the explosives. Hang tight, Beastie."*

As she waited, a few of the scarier visions began to dissolve, and in their place were greater outcomes of today. There was still the worst one, though. The one where Morcant won and she was enslaved to him forever. Yet she knew better than to let her fear take control.

Since Papa began training her, Sabrina had learned to dull the sharper emotions. She didn't always think before she reacted, but she was developing new skills every day. Patience. Critical Thinking. Clarity. Big words Papa used every day to instruct her in the ways of an Aether. She constantly prayed she was as good and fair as he was. Glancing at Morcant, she narrowed her eyes. As deadly when it came to dealing with enemies like *him.*

A sudden dark premonition struck her. Staving off a shiver, she jumped to her feet. If she'd have had time, she would've giggled and chased Morcant around the cell just to see him sweat. But she didn't. She had to save the others. Prevent them from coming their current route.

The door to the cell was locked, and the wires ran to another block of C-4 attached to the bolt. Should anyone open it, they would all be toast. Her captor had bragged about it, in addition to the spell he'd cast. Stating they'd never know, he quoted some old bug commercial about roaches checking in, but not out.

But *she* knew.

Morcant intended to allow Papa's team to enter, because he'd also applied an old Blocker tool to keep anyone from leaving.

Sabrina wasn't concerned. If he died, so did his stupid spell.

Frowning, she wondered if she was strong enough to kill him by herself. That had been one of her visions. If she did, she could end this, but her future would be full of haters. Jam-packed with those from the witch community who would forever be afraid of her. The Authority would never stop sending people to hurt her family, all to get to her.

"What are you doing, girl?" Morcant growled as she touched the door. "Get away from there before you blow your fool head off."

"You sound like you care, Mr. Thywyll," she said with a tilt of her head. Giving him a cold stare, she sneered like she'd seen Aunt Josie do. "Or is it that you would miss my Aether magic? You know, if you don't kill me yourself, it goes back to my Papa, right?" she taunted. "You know what no one tells you, Mr. Thywyll? That you have to have special DNA to keep it, and you don't. Too bad, so sad you're weak. You can't even pop a simple protection bubble. You're as stupid as your ability."

"Beastie." Warning evident in his tone, Papa said, *"Don't poke the bear in the cage. Morcant is a wild animal and unpredictable at best."*

Forgetting his number-one lesson in controlling her temper, she ignored him.

"Who eats bad thoughts?" she yelled at her jailer. "Dumb people! That's who!"

A satisfied light entered Morcant's mean, reptilian eyes, and Sabrina reigned in her outrage over his treatment of her family and her. Picking on him to distract him was one thing. Letting her fear and anger build was quite another, and it would give him the advantage.

She shrugged. "I'm sorry you're not very smart, Mr. Thywyll."

Fury washed over him, and he charged.

"Now, Ronan," she whispered, and flicking a finger, she disengaged the lock.

She'd have to reduce her shield by half to duck through the opening and get to her mother's body. By doing so, it would allow Morcant to get closer than he should.

As he was almost to her, she clenched her fists to her chest and called the C-4 to her. The suction sound made Morcant's beady eyes round. He didn't know that she'd already neutralized that particular explosive along with the ones closest to her.

When it was in her hand, she opened her arms wide. "Want a hug, Mr. Thywyll?"

He looked like he wanted to vomit. Sweat beaded his brow and dampened his hairline.

"You don't know what that can do, girl. Easy now, put it down on the ground."

With a scoff, she tossed it from hand to hand.

"Sabrina, I mean it. You'll kill us both."

"You don't think you deserve to die? You're a bad man, and you've lived too long."

Backing out the cell door, she called two more bricks to her and, in the process, watched him sway on his feet in terror. Good. He should know how all his victims felt.

"Wow! This is a lot of clay," she said to no one, flaring her eyes ridiculously wide. Infusing excitement into her voice, she said, "We could use it to model dolls." Grinning, she held one out. "Wanna play, Mr. Thywyll?"

"You're crazy!"

"'Mad as a hatter,' Papa says," she agreed with a nod. Her father said no such thing, but it was fun to turn the fear back on Morcant.

The wall behind him parted, but Sabrina didn't remove her gaze from him. It was important to keep him distracted for a little while longer. Just until Alastair could get behind him with his sword. Taking another step backward, she looked down the hall to see who it was she'd heard in the other cell earlier. To find the woman who had been in excruciating pain and was fighting against her suffocating fear.

Stomach plummeting to her toes, Sabrina made the mistake of looking past Morcant to Alastair.

When he met her eyes, his dark-blond brows collided.

Morcant was already turning toward the group of Sentinels crowding through the door.

"Get out!" she screamed. "Get out!"

But the few in the rear were too slow to react, blocking the others from escaping. Sabrina flung her hands upward, stretching the boundaries of her bubble to encompass everyone, including the prisoner down the hallway. The woman, who had been taken while she was out shopping for her husband's birthday present, was very important to Uncle Alastair and needed to be saved.

Unfortunately, Sabrina's actions removed the existing barrier between her and Morcant.

CHAPTER 31

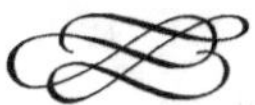

*A*n explosion rocked the room.

Damian did the unthinkable. He broke their ceremonial circle by jumping up and rushing toward the trapdoor. A second explosion knocked him off his feet, followed immediately by two more.

The whole goddamned building was going to collapse!

Scrambling for purchase, he dropped through the floor opening and ran for the underground passages his team had created, praying to the Goddess they were still there. The entire time, he shouted Sabrina's name.

A hand reached out of the smoke cloud and dragged him against the wall. The action triggered his fight mode, and he raised his arms to strike.

"Dethridge! It's me. Calm the fuck down."

"Creed? Where are the others? My daughter?"

"On the other side of the wall."

As Damian prepared to run, Creed stepped in his path. "You're not going anywhere near there until you chill out. I'm not an empath, and *I* can feel your worry." Dark brows clashing together, he voiced his concern. "You can't make him any stronger than he is,

Aether. We both know that. No matter what is going on with your family on the other side, you need to rein it in, man."

Creed was right. Damian knew that, but still, the struggle was real. Any parent would lose their fucking mind if they thought their daughter was at the bottom of a cave-in, and he was no different.

"How bad is the collapse? Has the building come down?" he demanded.

"That's just the thing. Other than the wall closing off and the ground shaking, everything seems to be intact. Think about it. You and I wouldn't be standing here if the building had fallen."

As the significance of Creed's words sank in, Damian allowed the truth to override his pressing need to get to Sabrina. *She prevented the cave-in!*

"I think so." Creed nodded, and his shoulders dropped marginally, as if he no longer needed to be on the defensive. "You good, Aether?"

"Yes. I'm good. Let's get on the other side of that bloody wall." Once again, he turned to go, but his clearer head prevailed. "Find whoever is left on this side and shore up the building, Caldwell. If Sabrina is holding all this at bay, everyone still faces danger until we can put magical supports in place."

"How do I do that?"

"Test the structure as if you were building a home from scratch." He sighed, seeing the confusion written on Creed's visage. "I can see you've never done that. Where the hell do you live?"

"I can hide better in a crowded city."

"I see." And Damian did. As a loner shunned by the witch community for a perceived injustice, Creed would avoid them in return, choosing to spend his life either among mortals or on the outskirts of the world, where no one else existed. Perhaps both. He'd have had no need to build a home like Damian's estate. "Fintan and Mack are in the maintenance flat. They'll know what is needed."

"I'm on it."

"I've no doubt." As Creed shifted to leave, Damian called his name. "Thank you for what you just did for me. I won't forget it."

With a nod, he left.

Inhaling and exhaling a deep, cleansing breath, Damian charged for the tunnel. There, he discovered Narissa and Jordan discussing their options.

"Give me your power, Siren," he told her.

The couple's brows shot comically high.

"Pardon the phrasing of that particular request. Please, Ms. Sullivan, will you loan your power to mine to get through the collapsed wall?"

"You can't do it yourself?"

"Yes and no. I could, but it would require all my concentration. This way, you're doing the concentrating, and I'm immediately prepared for what happens on the other side."

"So the correct way to phrase that would be, 'Narissa, I'm going to merge my magic with yours so you can create an opening. Be prepared when it snaps back and you're once again a weak woman as I step over the stones to get to my daughter.'"

With a wry smile, he nodded at her. "Something like that."

"Let's get to work, sugar."

Narissa positioned herself a few feet from the wall, and Damian placed his hands on her shoulders to amp up her abilities.

"Do you need to sing to draw out the Siren, or are you able to channel her without? I can conjure earplugs for both Jordan and I to fight the sound."

His comment was not to insult her, but to protect both Jordan and himself from the highly seductive song that could lure them under her spell. If she unintentionally trapped them, Damian would waste precious minutes fighting free of her mesmerizing draw.

"No, sugar. I've been around long enough to figure it out. My mama taught me the right way."

"Okay, go."

Her tentacles emerged, tearing through her slim black pants, shredding the material in the process. But Narissa had been prepared for that too, and new material grew from the old, preserving her modesty. With the added limbs, she drew power from all the elementals surrounding her, Damian included. Once she was amped up, he backed away, prepared to storm through the opening she was about to create.

His first sight of the other side sent him into overdrive, and he plunged through the rest of the debris like a supercharged bulldozer. Bricks and chunks of cement flew around him, and those fast enough to duck saved themselves the pain of being struck. The sound of stone on metal clinked and pinged in the air.

After an initial head count, he realized Alastair was missing from the group, as was the sword needed to decapitate Morcant once and for all. The bastard *would* die today. Damian would make sure of it.

"Let my daughter go, Thywyll, or I'll inflict suffering on you in ways that make Genghis Khan look like a fucking kitten."

With a knife inches from her throat, Morcant's mouth stretched into a grotesque smile. "When I kill her, you'll not be able to touch me."

"Then what are you waiting for? Do it and try me."

A flare of fear filled the other man's eyes, and he glanced around wildly as if expecting backup.

"Is now the time to tell you the Authority isn't coming to your aid?" Damian taunted, slowly skirting the half circle of his gathered team.

Tucking his hands into his slacks, he sauntered forward, appearing as casual as a tourist on a Sunday stroll through the park. He didn't fool anyone. Neither did he care to. Containing himself was key. He'd yet to meet his daughter's wide-eyed stare, fearing he'd lose control if he did.

"He can't move, Papa," Sabrina said calmly. "He's frozen like everyone."

Pausing, he turned back and noticed that although the Sentinels could move their eyes, that was *all* they could do. He frowned his confusion and faced his daughter. "Your doing, Beastie?"

She shifted her head slightly. "Theirs."

Following the direction of her gesture, he saw Alastair, Castor, and Ronan bent over the figure of another person. The lines around

Al's mouth and eyes were tight as if he were struggling not to give into deeper emotions. With Morcant present, Damian's guess was likely spot on.

"Why did they freeze everyone?"

"Because of the bombs," Castor called back. "We couldn't take the risk of another going off."

"And why is this place not a pile of rubble?"

"Ask your kid."

Damian looked closer. The strain of her stance was getting to her. Hands in the air, fingers spread wide, she appeared to be holding up the world. Finally, he understood.

"Beastie, I'm going to take the magical weight from you. When I say, you can relax, all right?"

"No, Papa. If I let go, the building will fall down."

"Even if I take over?"

"Yes."

"Okay. Tell me what you propose we do, my dear."

"Ronan and Uncle Alex need to let them go."

He shot a look at the two men in question. Ronan shook his head and pointed to Morcant, who held the knife to Sabrina's throat. If they restored time, the Arcane Devourer would kill Damian's daughter. If they didn't, they risked catastrophic consequences. Time should never be suspended for this long.

Moving to Morcant, Damian gripped the wrist with the knife, hauled back, and hit him with the force of a battering ram. His head snapped back with a crack. Neck broken, his head lolled to one side and any sign of life drained from his eyes. That Morcant would stay dead was a pipe dream, but it gave Damian working room.

"Can you decimate his soul?" Castor asked somberly.

"I can try. If it's sewn to his body, as I suspect, it will take more than my magic."

Easing the arm with the knife away from Sabrina's throat, Damian shoved Morcant away from her. His body fell against the wall and slid down to rest next to another.

Vivian.

Vacant eyes stared through him at nothing.

Stomach churning, he ripped his gaze away and cradled Sabrina's youthful face between his large palms. "How long has your mother been that way?"

A single tear escaped down her creamy cheek.

Too long.

"I see."

Inside, his heart crumbled to ash and his broken soul howled its grief. Outside, he remained stoic. He didn't have a choice.

Unable to disguise the anguish completely, his voice was raspy when he asked Castor, "Who's there with you?"

"Rorie."

Christ alive!

They needed either the Healer or to use the services of the Death Dealer, like Damian had planned to do for Vivian, but Trevor, like the rest of their crew, was a human statue. The whole goddamned situation was like a Jenga puzzle. One wrong block removed, and the entire thing would crumble. But where to start?

"Beastie, tell me what I should do."

"I can hold it longer, Papa."

"You shouldn't have to. Mack and Fintan have it covered. I'll send the Siren to—" Prepared to address Narissa and Jordan, Damian shifted as he spoke, immediately discovering their movements were locked, too.

"How?" he muttered to himself. They hadn't been there initially when time was halted. They shouldn't be party to the effect. "And how is it possible those two can hold it for this long?"

It defied reason.

"The Goddess," Sabrina's voice whispered through his mind.

Closing his eyes, Damian sent out feelers through the base of the tunnels and upward, through the building. Oddly, he felt no human life above their level other than his three team members.

"Uh, Beastie? Where are the humans?" He pointed up.

"I sent them to the docks, Papa."

"Sent them, as in mentally instructed them to go?"

She gave a slight shake of her head.

The blood drained from his face. Lightheaded, he croaked, "Please don't tell me you teleported a building full of people in the middle of the afternoon."

Sabrina crinkled her nose and dropped her gaze to her dusty shoe.

The Fates would kill her for certain.

CHAPTER 32

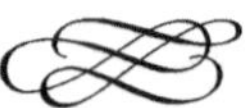

*J*umping into action, Damian went back to studying the structure of the building. The entire place was reinforced, probably better than the original construction. Creed and the Seers had done their jobs well.

Shifting his attention to the underground passages, Damian nodded his satisfaction. They, too, would hold. That only left the room they were in and the plethora of dynamite dotting the ceiling.

"They've repaired it all, Beastie. I'm going to start at the far end, by the easternmost wall, and work my way back here, dismantling the explosives. I just need you to hold on for five minutes, maximum." He touched her damp cheek. "Can you do that, my dearest heart?"

"Yes, Papa."

Ronan joined them, his underlying emotion grim, but his visage didn't show a sign of it.

"How bad is Rorie?"

"Sure, and she's halfway to dead. Morcant was after injectin' her with a slow-acting poison, he was."

"Can we save her?"

"Aye, if we knew what he gave her. Or maybe Blane can help. But we can't release the spell holding all this."

Ronan didn't need to inform Damian that Rorie would die and they might follow on her heels if the C4 wasn't disarmed.

"Right. Loman was an explosives expert, if I recall. Any chance you learned a thing or two?" he asked, infusing optimism into his voice. All he got for his upbeat attitude was a snort. "I had to ask."

"Aye."

"Creed will know, Papa."

"If we bring him down, he'll go the way of the others."

"You could go up."

The clinkity-clink of metal rolling along stone captured his attention. He caught sight of a signet ring circling Draven's shoe and smiled. The lack of sleep over the last days was befuddling his mind, and he shook his head over not coming up with the idea himself.

Digging into his pocket, he slipped the tanzanite conduit in place, crossed to Draven, and picked up the ring he'd somehow managed to dislodge from his own hand.

"Well done, Masters. Thank you." Once he had the Guardian's ring in place, Damian curled the man's fingers upward to lock it there.

"Anytime, friend," Draven telegraphed through their mental connection.

"Creed? Mack?"

"Here, Damian. The building is secure," Mackenzie answered for them.

"We have another problem," he replied tiredly.

"Yeah, and we heard all about it. But you're after facin' another problem, Aether," Fintan said. *"There's a new team of Sentinels linin' up outside the feckin' building."*

The desire to rage, to shout, "Enough already," was suffocating in its intensity.

"I can't think about them now. That's for you and Mack to defuse. I need Creed to tell me how to disarm these fucking explosives."

"I'd have to see one. I can't just tell you to cut the red wire like they do in the movies, Dethridge."

"I figured it was too much to hope for. Hang tight."

"Beastie, are you still holding strong?"

"Yes, Papa, but you have less than two minutes."

"Before?"

Her normally mischievous smile was nowhere to be found, and her grimace said it all. The Sentinels weren't only here for her. They were both in trouble. Isis hadn't been able to hold off the Fates as long as she hoped.

Striding to the nearest block of C4, he described it to Creed down to the last detail.

"Okay, so it is as simple as telling you to cut the red wire," Creed telegraphed, humor heavy in his reply.

Turning in a slow circle, Damian raised his hands, palms toward the ceiling, and projected light. When he was positive he'd illuminated the entire cavern, he spun again, noting and memorizing the position of every gray block. Holding the picture in his mind, he lifted his arm and quickly brought it down in a chopping motion.

All the red wires split simultaneously.

"You have all the best party tricks, cher."

"Ronan, Castor, reset time, and do it now," Damian ordered, running and sweeping his daughter into a tight embrace as far away from the threat as he could get.

"I knew you'd save us, Papa."

"I'm glad you did. I've aged another damned century," he retorted. "Jordan, please help Alastair with Rorie."

Rather than rushing over, the young man approached him, but his attention was focused on Sabrina.

"Did you see if any of the men had a needle?" he asked her.

"Yes." She pointed over Damian's shoulder at something behind him.

"Thanks!" In a flash, Jordan had the needle uncapped and was sniffing the contents. "Witchbane and"—he took another whiff—"oleander. Wicked!"

"Oleander? Isn't that a plant, sugar?" Narissa asked as she gingerly stepped over the wall debris. Tentacles retracted, her clothing was restored to its former glory. "How can a pretty pink flower be poisonous to a witch?"

"That's a good question, Ms. Sullivan." Jordan flashed her a boyish grin, and his eyes lit up in preparation of his explanation. "What makes the oleander plant toxic are the two potent cardiac glycosides: oleandrin and neriine. They're found in every part of the plant. Similar to digitalis, which you may have heard of because it's sometimes used as heart medication, these molecules manipulate the ion pump that controls heart muscle cells, increasing the force of heart muscle contractions."

"Yes, her heart's racing, but the room is filled with the smell of vomit, and she was curled up, holding her stomach when we got to her," Alastair stated coldly. His fear for his mate had risen to the surface and consumed his reason. The icy waves of his fury were lapping them.

"Yes, sir." Jordan tossed the needle on a tray and hurried toward Rorie's cell. "In addition to the cardiac issues, the oleander poison will cause cramping, nausea, vomiting, and—"

"We get it, son," Al snapped. "How do we heal her?"

"I've got you covered, Mr. Thorne." Jordan's youthful, lean visage and wide eyes gave the impression of an overeager puppy wanting to please its master.

"Mr. Brothers."

He shot Damian an inquiring look.

"You also mentioned Witchbane, son. Will it infect you if you treat Rorie?"

"No, sir." A wide, happy grin transformed his face. "I'm Medico and a Venenum Eater."

"In that case, please proceed."

"What the feck is a Venenum Eater and a Medico?" Ronan asked in an aside.

"Just what you see. A Healer is able to consume poisons that are toxic to everyone else."

"Grand."

"Indeed."

Confident Rorie would be fine, he nodded to Alastair. Damian had yet to put down Sabrina, and he was startled when she squirmed in his arms.

"Papa! We have to hurry. Mama is waiting to come back."

"Beastie…" How did he tell her there was no coming back after this many hours? Had they gotten to her sooner, then maybe.

Leaning in, his daughter sandwiched his face between her small hands. "She's *waiting*."

Heart hammering, Damian's breathing increased exponentially until he thought he'd hyperventilate. "Who?" he croaked past the tight ball in his throat. "Who do we need?"

She grinned. "Just you and Mr. Trevor. Like you did for Aunt Josie."

After delivering a smacking kiss on her mouth, he handed her off to Ronan.

"Blane!" he bellowed, dashing for Vivian's vessel. Two steps away, it registered that Morcant was missing. *"Goddammit!"*

Morcant's body hurt like a bitch.

Every muscle. Every bone. Every fucking cell.

His organs were a raging inferno, cooking him from the inside out. He needed sustenance. And soon!

The Aether's savage curse drifted to him, giving him the smallest of boosts before Damian managed to control his anger. It would've been nice to feed off that particular source for a bit, but that cagey sonofabitch was too restrained.

The sudden silence was eerie, even for someone as twisted as him. Peering over his shoulder, Morcant continued to inch forward as he ran his hand along the rough surface of the wall. Where was the damned latch?

A whisper of ill intent drifted to him, and he sniffed the air, hound-like, seeking the source. Perhaps if he was able to channel it, he could make good his escape.

As his fingers encountered a divot in the stone, he breathed a sigh of relief. Yes, he'd live to fight another day. Gleefully, he pulled the lever and waited for the mechanism to disengage. When nothing happened, he pulled it twice more.

What the actual fuck?

He wanted to yell his frustration, but if he alerted the others to his location in the passage, he was a dead man. No way would the Aether allow him to live one more hour of one more day. Morcant had sought to claim the ultimate prize, but failed magnificently in his quest.

"The Authority wishes you to attend them," a flat feminine voice intoned.

Good. The Authority's Red Guard would haul that bastard in and strip his power for assembling Sentinels without express permission. Damian was screwed every way from Sunday, and Morcant wanted to dance a jig on the man's perfect fucking face.

"Morcant Thywyll, you have been ordered to attend the Authority. Do you wish to comply?"

He jerked in surprise. They weren't here for the Aether. *They were here for him!*

"No, I don't fucking wish to comply," he snapped. "Do you take me for a fool?"

"We don't take you for anything," another drab voice replied.

Sniffing the air, he tried to ferret out their more complex feelings, seeking any ounce of negativity he could.

There was none!

How the hell was that possible? Had the Authority anticipated he'd drain them dry to regain his strength? In the process, giving them a drug or casting a spell to remove all feeling from the army they'd sent to retrieve him?

And they were many. *That* he could sense. Their heartbeats were in sync, which had made it hard to detect the others at first, but now he knew they were there, it was easier to discern one from the next.

Ten in all.

Oh, how the Authority must fear him.

"Why aren't you taking the Aether in?" he ground out. "He and that freakish child of his are the real problem."

"Please clasp your hands together and place your arms parallel to the floor, sir."

"No!" Trying not to give in to the panic, he tugged the lever again. "No, I don't believe I will. Not today. Go back and tell your masters Morcant Thywyll said to fuck off."

Another slight shift of energy came and went. Another instantaneous flash of ill intent. He raised his chin and sniffed.

Where. Was. It. Coming. From?

The skin on his neck tightened uncomfortably, and a chunk of his lank hair fell from his head, tumbled down his shoulder, then drifted to the floor.

He was decomposing.

In his desperation to feed the clawing hunger inside, he pivoted back and forth, a wild animal in search of prey.

Then it came.

"Ah," he said with a welcoming sigh.

But the other person's fury was short-lived, replaced by grim satisfaction.

The barest whisper of movement could be felt behind him, but it wasn't enough warning to save himself. Still, he tried, turning toward the oncoming threat.

Alastair Thorne's arctic stare was the last thing Morcant saw as his head was severed from his rapidly decaying body. His final fleeting thought was that he'd underestimated the man. Alastair was an unforgiving and lethal foe.

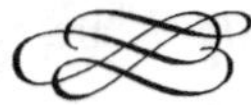

"Blane!" Damian barked. "Make sure that fucker is never coming back, please."

"I'm on it." Trevor jogged down the corridor toward Alastair, who remained unmoving as he stared coldly down at Morcant's decapitated body. With his abilities, the Death Dealer could obliterate the soul so it never came back. Morcant would be truly done with no chance to worm his way back and terrorize others.

"Al?"

He briefly glanced Damian's way, twirled the large claymore like a brawny highlander of old, raised it, and plunged the blade into Morcant's heart, for good measure. The dark side of Damian wanted to laugh with glee, but based on the shocked expressions of the Authority's cleanup crew, it wouldn't go over well.

"Perhaps the Death Dealer wasn't needed after all," he murmured.

Jordan Brothers knelt beside him. "He is to bring your wife back. But in the meantime, use this." Digging through his messenger bag, he pulled out a leafy object. Thin, it curled slightly along the edges and was veined through the center. Holding it by the stem, the

Healer instructed him to do the same. "It will bind her soul to her body to the earthly plane, and it will be easier to resurrect her."

"What do I do with it?"

"Oh, sorry. Just put it inside her mouth." With a grin and a wave, he darted back toward Rorie.

Today's youth.

"Tell me about it." Alastair muttered in passing. *"And thank you for the honor of killing that bastard,"* he added through their link. *"I'd love to do it a thousand times over for what he did to Rorie and Vivian."*

"Thanks for doing the heavy lifting. That sword weighs a ton." Damian allowed a small smile, then inserted Jordan's binding herb into Vivian's mouth. Stroking her hair, his gaze swept over her unsettlingly still visage. If he didn't know better, he could swear she was sleeping, but there was no life force present.

Shifting her body, he searched for a killing wound. Finding none, he faced his daughter.

"How did she... she..." He closed his eyes and willed back the building moisture.

"Her neck, Papa." Sabrina's solemn reply forced him to reexamine Vivian's body. Sure enough, there was slight postmortem bruising around her throat, but more importantly, he could feel the crushed bones of her cervical spine and the severed cord. From behind, he could sense the approach of the Authority's enforcers, but he ignored them as he cradled her body against him and repaired the damage.

As one, his entire group of Sentinels, with the exception of the Healer who was helping Rorie, formed a semicircle around him.

"I feel like there's going to be a rumble," Castor quipped with a wide grin. Throwing his hands wide, fingers splayed, he belted out a verse from West Side Story. "When you're a Jet, if the spit hits the fan, you've got brothers around. You're a family man!"

Alex was entirely inappropriate in the best possible ways. He could always be counted on for gallows humor.

"Why are you still lingering about?" he asked the newcomers, meeting the solemn gaze of the woman standing in front of the others.

"We have orders to bring in Sabrina Dethridge, sir."

With a small quirk of his lips, he lifted a brow. "Do you honestly believe I'd let you leave here with my daughter in tow?"

She audibly swallowed. Apparently, as the Aether, he was scarier than the Arcane Devourer.

With a side-glance toward Draven, she blushed.

Interesting.

"It's required, sir," she said, gamely continuing her mission.

Damian stroked the smooth skin of his wife's face, debating his next move. He could simply kill them all and be done with it, but the Authority would send more. Perhaps the gods and goddesses would lend their firepower to bring him down. It would be a recreation of his mother's defeat. Entombing him was the only way to stop him from returning to rain hell down upon their heads.

This wasn't the way he wanted it, but neither would he let his daughter be harmed. Sighing heavily, he eased Vivian's head from his lap and climbed to his feet. Damian stepped in front of the Authority's agent and clasped his hands behind his back.

She was clever enough to back a foot away, not taken in by his deceptively casual stance. "Please, sir. Our team doesn't want any trouble."

Draven approached, wedging himself between Damian and the woman.

"Your team will all be dead in less than ten seconds if you don't leave now, *cher.*" His lazy gaze traveled her striking visage, then continued down her body at an unhurried pace. When he met her eyes, he grinned. "But I'm happy to go with *you*. I may even let you cuff me."

"Damnit! He stole my line," Castor complained good-naturedly.

"Your flirting is not necessary, Mr. Masters," the Red Guard's captain replied crisply. Her chin shot up, and her expression cooled, but she couldn't hide the heightened color of her skin.

"Leave off, Masters." Damian touched his shoulder. *You're like a cat with a mouse,* he added telepathically.

Chuckling, Draven inched back, but he never removed his hawklike attention from the Authority's team leader.

Also interesting.

"Ms. Ellis." Damian smiled at her surprise. "Yes, I'm aware of who you are. Ms. Ellis, you may tell the Authority I will join them tomorrow morning at precisely nine a.m."

"But, sir—"

"I will have my daughter with me, as long as I receive assurances of her safety," he added coolly.

Her dark brows met over midnight-blue eyes, and she shot a frustrated look toward Draven before nodding. "All right, Mr. Dethridge. I accept your terms. Tomorrow, in Council Hall B, at nine a.m."

"Excellent. In the meantime, I suggest you take your crew and wipe the minds of anyone who may have witnessed the mass arrival of the building's occupants in the park. I assume you have that ability, yes?"

With a sharp nod, she gestured the others to precede her out of the tunnel. When they were outside of hearing range, she said, "You didn't hear this from me, sir, but you may want to bring any deities who are willing to go to bat for you and your daughter." She cast Sabrina a sorrowful look. "Tomorrow you'll face a tribunal, and your daughter's life hangs in the balance."

"Thank you, Ms. Ellis. I'll come prepared."

"My condolences on your wife, sir."

With a respectful nod, she exited.

"It was my singing, wasn't it? It always gets 'em." Castor walked away, humming.

Unexpectedly, Draven Masters burst out laughing. "I look forward to workin' with him in the future."

"Thank you for your service today, Guardian. It was more than I could've asked for."

"What do you intend to do about tomorrow, friend?"

"I've not gotten that far yet. My main concern is my wife. Everything else will have to wait until Vivian is back with us."

"Do you need the added power from us?"

"I don't believe so. Thank you." Damian called him back when the other man would've walked away. "I can't see what tomorrow holds, and I doubt Beastie can, either. But should we survive the tribunal, I will always be there if you need me, Masters. Tell the others the same, please."

A warm smile curled Draven's mouth, and he reached into his pocket, pulling out a coin. "Not my lucky one, but charmed all the same, *cher*. Keep it on you tomorrow."

The gold emitted a soft glow, and the strong enchantment attached to it was undeniable.

"What does it do?"

"You'll only see if your trial goes the wrong way."

"You have a store of these you keep on hand?" Damian asked dryly.

"Three, in total, and abso-fucking-lutely."

Crossing to Ronan, who still held Sabrina, Draven nodded politely. "If you ever need backup for the girl, I'm a shout away." After pressing an index finger to Ronan's temple, he laid a hand on his shoulder to steady him. "Sorry about that headache, friend. It's handier and untraceable."

Draven smiled down at Sabrina's drowsy face. "Thank you for your gift, *cher*. I'll treasure it always."

"Goodbye, Mr. Draven." She yawned and blinked up at him. "Miss Brooke is very nice."

"Miss—?"

"Sure, and she means Brooke Ellis," Ronan said. "Ya have to speak wee wild beastie to understand she's after settin' ya up with the woman."

Chuckling, Draven swirled his lucky chip over his fingers. "Ah, well, I'm sure she is, but I've had my one great love."

Sabrina smiled knowingly. "Do you know the soul can come back if it wants to?"

His expression was gobsmacked, and slack-jawed, he whipped around to where he'd last seen Brooke Ellis.

"Don't worry, Mr. Draven. You'll see her again," she assured him. Then, pressing a hand to her mouth, she shot Damian a contrite look. "I'm sorry, Papa."

"I think we'll forgive this one slip, Beastie. It's been a long couple of days."

"Can I go home to see Grandpa Nate now?"

"I, uh…" At a loss for words, Damian didn't know how to convey he found it impossible to deal with the fact she'd be out of his sight. Until the tribunal was over, and likely for a few decades to come, he'd not be comfortable if she wasn't in the same zip code.

"We can all go," Creed said, stepping out of the shadows. "To watch over her."

Damian had never known the man to smile in recent years, but he did as he looked at Sabrina, and it transformed him from austere to genial.

"It's safe, Papa," she assured him.

The word 'yes' wouldn't leave his mouth, but he managed a nod. "Is there anything I need to know about Trevor and I reviving your mother before you go?"

"No. Just like Aunt Josie, but longer." Sabrina patted Ronan's chest and pointed down. When she was on her feet, she ran to Damian and flung her arms around his neck as he bent to greet her. "Thank you for saving me, Papa. I knew you would."

He savored the feel of her warm body and the loving energy merging with his. Their bond remained unbroken. Parting from her, he held onto her shoulders, giving her a gentle shake.

"You're never to run off and scare me like you did, understand?" After she nodded, he said, "For today only, you can eat all the choco-late-chip pancakes your heart desires. Tell your grandpa I said so."

"He'll think I'm lying."

"You have your Sentinels to bear witness. He'll believe *them*," he assured her.

When she squinted at him with doubt, he chuckled. "Once, when

I was your exact age, I ran away from home. You know what he did after he found me?" Damian tucked a lock of her unkempt hair behind her ear. Likely she *did* know, but he said it anyway. "He hugged me so tightly I could barely breathe. Afterward, he made me blueberry pancakes, and I ate them until my belly ached."

Her engaging grin triggered his.

"Go get your pancakes, my love."

"Thank you, Papa."

She hugged him one last time and darted away.

Rising to his feet, he smiled at those gathered. "If one hair on her head is harmed, I'll kill you all. You'd better stay alert. She's quick."

The group scrambled after her.

CHAPTER 34

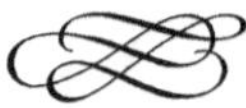

With the bulk of their numbers gone, the tunnels seemed cavernous and more threatening, somehow. Odd, that. Morcant and his two henchmen were gone, and the tribunal was a matter for another day, so there shouldn't be a sense of unease haunting Damian.

Yet there was.

He felt it beneath his skin, burrowing along his nerve endings, urging him to take note.

"What is it, Dethridge?" Trevor watched him warily. "You're on high alert. What's going on?"

"I don't know. A feeling, I suppose. As if all of this was too easy."

"You call today easy?"

"For me, yes." Again, he glanced around, unable to shake the perilous feeling. "You need to get out of here. Right now." Scooping his wife into his arms, he transferred her body to Trevor. "Go, Blane. Take her into the hallway, then teleport to my home."

Dodging through the wall opening, the Death Dealer was gone, and Damian jogged down the hallway to where Alastair, Castor, and Jordon remained to care for Rorie.

"We need to get out. There's something—"

Bulbs flickered, giving an idea of how dark the place would be in a blackout.

Damian retraced his steps, pausing to study the wiring leading to the ballasts housing the lights. Concentrating on sound only, he listened for the hum of electricity, the annoying buzz he'd spent years trying to block out after its invention.

The current wasn't normal.

A pattern disrupted the standard flow.

"Castor, if or when I say, freeze the room," he mentally projected.

Easing into a standing position, Castor dropped all pretense of teasing and raised his hands as he prepared for battle.

"Al, take your wife and Jordon out of here. Immediately."

Worry tightened the lines around Alastair's mouth and his sapphire eyes were solemn. *"I'd stay if it wasn't for Rorie."*

"I know. Go."

With the help of Jordan, Alastair got his mate on her feet and shuffled her out the exit.

"And then there were two," Castor said.

"Or more."

"How do you know?"

"I feel them. It's time for your escape, my friend."

"Fuck you, Dethridge. I'm not leaving."

"Alex—"

"No! You've saved my life, my nephew, his mate. Hell, you've saved just about everyone I know."

"Alex—"

"I'm not—"

"Alex! Shut the fuck up and let me listen!"

"You only needed to ask," Castor replied sourly.

Damian snorted before spinning in a slow circle. The threat was everywhere at once.

"Go."

"No."

"I'm about to level this room, Alex, and I can't do it with you here. Please go."

"What about you?"

He didn't say he'd be buried alive. He didn't need to.

"Fuck that, Damian. That's going to be a big hell no!"

"If you ever did what you were told, I'd die of shock," Damian muttered aloud.

"Meh."

To the troop of twenty-two warriors, he said, "Reveal yourselves. Cloaking does you no good in my presence."

"Jesus!" Alex pressed his back to Damian's in a show of unity as the Authority's enforcers came into sight. "All this for one man?"

"But he's no average man," Brooke replied as she stepped forward.

"Ms. Ellis." Damian looked past her at the hardened expressions of her fellow soldiers. "I thought we established I'd be visiting the Authority in the morning."

"It appears that's not good enough for Butthanger."

"Buttagier," he corrected absently, noting the moniker had stuck. "He sent you after me, knowing you would all suffer for the attack? Was this sanctioned by the rest?"

By "rest," he meant the Fates and Isis.

"I don't know. I'm simply following orders, sir."

"Hmm. Following those orders is a suicide mission, Brooke," he said gently. "Is it your intent to die today?"

"Your powers were supposed to be neutralized," she said. Her brows drew together as if she was confused as to why they hadn't been.

"This feels like a setup," Alex remarked. Damian glanced over his shoulder and almost laughed when Castor gave a come-at-me-bro grin to the nearest soldier.

"Do you take nothing seriously, my friend?"

"Why should I? It's only life or death."

With a slight shake of his head, Damian addressed Brooke. "Alex is right. This has setup written all over it."

Her concern was evident in the side glances she threw her Red Guard, and Damian could sense her heightening unease.

"Brooke, if I may?" At her nod, he approached her. "Let me paint the setting, and you can tell me if it's accurate. You returned to base and told Butthanger I'd bring my daughter in tomorrow for the tribunal." She made an affirmative gesture. "However, his jowly face wobbled as he sputtered his dismay?"

Her lips twitched. "Yes."

"Sorry, I was picturing the scene. Perhaps I went too far."

"Not at all," she replied. Her frown fell away as she fought a smile.

"Good. To continue. He bid you return and what? Arrest me? Try to kill me?"

"He said to use whatever force was necessary and that your magic would be reduced."

"But it's not."

Her gaze traveled the expanse of her team like a high-speed train, then settled on Damian. "Clearly, since you were able to sense us so easily."

"Clearly." He sauntered back to where Alex now rested with his back along the jagged stone wall, purposefully studying his nail beds.

"Alex, would you like to finish how this little scene plays out?"

Castor clapped his hands like an excited three-year-old. "Oh! I've been waiting for my turn."

Running a hand across his mouth, Damian hid his grin.

"Okay! So here's what's going to happen," Castor said, gesturing with his hands as if he were drawing everyone closer for story time. "You all are going to attack, per your ridiculous orders. The Aether, fully juiced, is going to wipe you all out with a simple flick of his wrist." He shot a faux exasperated glance Damian's way. "Keeping all the fun for himself, I might add."

"It's expedient," Damian quipped.

"Sure, but I never get to play."

"Whine, whine, whine."

Castor shrugged and faced Brooke. "What amounts to a one-minute skirmish won't kill Damian, but it will put a target on his back when he defeats all of you. He'll be labeled unstable, and all the deities, the Authority, and the Six will be forced to step in. They'll attempt to entomb him."

Brooke's midnight-blue eyes darkened with the realization she'd been a pawn in a game far above her pay grade.

"But they won't be able to," Damian stated with satisfaction. "Would you care to learn why, Ms. Ellis?"

Castor grinned.

After a considering pause, she nodded.

"He's got friends, *cher.*"

She spun toward the wall opening where Draven and Creed were looming. Although Masters's stance was deceptively casual, his companion's was not. Expression steely, Creed manipulated a ball of fire in his palm in a slow, menacing rotation.

"An Aether, a Traveler, a Guardian, and one pissed-off ex-employee of the Authority. What do you suppose your chances are, Brooke?" Alex asked pleasantly as if discussing the weather.

"You forgot the Wraith," Creed stated succinctly.

Draven nodded. "You can't see or feel her, but she's here, none-theless."

"My suggestion is simple, Ms. Ellis." Damian waited until she met his cool, no-nonsense gaze. "Forget this foolishness. Take your team and go home. Save their lives and your own."

Torn, she shook her head.

"I still intend to attend tomorrow's tribunal, my dear. Buttagier will answer to the others, and you'll be off the hook."

"You don't understand," she said. "We all face elimination if we return unsuccessful."

"So you're slated to die either way," Creed said flatly.

"There's another way, *cher.*" Draven shoved a few soldiers aside as he made his way to her. "You can disappear."

"Like you?" She scoffed. "Like Caldwell? Become traitors to the Authority?"

His expression hardened, and he stepped into her space, but Brooke didn't back an inch.

Whatever he'd intended to say would've been scathing, and for the sake of future relationships, Damian decided to defuse the situation.

"Or you can join our side, Ms. Ellis." Placing a calming hand on Master's shoulder, he recognized her false bravado as a ploy. Others were watching. Damian smiled at Brooke. "It's far more lively and entertaining if you decide you want to."

"Never going to happen." A flash of discomfort crossed her visage, and she touched a hand to her temple. With a nod for someone the rest of them couldn't see, she swirled her hand in the air.

"Return to base," she ordered in a hard voice. "Immediately."

One by one, the soldiers fell into line, forming two columns and marching in unison toward the door. Brooke lingered long enough to say, "Tribunal. Tomorrow at nine a.m. sharp. Any later, and a kill order will be issued, Mr. Dethridge."

"That isn't what this little show of force was?" Castor asked, his eyebrows at his hairline.

As she shifted to leave, Damian glimpsed her lips twitch. "It's all fun and games until someone gets on my bad side, Mr. Castor," she called out, not bothering to turn back.

"Now that's over, let's get to Ravenwood. I need to check on my children," Damian said heavily. He prayed this foolish stunt by Buttagier hadn't cost him his wife. If it had, the man would be unable to hide. Whatever rock he scurried under, he'd be found.

CHAPTER 35

$\mathcal{V}$ivian waited, not so patiently, for her husband to revive her. There was no way in hell she ever intended to leave her children despite the draw of the Otherworld. And it had been strong. The allure of peace and love, of no troubles, could tempt even the most resistant.

Yet the instant she died, she'd seen it all clearly. Her children needed her guidance. Especially Nate. Without her, he'd be tempted to ignore Damian's sage advice and run wild. Worse than his sister already did. That recklessness would lead him down unredeemable paths. Eventually, he'd square off against his sister, and they'd all lose out.

If Sabrina defeated Nate, her self-hatred would be limitless. Her father's affectionate nature would disappear, and their relationship would be strained for the remainder of their long lives. If Nate won, he'd make the Enchantress's reign look tame by comparison. Delaney, the only other person bonded to Vivian's son, would be unable to reach him on her own.

However, if Damian and Trevor Blane could resurrect her, if they could restore her mind and make her soul whole, the chances were better for Nate and the magical world as a whole. That went the same for the next day's tribunal. Damian and Sabrina had to survive it. The alternative was bleak.

"Why the delay?" Damian snapped, bringing Vivian's attention to the ceremony taking place.

"I have no fucking clue, man." With a shrug and a swipe at his forehead sweat, Trevor leaned his head against the wall where he sat, weary from the restoration process and hurting from the electrocution. "What did your kid say? Longer for her?"

"Yes." Grimness tightened her husband's features. "But you can't take another bolt, Blane. It'll kill you."

"I refuse to believe we can't bring her back. What are we missing?"

Josie, who'd been lingering in the hall, entered the room and sashayed over to Damian. Placing a hand on his bicep, she smiled. "The spark."

"I don't understand."

Vivian smiled. "Good girl, Josie!"

Her sister looked her in the eye and grinned.

Vivian nearly fell over. Or she would've if she had been inside her body. "You can see me?"

"Yes, Viv."

"You can see her?" Trevor and Damian parroted in surprise.

"Yes." After an exaggerated eye roll and a single-shoulder shrug, she sauntered over to the body on the bed. "I think it's from being on the other side as long as I was."

"Ask Vivian what we need," Damian ordered. His tone was as sharp and intense as his expression.

"I told you. The *spark*."

"Tell him what the spark is, sister," Vivian urged.

"I don't know that, Viv." A frown tugged Josie's auburn brows together. "Do you?"

"Nate. Nate's the spark."

"Baby or Guardian?"

"My son."

Josie relayed the message, and before she was finished, Damian was bolting down the hall toward the nursery.

Within seconds, he'd teleported back into the room, Nate cradled in his arms. "You may want to plug your ears for this," he warned. "When I wake him, he'll scream his head off. He felt the connection with Vivian snap earlier today."

"Tell Damian—"

"You tell him, Viv. Use me as a conduit to speak."

"It'll weaken you," she warned.

"I'll be fine," Josie assured her.

Meeting Josie halfway, she joined her energy to her sister's by clasping her hands.

"Damian, place Nate on his belly across my chest."

Appearing ill at ease, he did as instructed. "What's next, and let's hurry this along. Hearing your voice come out of Josie's mouth is most disturbing."

Vivian laughed, and both men looked visibly shaken.

"Kiss me, Damian."

His black brows snapped together so fast that Vivian would've bent double in her amusement had she not been tethered to Josie.

"I am *not* kissing your sister."

"Good. Because you need to kiss *me* to breathe life into my body. Just as you did when you woke me the day you came to retrieve Sabrina."

Lips turned up in a self-deprecating smile, Damian shook his head. "Of course."

"But how does the baby figure into all this?" Trevor asked.

"He's her tether to this side. The maternal love she feels for him is her reason for living. The spark."

Satisfied her husband understood what needed to be done, she released her grip on Josie, mentally wincing when her sister collapsed in a heap on the floor.

When Trevor opened his mouth to speak, Damian waved him off.

"Remember your family, Viv. Remember how much we love you and need you. How much Nate and Sabrina need you. Come back to us, fully restored, my love." Enchantment in place, he bent and kissed her.

The pull was instantaneous, and her soul snapped into place.

And fuck if every cell of her body didn't ache like a bitch.

She moaned even as she reached to wrap her arms around her son.

The muffled sound of Sabrina's sparkling slippers hitting the carpet runner heralded her arrival. She skidded to a halt just inside the door. Her eyes wide and focused on Damian.

"I forgot to tell you about the spark and that you had to kiss her, Papa!"

"We figured that out on our own, Beastie."

With a face-splitting grin, she ran for the bed, only stopping when she was at the edge. "Nate is going to be fine, Mama."

"Yes, and so are you," Vivian croaked past the lump forming in her throat. "I'm sorry you had to suffer Morcant and his men."

"It wasn't so bad. I knew Papa was coming for us."

"I always will," Damian said with a hard look. "Count on it."

"Since my job here is done, I'll leave you all to your reunion," Trevor said, using the wall as a brace to haul himself up.

As he rounded the bed, Sabrina stepped over Josie and met him. "I can give you a boost, Mr. Trevor."

"Your magical help scares me, kid." He smiled to take the sting from his words. "Give that boost to your aunt, and I'll help her to her room."

Within minutes, they were alone and snuggling together on the bed, one worn-out but happy family.

"If I make it to my next birthday, it will be a miracle," Damian teased.

Or perhaps he was serious, because they still had to face the Authority to argue for their lives.

"You need not go, Viv," he said quietly. "I can handle it."

"How did you know—ah! Our new connection."

He stroked the hair back from Vivian's temple as he watched Sabrina buss Nate's round cheek. "I confess, I like it."

"I do, too."

When he smiled, it warmed the places that still felt cold and lifeless. The areas where her fear resided.

"Tell me it's all going to be all right, Damian," she whispered, in deference to her sleeping son and drowsy daughter.

"It's going to be okay, Mama," Sabrina mumbled the assurance Vivian needed, never opening her eyes as she snuggled closer. "Papa is going to be too smart for them."

Damian nearly groaned aloud.

"No pressure," he muttered. Meeting Vivian's humor-filled gaze, he shook his head. "Sometimes, she has more faith in me than I do myself."

"That's a lot of faith," she replied. "You're pretty full of yourself most days."

He chuckled. She wasn't wrong.

Lying like they were, him on his side, facing her, with their children between them, he felt at peace. But tomorrow wasn't far off, and he would do whatever was necessary to convince the panel his daughter remaining alive was ultimately for the greater good of the witch community and the world at large. He probably should leave out the part that if they took her from him, hurt her in any way, he would peel the skin from their flesh and burn them over an open fire until they begged to go to hell for respite. But likely, he'd say it anyway.

Yes, perhaps he was full of himself, but a parent's love was no small thing.

"I'll stand beside you, holding the torch, darling."

"Sorry. I suppose my thoughts turned bloodthirsty."

"I'd say they were justified. Buttagier, or someone close to him pulling his strings, has it out for us. I'd like to know why, Damian."

"We'll learn the whole of it tomorrow, Viv. For now, get some sleep. You've been through a lot."

"And you haven't?"

"It feels as if this was all in a day's work for me." He smiled softly and leaned in to kiss her. "I've got to go check on Rorie and Alastair."

"Hurry back."

Hurry back. When they'd first met and fell in love, she was constantly telling him that. It never failed to fill his heart to overflowing that someone cared for him enough to want him around. The life of an Aether was lonely most times. Everyone feared him to varying degrees. Everyone but Vivian, Alastair, Castor, and Sabrina. Those who knew the true man behind the fearsome Aether persona.

"I don't fear you, Damian. I never should've, and I never will again."

"Unless I go crazy?" he couldn't help asking.

"Not even then," she assured him. "Seeing you with the children, with me, the lengths you'll go to protect all of us. Seeing and experiencing the angst you hide so well. Seeing the love you hold for all of us. How can I?"

He felt he should be truthful. "You'd be foolish not to have a healthy respect for what *could* happen, Viv. To use caution." Perhaps that was why it was easy to forgive her for leaving in the first place. He'd always understood how quickly a person could become unstable.

"My mother would've killed me." Emotionally vulnerable in a way he wasn't normally, Damian looked out the window, not truly seeing anything past the night sky. "Eventually."

"I don't think so." Vivian lightly gripped his jaw and brought his head round to meet her confident silver-blue gaze. "She defied the Darkness and held it at bay three times." Ticking off the incidents on her fingers, she said, "To allow Nathanial to escape with you before her takedown. To write and send a note through time that would ultimately save you and Sabrina. Then when she escaped her tomb and possessed Mack. She was unable to harm either of you. That's what a mother's fierce love does. A father's, too."

Wanting to believe she was right, he captured her hands and kissed her knuckles.

"I mean it, Damian. The bond you and Sabrina share is supernatural and stronger than any alive. You'd never hurt her, and I was foolish to believe you ever would." Her incredible eyes brimmed with tears. "So foolish. I'm not sure I can ever forgive myself."

"Viv." He brushed the moisture away with his thumb. "We've discussed this, and I forgive you. Please, please, let it go. Your pain causes ours," he said with a nod toward their children. "Free yourself from the past, and let's start anew."

Overcome, she nodded, but he heard the words she was thinking.

I love you so fucking much, Damian.

With a heart close to overflowing, he grinned and said, "I love you so fucking much, too, Vivian."

He rose, shifted Sabrina to the other side of Nate, and tucked pillows beside her.

After taking a moment to memorize the beauty of his family like this, he circled the bed, leaned in, and kissed Vivian properly. When he was done, she was breathless and her irises were lighter in her happiness. A witch's tell. He'd know she was content even if he wasn't empathic or had a special ability to hear her inner voice.

"Sleep, now, my love. I'll hurry back."

CHAPTER 36

The tribunal was packed. Rubberneckers in addition to the Authority members, the Fates, three deities, and the Witches' Council lined the stands. Every imaginable magical being was present, from Guardians to Healers and everything in between, all occupying the tiered bleachers behind those who would determine Damian's and Sabrina's futures.

Did they all want to see the Aether get his due?

Sabrina's fingers squeezed his, and he glanced down to see her staring up at him. Her pointy chin was raised and a questioning light was in her eyes, making her appear even younger than her ten years.

He winked.

Hands clasped tightly, they traveled the aisle and entered the round. There were two chairs, but Damian didn't sit. Instead, he lifted Sabrina up to stand on one so she was almost level with him. Brows arched in a display of arrogance and irritation, he slowly turned, meeting the eyes of those who were to be their judge and jury.

"Mr.—"

He held up a hand, cutting Buttagier off.

"Centuries." Damian had said the word softly, but the acoustics and a boost of his magic caused it to echo. "That's how long I have served the witch community. How long I served gods, goddesses, the Fates, and both councils. *Centuries.*"

"We know—"

"I'm not finished, Butthanger," he snapped. The furious slap of energy behind his comment caused the other man to hiss in a breath. "Do not interrupt me again."

A low murmur reverberated around the chamber, and many sat wide-eyed and fearful.

As they should.

"For centuries, I have served without complaint. I've accepted every task, faced down every villain, Morcant included, and I've always done as you've requested." Pausing, he ran a hand down Sabrina's black curls, lightly kissing her temple to show his affection. "But now, you dare force my daughter to stand trial. For what, I ask you? For being too powerful? For possessing the ability to see through your black hearts to the ugliness in your tainted souls?"

Buttagier was sweating with his need to speak, but a deep respect for Damian's retaliation held him in check.

"What has she done that is so wrong? Saved lives?" Slowly, he scanned the crowd. "She's saved mine multiple times."

The Fates, known as the Three Sisters of Fate, rose as one. Each was different in looks from the next. Had someone dared racially profile them, they'd be considered unique women of shape, size, and ethnicity, representing all humans on the planet. But they *were* blood related.

It made Damian laugh to know people were so ignorant in their belief that one's skin color defined a person. Or that where they were born in the world made them better than another. It didn't. It was all circumstance. One of those three rulers decided which body a soul should inhabit and where they should reside on Earth, and for how long. All under the guise of some greater plan.

And it was ultimately those three women who would have the final say in Sabrina's and his futures.

None opened their mouth, yet their voices blended together in a chorus of worldly accents as they spoke.

"The child possesses unimaginable magic, Aether."

"I'm well aware."

"She is more powerful than any human should be," they said.

"And yet, you were the ones to give her that power," he replied silkily. "Did you gift it so you could take it away? To force us to stand here today as you strip us of our magic and our lives?"

"No one has mentioned stripping *you* of your magic or your life."

With a humorless smile, he shifted to stand in front of Sabrina. "You'd need to do both to hurt my child, Sisters of Fate. You know I'll never allow harm to come to her while I'm able to draw a breath."

As one, they teleported into the round and formed a semicircle around him.

Reaching back, he gripped his daughter's arm and pulled her to him, silently urging her to hold on. They presented a united front.

"Send the child to us."

"No."

"Your defiance will make this harder, Aether."

He was well aware, but he allowed his arrogant stare to speak for him.

"If I may consult with the accused?" Isis rose to her feet, commanding attention.

A slight bow of his head was his acknowledgment, though Damian didn't remove his focus from the Fates.

She teleported, positioning herself beside him, facing the others. A show of support for a father and daughter who still held her favor.

"Exalted One," he murmured.

"Beloved. I see you've gotten yourself into a pickle—is that the expression?"

"Yes, I believe it is," he replied with a chuckle.

"Nathanial is fond of pickles."

His bark of laughter couldn't be contained. Isis had referenced

Nate's favorite novelty socks. They displayed a plump, smiling pickle with the words *"Kind of a big dill"* beneath it. In this setting, Damian didn't dare correct her or say it was Nate's *wife* who likely preferred pickles. Her husband's pickle, to be exact.

"When this is over, you will explain to me why you laughed, yes?"

"I will, indeed, Exalted One."

"Excellent." With a regal nod of her dark head, she lowered her voice. "Ask them of what Sabrina is being charged. They cannot take her magic without formally charging her."

Damian followed her lead. "Sisters of Fate, I'll need you to clearly state what the charges are for this tribunal. So far, it seems like you are a bunch of scared children."

Isis cast him a sharp look, and her tone was irritated when she said, "I didn't tell you to elaborate, Aether."

"That was on me. My bad."

Compressing her lips, she nodded, and Damian received the distinct impression she was trying to contain her humor.

"She is charged with issuing magic without license," a council member called out.

"To whom?" he asked.

"To the Guardian," the Fates intoned.

"You'll have to be more specific. My daughter has restored powers to only two Guardians with the express permission of the Goddess Isis and the Goddess Anu. Those Guardians are Ronan O'Connor and Dubheasa O'Malley."

Sabrina patted his chest, a signal for her to get down.

It went against every fiber of his being to release her, but he did anyway.

Fearlessly, she approached the Fates, and Damian's heart swelled with love and pride.

"You aren't talking about Ronan and Dove," she said, not intending it to be a question. "You mean Mr. Draven."

"Draven Masters, yes. He is a traitor of the Authority, and you have aided him in eluding us, Sabrina Dethridge," they told her.

She laughed.

Christ Almighty, she had the nerve to laugh in the combined face of the Fates.

Dropping his head back, Damian looked to the heavens and prayed like he never had before. If there was another being overseeing this farce of a trial, one with greater power than all who resided here this day, he hoped they could hear him and grant mercy.

"Why do you laugh, child?" one of the Sisters asked curiously, stepping forward to meet Sabrina.

"Because you're funny. Mr. Draven isn't a traitor. He will answer your challenge and save the Authority."

The dainty Sister who'd questioned Sabrina frowned and returned to the other two. "What is this she has stated?"

From nowhere, a thread appeared. It was rope-like in thickness, but it sparkled with an iridescent glow from within. Markings resembling slashes and symbols peppered its entire length. As Damian, along with all the attendees, watched with rapt attention, the thread grew longer and additional marks burned into the new section.

Expressions varied in their shock, they faced Sabrina.

"Did you do this, child?" the taller Sister to the right demanded.

Sabrina shrugged one shoulder. "It will happen, but only if he isn't put in jail."

"You cannot alter the future, Sabrina Dethridge. This is forbidden and why you must have your abilities removed at once."

Obstinate to the end, his daughter crossed her arms and lifted her chin. "No."

The wind was knocked out of him, and Damian's first instinct was to fall to his knees and beg.

CHAPTER 37

After catching his breath, Damian followed Beastie's lead and approached the group, more than thrilled to see Isis join him.

"I would humbly request you not remove her magic, Sisters of Fate," Isis stated. "The Dethridge power is woven into her DNA. You risk harming the child or her possible death, should you try."

"She willed her magic into existence!" someone shouted from the audience.

"She is too powerful!" shouted another.

Murmurs of approval ran through the crowd, and Damian's unease began to build in earnest.

"How ironic you all condone a witch hunt, considering you are all witches and warlocks," he replied, addressing the crowd in a booming voice. Turning in a circle, he lifted his arms and gathered molecules from the atmosphere, tugging at the magical essence of those around him, with the exception of the deities, the Fates, and his family.

"Do you feel that?" he called out. "I've had this ability my entire life. My. Entire. Life. For centuries. But have I used it? Never for my own gains, and only when demanded by those in charge."

"You lie!" a heckler called.

Extinguishing the drawing spell, Damian dropped his arms to his sides. "Please explain."

Buttagier unrolled a parchment. "In recent years, you've murdered Moira Doyle, Loman O'Connor, Morcant Thywyll, and… Morgan Black." He inhaled deeply as he tossed the paper aside. "There have been others. Deny it if you will."

Even knowing it would sentence him to purgatory and his daughter to the whims of the Fates, Damian couldn't speak false.

"Answering to recent circumstances, yes, I did eviscerate Moira Doyle," he replied with a nod. "However, Loman O'Connor and Morcant Thywyll were not by my hand."

"You sanctioned it, which is the same thing," Buttagier said with a smug expression. "And you didn't deny murdering Morgan," he sneered in his anger.

"I did sanction those deaths, and yes, Morgan was at my hand. He was complicit in the kidnapping of my child and the temporary death of my wife. I will destroy anyone who seeks to hurt my family." His tone was lethal, as was the look he cast the others. "My job, as defined by those higher than me, is to maintain balance in our community. All three of those people were deranged and sought to harm others by channeling magic that was not theirs to use."

"You did it for the Oracle," another called out.

"Yes. Had anyone gained what she possesses and, through her, what I possess, they could destroy you all. Are you too stupid to see it? Too blinded by your fear of me? Me, who has never sought to hurt a single one of you."

"But your mother did!" Buttagier snapped. "What's to stop you from doing the same?"

Isis waved a hand. "The Darkness has been contained. By our current Aether, I might add." Crossing to Sabrina, Isis laid a hand on her delicate shoulder. "Also with the assistance of this child you would seek to harm."

The crowd noise increased as they all conversed among themselves. Some whispered fiercely as their neighbors leaned in, all keeping their eyes on the group in the round. Others were louder, appearing to argue in favor of him and his daughter.

Damian felt the building energy behind him.

One by one, the spectators fell silent as they focused on whoever approached him.

The first to reach him were his lifelong friends.

"Alexander Castor. The Traveler," he said, introducing himself with a cocky grin and a wink for the Fates.

The man beside him snorted and stepped forward. His tone was as arctic as his stare. "Alastair Thorne. Morcant Thywyll died at *my* hand for poisoning my mate."

The Guardian ambled forward, his duster billowing behind his long, lean frame as he rolled the ever-present chip across his knuckles. Giving Damian's pocket a significant look, Draven locked eyes with him.

"Draven Masters. The apparent traitor to a broken system." He didn't bother to raise his voice, but his raspy Cajun accent carried to the stands regardless. "The Guardian whose powers the Oracle saw fit to fuse to my DNA. I trust her predictions, or I wouldn't be here today."

The next two in line took his place at the center of the round.

"Trevor Blane, and this is my brother, Simon."

"We're the resident Death Dealers," Simon told them. "We are the two responsible for obliterating Loman O'Connor's soul."

"He had it coming," a woman called out. "Evil fecker kept us imprisoned on an island to steal our abilities. These men liberated us, they did!"

With a polite nod, Simon put his hand on his brother's shoulder and guided him to the side so the next visitor could introduce themselves.

"Creed Caldwell."

The response was deafening. Labeled a betrayer and enemy of the Authority, he was risking his own life to stand up for Sabrina.

Creed's gaze sought hers, and he nodded his deep respect.

"Having seen what this child was forced to endure, I believe I can do no less by appearing here today in support of her."

Red Guards rushed the round, and Damian positioned himself between them and Creed. "He is under my protection."

"You realize that makes you an enemy of this establishment, Dethridge. Correct?" Buttagier called out triumphantly.

"Does it? Or does it make Caldwell an ally?"

In a nervous gesture Damian could feel halfway across the chamber, the lead council member's gaze darted around, testing to see who had his back.

No one.

With a half smile, Damian shook Creed's hand. "Thank you for risking your life, both today and yesterday, when it mattered to save my family and Aurora Thorne."

The remaining Sentinels who had banded together to assist him shuffled forward and introduced themselves. All received his undying gratitude for the show of force.

Most surprisingly, others emptied the bleachers to join the group at his back. There were those he recognized, had assisted at some juncture in time, and those he didn't. Some bore a fleeting resemblance to witches whose lives he'd saved in the past but who had finished their life cycle and moved on to the Otherworld.

Two-hundred-plus years was a long time, and his magic had touched many for the better.

One individual pushed his way center stage, met Damian's curious gaze, and stuck out a hand. Startled, he responded in kind. "I don't know you or what I may have done to help."

"You took my father's life. Or, according to you, had a hand in it, anyway." The young man's chin came up. "Thank you for saving my mother and me, sir. He was a truly horrible person."

"Who was your father?"

"Morgan Black. I'm Virgil Black."

"He's Mr. Creed's nephew, Papa," Beastie replied promptly.

"Half," the blond-haired boy corrected. "I'm his half nephew."

Not so oddly, the young man resembled Creed Caldwell when

he'd been that exact age. "I'm glad you view Morgan's demise in a positive light, Virgil."

"I do, sir."

"We all do," Isis said. "And that is why this tribunal is finished. It's clear to me, as it should be to you, that the Dethridge family serves the side of good."

"But the girl!" Buttagier cried.

Sabrina skipped toward him. Staring at him from her position below, she seemed small. Fragile in the face of the councilman's outrage.

"Morcant Thywyll was a bad man, Mr. Buttagier," she told him in a calm, steady voice. "But you sent him after me. I know why, and I'm not mad at you."

Red-faced and sweating, he ran a pudgy hand through his thinning hair. "I don't know what you're talking about, girl."

"Yes, you do. Morcant was never going to keep his promise to you."

Cupping her hands together, she scrunched her face in concentration. An inch-sized sphere appeared, visible through the gaps between her fingers. Purple beams shot in all directions as the sphere grew to the size of a baseball. When Sabrina was done, she tossed it to Buttagier.

"You can see it's not Papa's fault."

The crystal ball was faceted, and as it replayed the scene in the apartment of 1C, it showed Damian's ruthlessness in dealing with Morgan Black.

"He didn't have to die! I could've reformed him." Furious tears flooded the councilman's eyes.

"No, sir. You couldn't," she said simply. "He was afraid of Morcant, just like you. But unlike you, it made him happy to hurt children."

"Your father didn't give my boy a chance. Why should I give you one?"

Fuck.

Damian closed his eyes and hung his head. The man with the

scar and yellow eyes had bore no resemblance to Buttagier. Neither did they share a name. How the hell was he to have known?

"Your *son* set explosives along the tunnel's ceiling. Enough to level a city block, Buttagier," Creed Caldwell stated. "Innocent mortals. It seems you chose the wrong bastard to love. You picked the bad seed, *Father*."

"Enough!" the Fates cried out. "We care not for the procreation of others or their petty squabbles. The child is too powerful to remain in possession of her abilities. They shall be removed."

"No!"

Damian surged forward, with his group of Sentinels at his back.

But they were too late.

CHAPTER 38

Thunder boomed, and the floor below them shook as a metal cage emerged from beneath the marbled tiles. It encircled Sabrina, and sigils burned into the bars with a sizzle and pop. Damian recognized most of the enchantments, having encountered them throughout his lifetime. They were eerily similar to the ones created to entomb his mother and contain her magic inside the garden walls.

Memories of Sabrina's birth, of her first steps, along with other special moments that were imprinted in his mind and on his soul, began fading.

A sick realization gripped him.

They intended to take her from him in *every* way!

"Beastie!" he roared.

A sweeping wave of his arms sent people tumbling out of his path as he raced for his daughter. The Fates cried out their affront as if surprised he would dare attack them.

But he'd dare anything.

"I'll not lose you. I'll not lose you," he cried. Gripping the bars, he screamed his pain, both internal and external, as the enchantment seared the flesh from his hands. The agony caused his emotions to riot, and his power, amplified by his heightened state, turned destructive.

Dust showered the occupants of the chamber as the entire building rocked on its foundation.

Columns crumbled, and terrified screams rang out.

The supernatural illumination flickered out, plunging the entire place into darkness.

"Fools! He'll kill us all!" Isis shouted over the noise. "Stop this at once!"

Tuning out the noise, Damian called to his daughter. "When I tell you, teleport to safety, Beastie. Do you understand?"

"No, Papa," she said tearfully. "You have to stop this."

"I'm trying. I—"

"No! You have to let me go now."

"Never!"

She sobbed her grief and collapsed on the floor of her prison. "They will kill you. You have to stop."

"Not until you are free," he told her raggedly. The urge to gag was strong, but he doggedly ignored the smell of his charred flesh as he used his enhanced strength in an attempt to part the bars. They barely budged. "Goddamn it!"

"Please!" she cried. "Please, Papa. They will kill you. They will—"

Reaching through the bars, he extended his blistered hand for her to grasp. "I've told you. You're my heart. I cannot live without you."

Alastair staggered up to the cage, Castor beside him.

"Tell us what we need to do."

"Don't let me forget her." His eyes burned as his vision of her blurred. "Don't let me forget about her. They're going to try, but don't let them. I promised her."

Nathanial and Evelyn appeared on the other side of the cage, each looking as if they were ready to destroy the world in their outrage.

"Help me, Dad," Damian croaked. "Help us."

"That's what I'm here for, my boy."

"That's what we're all here for, *cher*." One nod from Draven had all the Sentinels joining hands as they formed a circle around Sabrina, Damian's parents, his best friends, and him. "Hold the line," the Guardian ordered. Bending, he said, "The others are only a show of force. None of us are powerful enough to fight the Fates. But you can."

Unable to respond, Damian frantically wracked his pain-ridden brain for a solution.

"Remember the coin, friend," Draven told him through their telepathic connection.

Heart in his throat, Damian plunged his damaged hand into his pants pocket and removed the token Masters had given him the day before. The one he'd impulsively grabbed before leaving home that morning. *"What—"*

"It's a promise owed. Hold it up."

Jumping to his feet from where he'd been kneeling, Damian lifted the coin high above his head.

"Call in the debt from the Fates, and do it now, Aether."

It was then that he recognized the significance of what he held. The desire to laugh his joy, to kiss Draven on the fucking mouth, and to dance in celebration, all hit him at the same time.

"Save the kiss for your wife, friend."

With a snort and a shake of his head, Damian shouted the words, "Sisters of Fate, I'm calling in your debt."

The silence, immediate and eerie, registered through his ringing ears. Everyone, with the exception of the Fates, Damian, and Sabrina, was suspended in time.

"It belongs to another," they intoned.

"He passed it to me of his own free will."

They conversed with each other outside of his hearing as the dainty Sister watched him with something akin to pity coated with wariness.

"I wish my daughter set free. From now to forever, she is never to be subjected to your ridiculous tribunals again."

"Not with her powers intact."

"She is no threat to you or this community," he insisted.

"With each day, she grows stronger. She cannot be left unchecked."

"*She's not!*" he retorted angrily. Seeing their averse reaction to his fatherly indignation, he checked his temper. "She's not unchecked. Yes, she grows in strength, but she also grows in compassion and wisdom. With all the visions of future outcomes she's received, all those that constantly flit through her mind regardless of how ghastly, she never shies away. Instead, she gains understanding. My daughter possesses a far better soul than the four of us combined." Dropping his arm, he gazed down at the glowing coin. He frowned as the same sigils from the bars imprinted themselves on the flat surface. Lifting his head, he saw the diminutive Sister's triumphant smile before she carefully smoothed her features. But her silvery stare bore into him as if she wished to impart knowledge.

Opening his mind, he sought her out.

"*Throw the coin at the cage. There are no restrictions to the debt owed,*" she said within the confines of his mind. "*My sisters merely seek to test your commitment.*"

Huffing out a breath of disgust, mainly at himself for not recognizing the game for what it was, Damian tossed the coin up. As it fell, continually twisting to show the heads of the Fates on one side and the sigils on the other, Damian once again absorbed the magic from those present. Then, in a single push from what he'd gathered, he batted the coin between the bars, where Sabrina plucked it from midair.

Kneeling, she pressed it to the center of her prison floor.

Around her, the cage dissolved into a molten pool of metal. It splashed and spit as if angry to lose its beautiful canary.

"Papa!"

Leaping over the liquid border, she ran for him.

And he was there to catch her.

"Butthanger has been relieved of duty."

Damian looked up from his poker hand and grinned at Alastair. "Excellent."

"He wasn't a bad man, Papa," Beastie said, pointing to the card he should throw away.

Creed Caldwell snorted into his drink as he folded what he'd been dealt. "Just be glad you got the father you did, kid. Mine wouldn't be trying to pry bars apart with his bare hands to save me."

"Linc's going to be glad because *you* will."

They all paused the play to stare at her.

"Who's Linc?" Creed asked as he carefully set his tumbler on the table.

With a naughty grin on her elfin face, she drew an arch above them. After a glittering soundproof bubble encased them, she said, "Your son, Mr. Creed."

"Just Creed, and sorry. I don't have any children. I make damn—er, darned sure—er..." With a scowl at Damian, he growled, "How am I supposed to say it?"

Not bothering to control his laughter, Damian hugged his daughter. "Creed has no plans to marry, Beastie."

"Not right away, but he will."

"Fat chance," Creed muttered under his breath as he climbed to his feet. "Am I allowed out of the glitter dome, or what?"

Sabrina snapped, and they were showered with iridescent purple flecks. The bulk of which covered Creed.

"That's mean, kid."

She grinned and shrugged.

"Your mother is going to be cross, my love. She despises glitter on the carpet," Damian warned.

"I'll clean it up. And you should fold, Papa. Uncle Alastair will win this hand."

"You're going to make me go broke, child," Alastair said with a deep chuckle.

"But you won."

"There is a nuance to bettin'. It's called bluffin', *cher*." Crossing to the table, Draven Masters brushed the shimmering debris from a club chair, then sat down. Palms flat, he called the deck of cards to him, then proceeded to shuffle, never taking his amused gaze from Sabrina. "Sit, *ma petite amie*, and I will teach you what you need to know."

"Will Blane be joining us tonight?" Alastair asked as he arranged his new hand.

"He's been assigned a job." Before the others could ask, Damian jumped up and kissed Sabrina on the crown of her head. "My wife has summoned me, gentlemen. I must answer the call." To his daughter, he said, "No cheating or revealing what everyone is holding. They may not know what you're doing, but I do. It's bad form, Beastie."

She giggled.

"We're only playin' for candy, friend." Draven tossed in the two Pixy Stix ante.

"Have you ever seen a magical child sugared up, Masters?" he asked with a wry chuckle. "It isn't pretty."

"As evidenced by the glitter bomb," Creed called from the sideboard where he was refilling his drink.

With a wide grin for his friends, new and old, Damian hurried from the room and up the stairs. When he entered the primary suite, he inhaled sharply.

"Ah, Viv. You take my breath away."

Perched on the bed, with her back to the headboard and with her smooth legs—encased in lacy white stockings and secured with garters—bent under her where she knelt, Vivian spread her arms wide. The frothy white lingerie gave the impression of an angel's wings, and her exposed breasts played peekaboo through the long strands of her tumbling platinum hair. Her grin was devilish, at direct odds with her celestial appearance.

"Do you know what day it is? What time?" she asked teasingly.

He did.

Frowning, he shut and locked the door, then strolled to the bed as if he had all the time in the world. When he reached her, he crossed his arms and tapped his chin as if struggling to recall.

"What day… hmm… let me see…"

A pillow hit him square in the face.

Laughing, he dove for her, rolled, and drew her down atop him. "Of course I know," he assured her with a hard kiss. "Today is the anniversary of the day you showed up at my door for the first time." He trailed her creamy skin with his fingertips, running them over her forehead, brushing her brow, then down her smooth cheek to caress her lips. "Long after I'm dead, I'll still remember."

She seemed melancholy when she asked, "Did you ever believe our lives would turn out this way? That night, when you told me you intended to marry me, did you see all of this?"

"I've never expected our lives to be easy, Vivian. But if asked, I'd say ours is the greatest love story ever told."

"Like a favorite love song," she said softly as she caressed his mouth. "The kind that never gets old and makes you want to play it on repeat."

"Solid gold. One that will never go out of style and makes you smile whenever you hear it."

"Yes," she agreed as she nuzzled the column of his throat.

"At least we're not one of those heartbreaking country songs, and I'm not mourning the loss of my pickup truck over my woman," he teased as he shifted to allow her better access.

She lifted her head. "How do *you* know about country songs?"

"I hit a dark period when you left."

Laughing, she straddled him and ripped his shirt apart, scattering buttons. "It had to be pretty dark if you know about pickup trucks in place of Bentleys, Porches, and Land Rovers, darling."

"I believe our soundtrack will forever be beautiful and never grow old."

Her smile was blinding. "Yes. I believe it will."

"How do you feel about more children?" He asked, parting the frilly material to play with her pert nipple. Her moan traveled straight to his groin, and he groaned as she ground her pelvis against his.

"The two we have aren't enough for you? I don't know how many more tribunals we have in us, Damian." She held his head away from her to meet his gaze. "When I saw the cage... the burns on your hands..." Releasing him, she gripped his wrist and pressed her cheek into his healed palm. "It was like watching a horror movie through that scrying mirror. I thought I was going to lose you both. I was getting ready to teleport there when I saw the Sentinels gather. Thank the Goddess for Draven's coin."

"Clever planning on his part. A contingency I should've been prepared for, but wasn't." Shifting to a kneeling position, he cradled Vivian's beloved face. Ducking to meet her solemn eyes, he smiled. "But what's life without a little risk? How can we appreciate these finer moments if we have nothing to lose?"

Snorting, she wrapped her arms around his neck and drew his head down to hers. "Well, I suppose if you don't feel too old to have a few more—"

She screamed a laugh as he tackled her to the mattress.

"I'll give you old, woman!"

"That's what I'm hoping," she replied with a bawdy grin.

EPILOGUE

SIX YEARS LATER

$\mathcal{P}$eas landed on Damian's plate, or rather, they formed as if conjured, and he knew the culprit.

Beastie.

He grinned as he looked up and met her sparkling gaze. At sixteen years old, Sabrina was still a handful, but she'd assumed the role of protector to her three siblings, Nate, Charlotte, and Asher. That meant helping them dispose of whatever they didn't care to eat.

Like peas.

Four years old and the most outrageous of all the Dethridge clan, Asher despised anything green. Ironic, since he was an earth elemental. When he wasn't sticking cut-up vegetables up his nose in preparation for a fantastical blowout, he tended to dump them on the floor for the Hellhounds to devour. Both actions thrilled Lottie, who, as her brother's personal cheerleader, always clapped and shouted from her highchair.

Their house had been filled with chaos for the last half decade, but only in the best possible way.

Damian's gaze traveled the length of the table, touching on all the people gathered for Sabrina's sixteenth birthday celebration. There was Trevor Blane and his new bride at the far end of the room, trading heated looks across their wine glasses, as they conversed with Castor and his new fiancée. A handful of the Thornes had shown up for dinner, and more would be arriving for the ball Vivian and Sabrina had insisted on hosting. Additionally, his trusty Sentinels and their mates, a few with children in tow, peppered the dining room.

Over the years of working together, of facing endless trials and tribulations, they'd all formed unbreakable bonds. Friends to the end, although they *did* bicker on occasion. Those brave men and women would always have his back, as Damian had theirs.

Giggles drifted to him, and he immediately recognized the source—Beastie and Chloe. Two beautiful young women, soon-to-be heartbreakers in multiple ways. Sabrina's two best friends flanked her, and Damian noticed ever-thoughtful Aeden O'Malley was as quiet as ever, attentively listening to the girls as they chatted away about whatever it was teenage girls found interesting. Every once in a while, the young man would sneak a glance at Ronan O'Connor, his hero and the person he strove to be like. The Guardian who had saved his life once upon a time and who continued to watch over him.

Whenever Aeden became too distracted, Sabrina absently touched his arm and gave him a winsome smile. Of course, he responded in kind, and whatever connection the two had was strengthened with each silent glance.

"Do you think they'll marry one day?" Vivian asked Damian as she scooped the peas from his plate and redistributed them on the floor for the dogs to noisily snarf down.

"Please. I'm not ready to think about Sabrina having a boyfriend just yet."

"There will probably only be Aeden. She calls him her forever friend," she replied with an amused smile. "Although I'd like for her to experience the world before she settles down."

"She already has, Viv. In her mind, she's seen it all. Continues to see it all."

"Still, she should be free to explore other relationships when she heads off to college."

"I'm sure she will. It isn't as if Beastie is shy," he said with a chuckle.

Vivian looked around the dinner table and sighed. "Should we tell the kids there's pizza on the terrace? I fear this meal has gone to waste."

"Lottie and Asher will be happy to be rid of their peas."

They shared a grin.

"You can't say I didn't warn you about future trials, tribulations, and tribunals, darling." Vivian gave him an arch look. "You'd better start figuring out how to get Asher out of trouble now. If any of your little monsters are going to wind up in hot water, it's going to be him."

His bark of laughter turned heads. Leaning in, he nuzzled the delicate shell of Vivian's ear. "Oh, they're mine now? Hmm. I remember the conception of each one, and as I recall, we were both participating in the act. With vigor."

That she could still blush after all these years together delighted him and filled him with happiness.

"Shush, you!" But her scowl was laced with humor. "Is it horrible to say that I dread the day Asher comes into his powers?"

"No. On that, we are in complete agreement."

Since the day of Sabrina's tribunal, Damian's abilities had been restored to full strength. Any glimpses of the future included. Yes, Asher would be a challenge, but no more so than Sabrina and Nate were or than Lottie would eventually be. They were all spirited children with minds of their own. Testing boundaries was second nature. They would all thrive, however, eventually becoming assets to the witch community, as would their children and their children's children.

And one day, when it was time for Damian to move on to the next world, he'd give what remained of his formidable powers to the daughter he adored beyond measure.

His firstborn, Beastie.

"What has you thinking so hard, darling?"

"You can't tell?" he asked with a loving smile.

Her silvery blue eyes lit on him, and her mouth curled ever so slightly. "I didn't want to be a creeper and read your mind."

Trailing his knuckles along her smoothly defined jawline, he tipped her chin up and dropped a light, lingering kiss on her lips.

"Creep away, my love, but be prepared for shockingly wicked thoughts."

She laughed as she stood. "Fine, don't tell me. I have pizza to conjure."

"I'll help." Rising, he clasped her hand and lifted it to buss her knuckles.

Once they were out on the terrace, his attention was drawn to the memorial garden he'd erected toward the back of the estate. For now, those iron gates housed a private park, but one day, it would serve as their family plot.

But not for hundreds of years yet.

The Dethridges still had a lot of work left to do.

Thank you for taking the time to read *THE AETHER*. I hope you loved it enough to continue the series with book 2, *THE DEATH DEALER*. You're going to enjoy Trevor and Soleil's opposite's attract story. And don't worry, because you'll see more Damian and family, too.

PREORDER THE DEATH DEALER

If you're *really* feeling it, you may want to secure your copy of *THE SEER* while you're there! Fintan and Taryn are sure to delight.

PREORDER THE SEER

If you never want to miss a release or sale, be sure to sign up for my text alerts. Currently for North American residents only, but the UK and Ireland will be coming soon.

Text **JOIN** to **1-877-795-1526** to subscribe.

Also, if you haven't already subscribed to my newsletter, http://www.tmcromer.com/newsletter, or joined my Facebook reader group, Cromer's Carousers, I encourage you to do so. It's the best way for you to stay current on upcoming stories and receive bonus content for available books.

ALSO BY T.M. CROMER

The Sentinels of Magic Series:
THE AETHER
THE DEATH DEALER
THE SEER

The Thorne Witches Series:
SUMMER MAGIC
AUTUMN MAGIC
WINTER MAGIC
SPRING MAGIC
REKINDLED MAGIC
LONG LOST MAGIC
FOREVER MAGIC
ESSENTIAL MAGIC
MOONLIT MAGIC
ENCHANTED MAGIC
CELESTIAL MAGIC
EVERLASTING MAGIC
CAPTIVATING MAGIC

The Thorne Witches: Happily Ever Afters Series:
ENDURING MAGIC
BOUNDLESS MAGIC

The Unlucky Charms Series:
PINTS & POTIONS

WHISKEY & WITCHES

BEER & BROOMSTICKS

COCKTAILS & CAULDRONS

WINE & WARLOCKS

HIGHBALLS & HEXES

MIMOSAS & MAGIC - TBD

The Angels of Legend Series:

LUCIFER

GABRIEL

The Holt Family Series:

FINDING YOU

THIS TIME YOU

INCLUDING YOU

AFTER YOU